PRAISE FOR AMELIA GREY'S NOVELS

A Little Mischief

"Amelia Grey's novels are wonderful to read and this latest story is no exception. This tale was full of laughter, love, and lots of fireworks . . . Reading Amelia Grey's novels is much like getting an unexpected gift, fun surprises from the moment you open the cover until you turn the final page. Treat yourself to a gift today!"   —*Affaire de Coeur*

"A wonderful adventure story with lots of twists and turns."   —*Rendezvous*

"If you like Amanda Quick, you will absolutely *love* Amelia Grey. I read this book in one sitting. It was fun, fast-paced, and very sensual . . . I enjoyed this book very much and am making it one of my favorite picks for this fall."

—*A Romance Review.com*

"Filled with witty banter . . . that kept me laughing out loud . . . For anyone who loves romances rich with laughter, *A Little Mischief* is not to be missed."

—*Romance Reviews Today*

continued . . .

A Dash of Scandal

"Absolutely charming . . . a wonderful, feel-good, captivating read."
—Heather Graham

"Fans of Regency romance will relish this amusing tale . . . delightfully cheerful."
—*Midwest Book Review*

"Such a tantalizing and funny read, you won't be able to put it down."
—*Rendezvous*

"For a light, humorous, and tender love story with an element of mystery, spice up your reading with *A Dash of Scandal.*"
—*Romance Reviews Today*

Never a Bride

"Will keep you up all night—praying for a wedding. Fresh and original and destined to be a keeper. Charming and delightful—a must-read."
—Joan Johnston

"A delightful Regency romp. You'll have lots of fun with this one."
—Kat Martin, author of *Desert Heat*

"An uplifting, wonderfully sensual story. I hated for it to end."
—Meryl Sawyer, author of *Lady Killer*

"Readers will be quickly drawn in by the lively pace, the appealing protagonists, and the sexual chemistry that almost visibly shimmers between them in this charming, light-hearted, and well-done Regency."
—*Library Journal*

"Witty dialogue and clever schemes . . . Both of Grey's vivid characters will charm readers."
—*Booklist*

A Hint of

Seduction

Amelia Grey

BERKLEY SENSATION, NEW YORK

THE BERKLEY PUBLISHING GROUP
Published by the Penguin Group
Penguin Group (USA) Inc.
375 Hudson Street, New York, New York 10014, USA
Penguin Group (Canada), 10 Alcorn Avenue, Toronto, Ontario M4V 3B2, Canada
(a division of Pearson Penguin Canada Inc.)
Penguin Books Ltd., 80 Strand, London WC2R 0RL, England
Penguin Group Ireland, 25 St. Stephen's Green, Dublin 2, Ireland (a division of Penguin Books Ltd.)
Penguin Group (Australia), 250 Camberwell Road, Camberwell, Victoria 3124, Australia
(a division of Pearson Australia Group Pty. Ltd.)
Penguin Books India Pvt. Ltd., 11 Community Centre, Panchsheel Park, New Delhi—110 017, India
Penguin Group (NZ), Cnr. Airborne and Rosedale Roads, Albany, Auckland 1310, New Zealand
(a division of Pearson New Zealand Ltd.)
Penguin Books (South Africa) (Pty.) Ltd., 24 Sturdee Avenue, Rosebank, Johannesburg 2196, South
Africa

Penguin Books Ltd., Registered Offices: 80 Strand, London WC2R 0RL, England

This is a work of fiction. Names, characters, places, and incidents either are the product of the
author's imagination or are used fictitiously, and any resemblance to actual persons, living or dead,
business establishments, events, or locales is entirely coincidental.

A HINT OF SEDUCTION

A Berkley Sensation Book / published by arrangement with the author

PRINTING HISTORY
Berkley Sensation edition / September 2004

Copyright © 2004 by Gloria Dale Skinner.
Cover art by Wendi Schneider.
Cover design by George Long.
Interior text design by Julie Rogers.

ISBN: 0-425-19802-2

BERKLEY® SENSATION
Berkley Sensation Books are published by The Berkley Publishing Group,
a division of Penguin Group (USA) Inc.,
375 Hudson Street, New York, New York 10014.
BERKLEY SENSATION and the "B" design are trademarks belonging to Penguin Group (USA) Inc.

PRINTED IN THE UNITED STATES OF AMERICA

10 9 8 7 6 5 4 3 2 1

*This book is dedicated to Kathy Baker
for suggesting the title.
Thank you.*

One

"Oh, for a horse with wings," that I might fly from one party to another as the Season is upon us. This column shall continue to fill your lovely heads with nothing but delicious gossip from our most popular and our most notorious members of the ton. Should we begin with the blithe Lord Chatwin, who has let it be known again this year that he is not looking to make a match? But what about the other half of the Terrible Twosome? Is Lord Dugdale looking?

Lord Truefitt
Society's Daily Column

"MERCIFUL HEAVENS, CATHERINE, it's not only dark as midnight here in the park, it's freezing cold, too. It's simply uncivilized to be out before daybreak."

Catherine Reynolds looked over at her widowed half sister who rode beside her on a temperamental mare. In the months Catherine had been in London, she'd ceased to be shocked by Victoria Goosetree's constant complaining. Though the older woman would never breathe an improper word in public, she was more than ready to speak her mind in private.

"You'll warm up soon, Vickie. I think just before dawn is the most beautiful time to be outside on a horse."

"The devil it is," Victoria grumbled as her mare snorted. "I can't see a thing and I don't think it's safe."

"You can't see anything because you're not looking, and with Mills riding behind us we are perfectly safe," Catherine said.

She took a deep breath, filling her lungs with the crisp mist of air that wafted across their path. She caught the scent of wet foliage and sighed as it reminded her of home. Their groom remained quiet as he rode behind them, and when Victoria wasn't talking Catherine could relax and enjoy the peaceful early morning sounds of Hyde Park.

"How much longer are we going to ride?" Victoria asked.

Catherine smiled to herself, remaining patient. Her mare nickered and shook her head as puffs of warm breath snorted from her nostrils. "We've been on the horses less than fifteen minutes."

"Feels like hours to me. I allowed you to talk me into this for today, but I don't think I should like to do it again."

Catherine laughed but not loud enough that her petulant companion could hear. It was cold, but that didn't bother Catherine. Having grown up near the northern coast, she was used to a climate where the chilling dampness never seemed completely to go away.

"You're the one who insisted that I shouldn't ride during the day when it is much warmer," Catherine felt compelled to say.

Vickie snorted louder than the horse she was riding. "I was only trying to impress upon you that young ladies who are looking to make an excellent match shouldn't sit a horse in any park during the Season."

This was yet another reminder of her half sister's belief in doing one thing in public and another in private.

"You should only be seen riding in an open carriage with a viscount, an earl, or perhaps a handsome marquis by your side. I don't know why I allowed you to talk me into riding before daybreak. My feet are numb."

Hyde Park was beautiful dressed in the magical misty-gray of predawn. Shadowed sky light filtered through tree branches and shone down on them. Shards of pink, gray, and dark blue were about to be born on the horizon, and Catherine looked forward to enjoying the birth of sunrise.

She had been in London over three months, and it seemed as if she had done nothing but be fitted for ball gowns and more ball gowns. She considered the amount of clothing ridiculous Victoria insisted she have for the start of the Season. And gowns were only the half of it. A lady had to select just the right gloves, bonnets, fans, and hand-kerchiefs, too. No one needed that many things to wear.

"Perhaps if we rode a little faster you'd warm up," Catherine said, hoping to find a way Victoria could enjoy the outing. "How about it? Are you ready to let the horses trot?"

"I'm not sure I can. This horse doesn't seem to be well schooled."

Vickie's mount nickered and stomped as if agreeing with her comment.

Catherine reached down her gloved hand and patted the warm, firm neck of the spirited animal she rode. Her mount needed no prodding. Vickie was right that the hacks

Mills had hired at a nearby livery weren't well trained for riders.

Vickie's mare was old and cranky, constantly fighting the bit, while Catherine's mount pranced restlessly beneath her like a young filly not saddle worn. But to Catherine, any horse was better than not riding at all.

"Perhaps your horse senses that you are unsure with her, and she's taking advantage," Catherine suggested. "You need to take control. A canter will take some of the wind out of her. Tighten up on your reins like this and let's ride."

"Very well," Victoria mumbled. "I'll try anything to warm up."

"Good. That's the spirit." Catherine gently urged her mount to pick up the pace. She turned back to Mills and motioned for him to follow.

Catherine had an excellent seat, having ridden since she was a young girl. She'd been forced to leave her favorite horse at her home when she made the trip to London by private coach.

Victoria was sixteen years Catherine's senior, and with no close male relative, it was Victoria's job to see that Catherine made an acceptable match before the Season's end. But what Victoria didn't know was that Catherine hadn't come to London in search of a husband; she had come in search of her father.

Her real father.

She had three clues. The names of three men. She knew one of them was her father, and she intended to find out which one had refused to marry her mother more than twenty years before.

After the man whom she and everyone else always believed was her father, Sir Patrick Reynolds, passed away a year ago, Catherine had found her mother's journal among a box of books in the attic. The diary was in deplorable condition. Over the years dampness had eroded and smeared the ink in many of the entries and rodents had chewed up many of the pages.

But in the readable passages of the neglected diary, Catherine had come to know her mother's deepest secret: The man she had married was not the father of the child she was carrying.

And that child was Catherine.

Lost in thought about her true mission to London, Catherine hadn't realized that Victoria and Mills had fallen behind her until she heard a cry of help. Catherine had a difficult time reining in her horse but finally slowed the animal. She turned the mare around and headed back to find out why Victoria had stopped.

"What's wrong?" Catherine asked as she halted her mount beside her sister. "Are you all right?"

"Yes, I'm fine, but something has happened to Mills."

A moment of concern flashed through Catherine. She didn't see Mills behind them, so she immediately headed back the way they'd come.

"Over here," she heard the groom call out.

It was difficult to make out much of anything in the darkness, but Catherine could see that Mills was not on his mare. He was lying on the ground. She and Victoria stopped their horses. Dismounting from a sidesaddle was difficult, but Catherine managed to kick free of her stirrup and jump down from her mount.

She hurried over to the man and asked, "Are you injured?"

"My horse stepped in a hole and we went down. I think I broke my leg."

"Sweet mercies," she whispered. This was all her fault. "Just lie still. We'll take care of everything."

Victoria knelt down beside Catherine and asked the groom, "How bad are you hurt? Can you ride?"

"I don't think so. I can't move my leg and my horse is limping, too."

Catherine had to come up with a plan of action fast. She looked at Victoria and said, "You stay here with Mills, and I'll ride back and get the carriage for him."

"I can't let you ride alone in the park!" Victoria protested. "Not only is it too dangerous, it would be scandalous."

"Nonsense," Catherine said. "This is not the time to worry about either of those things. Mills is hurt. Besides, it's no longer pitch dark. I'm a much better and faster rider than you. I know exactly how to get back to the carriage. I can return in half the time it would take you."

Catherine watched Victoria's brown gaze look down at the injured groom.

"I must have your promise that you will not stop for anyone or anything until you get to the carriage."

"You have it," Catherine said without hesitation.

"Then be off. Ride fast but be careful. It won't do for you to be seen riding in the park unescorted even for a short time or for so worthy a cause."

"I promise to be careful. Now come help me mount."

With Victoria's help Catherine managed to climb back onto her horse and head in the direction where they left the carriage. She often rode alone on the hills and countryside where she'd grown up, and she had learned early to always be aware of her surroundings so that she could find her way home.

Catherine let the mare have her head and galloped through the fading darkness. The chilling wind stung her cheeks and watered her eyes, but she kept up the fast, ex-hilarating pace, feeling free for the first time since coming to London.

The ribbons of her riding bonnet loosened and the wind blew it to the back of her shoulders. For a moment she felt as if she were back in her village on her favorite horse chasing the dawn.

Suddenly another horse and rider shot out of a side path right in front of her.

Catherine tugged hard on the reins, jerking up her horse's head. The mare reared in panic. Catherine lost her stirrup, and the leather went slack in her hands as the frightened animal came down hard on all fours, and then reared again.

She felt herself falling backward. She tried to grab hold of the horse's neck, her mane, anything to try and calm her mount, but the animal was too frantic.

One moment Catherine was tumbling down, and the next she sprawled on the cold ground flat on her back.

Catherine didn't know if she was breathing. She knew her eyes were open, because she saw the grayish-blue sky swirling above her.

She hadn't been unseated in years and it stunned her.

Suddenly a man loomed over her. "Miss? Miss, are you injured?"

She blinked to clear her blurred sight and managed to focus on the man's face. The first thing she saw was dark, dark eyes filled with concern. She wanted to tell him that only her pride was wounded, but for some unknown reason air seemed trapped in her chest, and she didn't have the breath to speak.

The man poised above her had hair as black as his eyes, and it fell attractively across his broad brow. Her gaze moved down a nose that narrowed at the bridge, making him look ever so handsome. High, angular cheekbones and his clean-shaven chin and jaw looked strong and square. His mouth appeared wide and his lips were full and well defined. They showed the same concern she saw in his eyes.

She knew he spoke to her again, but she remained still, gazing into his handsome face, feeling intrigued and captivated by the strange sensations going on inside her. Was it the intensity of his gaze that did confounding things to the rhythm of her heart, or was the fluttering caused by her fall?

He reached down and shoved one arm beneath her back, and he hooked the other under her legs, lifting her from the ground. Her muscles flinched at his touch more from surprise than fright that she might be in any perilous danger from this stranger.

Catherine felt strength in his arms and the immediate warmth of his hard body pressed against her hip. His impressive, masculine power embraced her as if she weighed no more than a quill.

The scent of shaving soap and leather awakened something soft and feminine inside her, and for a moment she had an intense desire to cuddle into the warmth of the strong arms that held her.

It wasn't until he started walking that her common sense returned.

"What are you doing? Please, sir, put me down."

His arms tightened firmly about her at first, but she pushed at his chest, saying louder, "Unhand me, you scoundrel."

She kicked her legs and squirmed until he set her down on her feet.

Catherine realized she stood far too close to this tall, lithe, wide-shouldered man whose breathing was as fast and rippled as her own. She was quite embarrassed she'd been thrown from her horse, and she tried to restore her dignity by taking a deep breath and pulling on the hem of her black velvet riding coat.

Her gaze locked on his. Catherine's stomach did a slow flip.

"What do you mean by touching me, and where do you think you were taking me?"

His full, feathered eyebrows drew together in a curious expression and framed eyes that shone clear as dark amber glass in the ever brightening light of day.

"I thought you were hurt. I was going to place you on my horse and go for help."

His voice was low, soothing, and as handsome as his face. A glow of unexpected pleasure filled her, causing her stomach to tingle.

There was something compelling about him, and that caused her to be wary but not frightened.

She took a step back and said, "I don't need help, sir. I'm not harmed."

"I'm glad to hear that, miss; however, I didn't know that at the time I offered assistance. My apologies."

Catherine brushed a strand of hair away from her face and took a calming breath. This was not a situation in which she'd expected to find herself.

"If you hadn't come racing out from under the trees like Lord Pinkwater's ghost was after you, you wouldn't have spooked my horse, and I wouldn't have landed on the ground."

He stood looking at her with the right amount of self-importance. She could see by the cut of his fine broadcloth riding coat there was no doubt that a gentleman stood before her and quite possibly one of the titled few.

"You are correct, but how was I to know there would be such a lovely young lady in the park on a horse galloping out of control, especially so early in the morning?"

Catherine shuddered in outrage as she pulled her bonnet back on her head, settling it in place.

"I beg your pardon, sir. I'm a very good horsewoman. My mare was not out of control. We were racing the wind."

A disarming rogue's grin lifted one corner of his mouth. "Racing the wind?"

Her statement had amused him, and that didn't sit well on Catherine's ignited temper or her bruised ego. "And I might add that I was winning."

The stranger threw back his head and laughed.

His laughter was appealing, deep and rich with indulgence. The wide smile on his face, showing even white teeth, made him even more handsome, and something that felt very much like pleasure curled deep inside her. This man stirred feelings in her that she'd never been made aware of before.

She couldn't imagine why she had made that ridiculous comment. She was making things worse for herself, not better. It wasn't like her to get flustered over anything, certainly not a man.

Suddenly she very much wanted to know who he was. She opened her mouth to ask him to identify himself when she remembered Victoria's parting words and Catherine's promise to her not to stop. What was she doing standing here and allowing this man to fascinate her when she needed to get the carriage to Mills?

Catherine had to make a hasty retreat.

She looked around where they stood but saw only the stranger's gelding. "If you are quite finished with your merriment, would you please tell me where my horse is so that I can be on my way?"

He cleared his throat and quickly wiped the grin off his face as best he could and answered, "I'm afraid she ran off after throwing you."

She gasped. "You let my horse run away?"

"Forgive me for having more interest in whether you were hurt than if your mount hightailed it out of the park."

"Merciful goodness," she mumbled to herself as she took in a deep breath, realizing her ribs were sore and her head was pounding.

What was she going to do? She must get to the carriage and take it to Mills and Victoria. It was best she not tell this stranger about her sister. Victoria was strict about her rules, and she would not approve of Catherine talking to this man no matter the unusual circumstances.

"Might I add that a proper young lady should not be out riding alone," the man added.

"I wouldn't be alone and at the mercy of a stranger if you hadn't frightened off my horse. Now, sir, I need to borrow yours."

She reached for the reins he held in his hand and just as her fingers would have closed around the strips of leather he whisked them from her grasp.

An inquisitive expression settled across his face. "Are you daft? I can't let you have my horse."

"Why not?" Catherine asked in her most sensible voice. "I'll return him."

That handsome, roguish grin returned to his face, and Catherine knew without a doubt that under different circumstances this man could do what no other man had ever done—capture her fancy.

"For one, he's not accustomed to strange riders. The other is that no gentleman I know would give a lady his horse."

Fighting her attraction to the man and beginning to feel more her confident self, Catherine said, "So you have no concerns for my needs although you nearly collided into me, causing my mare to unseat me and run off. What kind of gentleman are you, sir?"

He bowed and said, "One who will put you on my saddle and walk you to wherever it is you need to go."

"Rubbish. That is completely unnecessary and will waste time for both of us. You need have no fear I shall harm myself or your horse. I have managed untrained horses before."

"Yes, I see how well you handle horses."

Catherine's blue eyes widened. His retort stung. "Must I remind you that you are the one who rode out in front of me?"

"No. But I must say again, I've never had to worry before about a lady riding on this path so early in the morn."

Catherine opened her mouth to tell him about Mills, but thought better of it. There was still a chance she could keep Victoria from knowing she had talked to this man.

"Sir, I'm on a serious mission, and I don't have time to argue with you over who is at fault for my current predicament. I really need to borrow your horse."

With that, she reached for the reins again and this time her hand covered his.

They both wore gloves, but that didn't keep Catherine from feeling a shock of awareness as her fingers closed over his tight fist. Teasing warmth prickled across her breasts and settled low in her stomach. She was sure she'd never met a man who stirred up her senses like this one.

By the look in his eyes he also felt the same strange sensations. His dark gaze looked deeply into her eyes before sweeping down her face, past the front of her riding habit, down to her waist and back up to her eyes. A strange thrill skittered through her.

"I daresay I've never met a young lady as bold and as unconventional as you."

She let go of his hand as quickly as if it'd been a hot poker.

"And I've never met so stubborn a man. Sir, I don't have time for your obstinacies. There is something I must take care of immediately and I can't do it without a horse."

"Tell me where it is you wish to go, and I will help you onto my horse and walk you there."

"That will take longer than I have. Merciful goodness, you try my patience."

That enchanting smile played along the corners of his lips again. "And you've worn on mine."

The daylight brightened the sky to a light powdery shade of blue. He was obviously as strict about rules as her half sister. He would not be swayed from doing the proper thing.

She'd lived all her life in the country, but she'd often read about the rigid rules of London society, getting old copies of the *Times* and other broadsides when the mail coach came to her town. She knew there was nothing to do but get on the horse and let this man lead her to the carriage. She could only hope that Victoria would not consider her reputation ruined for talking to this man.

"Very well, if it is the only way I can leave immediately, I'll acquiesce to your wishes."

He bowed. "Thank you."

She looked into his eyes and held out her gloved hand.

Their gaze held for a moment longer than was necessary and Catherine's breaths grew uncommonly short. A heat she couldn't explain coiled deep inside her abdomen and rose up to tighten in her chest.

He ignored her hand and instead, settled both his around her waist. They were strong, and comforting. She shivered with pleasure at his firm touch and her arms immediately went up and her hands grabbed onto his broad, firm shoulders so she could help steady herself.

Catherine liked the feel of his body beneath her hands. She liked the warmth that emanated from him and flowed to her.

He boldly took hold of her, lifted her off the ground and onto the saddle. Her black velvet skirt pooled around her legs as she tried to fit her bottom sideways into a saddle made for riding astride a horse. With deliberation, he took the stirrup and was attempting to shorten it to fit her.

Catherine looked down and saw the slack strips of leather in his black gloved hand.

Temptation rose up inside her.

Should she?

Without further thought she reached down and grabbed them from his grasp.

She glanced at his eyes and saw a flicker of shock just before she kicked the horse's flank with the heel of her boot and shot past him.

Catherine held on tight and didn't turn around as she quickly put distance between herself and the handsome stranger.

Two

She had the face of an angel, the tongue of a shrew, and the heart of a thief.

John Wickenham-Thickenham-Fines, the Fifth Earl of Chatwin, bent double in the park. The chase had wrung him. Exhausted him. He placed his hands on his knees trying to suck in enough wind so he could keep going, but it was no use.

He'd had too much to drink and not enough to eat to run like the devil was after him. And the fact that he'd been up all night gambling with his friends didn't help, either.

Besides, his horse and the lady were long out of sight.

"Damnation," he managed to whisper between deep gulps of chilling air.

Who the hell was she? And what was she doing out at dawn anyway?

She'd been outspoken, bold . . . and refreshing. Refreshing? Where the hell had that thought come from? She'd stolen his horse!

She wasn't refreshing, she was a highwayman.

But even as the thought filtered through his mind, a smile slowly eased across his face. A beautiful, intriguing horse thief. Who would have thought it? A slow chuckle rumbled in his throat as he straightened.

Damned if she hadn't gotten his attention in a heartbeat.

He had been trying to make amends for nearly ramming into her, trying to be a gentleman in every way, and she'd hoodwinked him like no one else ever had.

He laughed out loud and shook his head in bemusement.

What kind of young lady had the nerve to steal a man's horse right from under his nose? Obviously, one who had no fear of being caught or the dread of being punished if she were apprehended.

And obviously one who did not know who he was.

She was lovely with French blue eyes, a small nose, and full generous lips that were made for kissing. Yes, soft and sweet and long and deep kisses that satisfied all the way to the soul's core. An unexpected yearning of desire splintered through him and confused him.

No woman had ever confused him, but this one had. She'd met his gaze without flinching and ridden off on his horse as if she were his master.

Had she bewitched him? He shook his head.

No.

Yes.

Maybe he was just light-headed from all the wine he had consumed over the course of the night. Maybe he was just tired and not thinking clearly from lack of sleep and chasing after the fastest horse in London. Anything was better than thinking he had been seduced by a golden-haired angel who had stolen his horse.

How could he be captivated by her?

John couldn't believe he'd actually let the young lady outfox him. He shook his head and chuckled again. By her clothing and her speech he'd known she was a lady of quality, but what was she doing out before daybreak?

Alone?

Was she someone's wife, someone's mistress, or just a mischievous miss?

Something told him she wasn't a titled man's mistress. Even though she had been quite bold, he sensed innocence in her that women of pleasure no longer had. She didn't look at him as a lady who'd known the intimacies shared between a man and a woman.

And if there was one thing John knew well, it was women.

Stealing his horse wasn't the only reason she caught his attention so quickly. Her challenging replies had stimulated him more than any woman he'd ever talked to. But what was even more astonishing was that she didn't seem the least bit impressed with him. That was certainly a change from most of the young ladies he met.

Whatever her purpose for being in the park, she certainly didn't want him knowing about it, or she would have let him take her where she was going. She mentioned she had a pressing mission, yet he observed no fear in her. But something had made her take his horse, and that fascinated him.

And that's what made him want to know more about her—after he got his horse back.

She had to be the excellent horsewoman she'd claimed

to be to handle his gelding. The General wasn't an easy animal to master, and he didn't usually accept unfamiliar riders. She obviously had a way with horses.

There had never been a lady John couldn't instantly enchant until now. This lady had not been interested in his charm.

Her only interest had been in his mount.

She had been self-assured and more than capable of taking care of herself. He didn't think a woman had ever caught him so unaware before. A sly smile returned to his lips. Unlike all the other young ladies he'd met over the years, this one had ensured that he would try to find out more about her.

Everyone in London knew how he valued his horse. Either she didn't know that or didn't care.

Maybe that was what made her so appealing that he wanted to know more about her. Her saucy tongue had pleased him and made him laugh.

For ten years he'd been known as one of the Terrible Threesome, which had now been reduced to a twosome. Chandler Prestwick, Earl of Dunraven, had married during the Season last year. Much to John's surprise, the love-bitten fellow actually seemed happy as a bird singing in a tree.

The gossip sheets hadn't let up on John or his good friend Andrew Terwilliger, the Earl of Dugdale, though he had to admit that the gossips were hardest on his friend about his light pockets, a subject John had never discussed with him. Andrew always seemed to have enough money whenever he needed it, so John didn't intrude.

John raked his hand through his hair and breathed in deeply as he looked around him. The early morning fog patchworked the park like a tattered blanket. His breath warmed the chilly air as daybreak continued to lighten the sky.

He had to think about what he was going to do. He'd been racing Christopher Corey, the Marquis of Westerland, and winning until he'd run right into the path of that lady.

Now, the Marquis would win the race and the money John and his friends had wagered. But that was the least of his worries.

John couldn't rejoin his friends on foot. How could he tell them that he'd been duped by a lovely young lady who had stolen his horse? His pride was already a bit bruised about that. They would never let him live it down if they found out.

Hyde Park covered over six hundred acres. There was no way he could walk it and try to find her. She could be anywhere. It would be more likely that his friends would find him before he found her.

The best thing for him to do would be quit the park as soon as possible. He needed some time to clear his head and think. He'd get another mount and come back later, after his friends left the park.

He'd started walking toward the east rim of the park at a fast pace when he saw his best friend Andrew Terwilliger and two others ride out from under a stand of trees and head straight toward him.

"Damnation," John muttered.

It was too late to try to hide behind a tree. It was clear by how fast they were riding they had already seen him. If it had only been Andrew approaching him, he would have jumped on the back of Andrew's horse and asked him to get him out of the park as fast as possible. But with the talkative Phillips and quiet and studious Wilkins with him, that would be impossible.

What was he going to say to them? He had to come up with a good story about why he was afoot, and he had to do it quickly.

"John, are you all right?" Andrew asked as he and the other two men pulled their mounts up short beside him.

"Yes, yes. I'm fine." John pretended to be dusting off his fawn-colored breeches.

Concern etched lines around Andrew's eyes and along his forehead as he looked John up and down. "Did you get thrown?"

"Well, not exactly," John said truthfully, "but my horse seems to have run off."

"I knew something must have happened when Westerland made it back to the starting point before you and won the race. There's no way that hack of his could have beaten The General."

"What in the devil's name happened to you?" Phillips asked as his large eyes searched the surrounding area of the park.

John looked up at the youngest and shortest of the three men. He should have known that if anyone was going to press the matter, it would be Phillips.

"My horse was spooked and, well, here I am," John said.

"What spooked him?" Phillips asked.

An intriguing young lady.

John cleared his throat. "I'm not sure."

"It's not like The General to throw you and run off," Phillips said, refusing to let the matter drop.

"Yes, you're right. It's not." John refused to give more information than that.

"So really, John, what do you think spooked him?" Wilkins spoke for the first time, after having studied the situation. "Do you think a wild boar roamed into the park?"

John looked up at his heavyset friend who had a spotty complexion and thinning dark hair. "No, nothing like that, I'm sure."

"It was probably just a shadow," Wilkins said. "Sometimes at dawn long tree branches can look as if they're grabbing for you."

"What are you talking about, Wilkins?" Phillips asked with a scowl on his face. "That's nonsense."

"I'm only saying it could have been a low branch, or maybe a large bird flew out of a tree and spooked his horse. Yes, that is probably what happened," Wilkins insisted.

John needed to get away from Phillips and Wilkins and find the lady and The General before anyone else did.

"Andrew, if you'll give me a hand up behind you," John said, "we'll go find The General."

John reached for Andrew's hand to climb up behind him. But before his hand made contact with Andrew's, John heard horses' hooves pounding on the hard-packed ground behind them.

He lowered his hand and turned. Christopher Corey, the Marquis of Westerland, was racing toward them on his newly acquired jet-black stallion.

John made a small, short sound that was almost a laugh, and then swore under his breath again. What else could go wrong?

The Marquis was one of the few men that John didn't get along with. It had all started last year when John flirted with a young lady Westerland later claimed he was serious about. When the young lady declined Westerland's attentions in favor of John's, a rivalry was born that had yet to be put to rest.

To add insult to injury, later that same year, Westerland's father had approached John, offering him his daughter's hand in marriage. John had politely refused even though the duke was offering a large dowry.

As the Earl of Chatwin, John had more than enough income from his estates, and a generous dowry wasn't going to convince him to be leg-shackled. He enjoyed his freedom and had no desire for the responsibilities of a wife and heir. He had plenty of time for that.

John usually stayed clear of Westerland, but last night the Marquis was insistent that his new stallion could beat The General, who was merely a gelding, but the fastest gelding John had ever seen. He'd paid a huge sum for the animal, but he'd been worth every shilling, winning every race—until today.

And all because of a mysterious blue-eyed miss.

When John had had enough of the braggart Westerland, he'd set out to prove him wrong and would have if the lady hadn't ridden into his path.

But right now John had to stop thinking about her and come up with something that would get him out of this awkward situation with some of his dignity intact.

Westerland pulled his horse to a stop in front of the other men and very close to where John stood. The stallion nickered and stomped.

A knowing grin lifted one corner of Westerland's thin lips as he looked down on John. A nasty twinkle sparked in his eyes.

"What happened?" he asked.

"His horse threw him," Phillips answered, though it was clear Westerland had been speaking to John.

"He was spooked," Andrew said, speaking up to defend his friend before cutting his eyes around to Phillips and giving him an irritated glare.

Westerland laughed and brushed a strand of his neatly trimmed blond hair from his forehead. The dandy wore his shirt points so high and his starched-stiff neckcloth so intricately tied that John wondered how the poor man kept from hanging himself.

"The great General? This magnificent gelding I've heard so much about since I returned to London was spooked?" He gave John a mock incredulous stare. "By what, pray tell?"

"A large bird," Andrew said. "You want to make something out of it?"

Westerland sneered at John before looking over at Andrew. "I don't need to. The horse said it all by tossing his master up in the air like a worthless sack of rubbish. Splendid." He laughed again. "What kind of bird did it see? A bloody flying bat from hell?"

John gritted his teeth and held his retort. He couldn't let Westerland goad him into saying something he'd regret. The least said about this matter the better. He had to change the subject from The General.

Thinking quickly, John looked up at Westerland and asked, "Did you think I was going to run out on you and not pay my bet?"

"Not for a moment. You don't know horseflesh, but I've never known you to run out on a wager."

John remained quiet but didn't take his eyes off the Marquis.

Westerland continued. "I came looking for you because Mallory just swore to me that he saw a lady riding your horse. I thought for certain he had spent too much of the night drowning in a tankard of ale and that he must be seeing things, but now that I see you're horseless, I'm wondering if I was wrong."

John's stomach tightened, but he made sure his face didn't show any sign of the struggle inside him. If he ever got his hands on that delectable miss, he would personally strangle her for putting him in this predicament.

"A lady, riding Lord Chatwin's horse, you say?" Wilkins questioned and then looked to John and asked, "Do you really think that's true?"

"Of course not," Andrew said.

"What if she found your horse and just took him?" Phillips asked.

John forced himself to remain quiet and let his friends do the talking. He was hoping they would muddle the situation enough to confuse everyone.

"There is no lady on John's horse," Andrew insisted calmly. "Mallory is full of horse dung. What woman do either of you know who could ride that beast? Besides, it is too early in the morn for a lady to be out in the park, and even if she was, she wouldn't be alone and she wouldn't just happen to get on a stray horse and ride him." Andrew chuckled. "Can't you tell that Mallory was just fooling with Westerland?"

"Maybe. Maybe not," Westerland said, allowing his stallion to paw the ground menacingly close to John's feet. "I think there are a number of ladies who could ride Chatwin's gelding, but I'd like to see the one who could master my stallion."

John didn't flinch but was seething inside that Westerland encouraged his mount's aggression.

"Perhaps we should fan out over the park and find the earl's horse and see if there really is a mysterious lady rider," Westerland said.

John knew he should be a man about this and admit what happened, but something inside him wouldn't let him divulge that a female, no matter how beautiful and intriguing, had outfoxed him. And the last thing he wanted was for these men to be out looking for the lady and The General.

If he didn't make light of this now, every one of them would want to ride the entire six hundred acres until they found his horse.

He reached into his pocket and pulled out a small coin purse. He tossed it to Westerland, who caught it against his chest with his gloved hand.

"There's your money," John said. "You won fair and square. Enjoy it."

"Thank you, Lord Chatwin," he mocked. "I shall enjoy spending every pound."

"Here's my bet, too," Wilkins said, and he dropped a few coins into Westerland's outstretched hand.

"I might as well pay up, too," Phillips answered and added to the coins.

John heard every clink of every coin as they puddled in Westerland's gloved palm.

Everyone looked at Andrew.

"Sorry, old chap, my pockets are to let at the moment. I had faith my dear friend of fifteen years wouldn't let me down. I'll have to settle with you later in the day."

"I'll be around," Westerland said, dropping the loose coins into the pocket of his waistcoat. He then looked at

John again and patted his horse's thick neck. "If you have the stomach for a rematch, let me know."

A sizzle of impatience assailed John. "You can count on it," he said tightly. He intended to get back every last ha'penny.

"Well, if a lady is really riding your horse, I'm not so sure you'll want one." He laughed and turned his stallion around but stopped abruptly. Twisting his head back to see John, he said, "Let me know if you ever get him back."

Then Westerland galloped off, the stallion kicking up clods of dirt.

Wilkins spit on the ground, and then said, "He's such a guttersnipe."

"Yes, a real bastard. Too bad The General didn't beat him," Phillips added.

"Don't worry, fellows," Andrew said in a more cheerful tone. "John will beat him next time and we'll get our money back."

John appreciated the faith his friends had in him. He hated like hell that he'd let them all down, especially Andrew. They'd all lost a considerable sum because of that lady, and John suspected Andrew didn't have the money to lose.

"Do you want us to help you look for your horse?" Wilkins asked.

"No, thank you," John said. "He can't be too far away. You and Phillips head home. Andrew will help me find him."

The men bid their farewells and John watched them ride away.

Andrew glanced down at John as his brows drew together in a frown. "Now, are you going to tell me what the devil happened to The General?"

"Bloody hell." John shook his head and chuckled. He didn't know when he'd been so outdone by anyone. "I might as well. A young lady, no doubt the one we just heard about, stole him right out from under my nose."

Andrew gave him a rueful glare. "No. You're blaming me. Are you sure?"

"Damnation, Andrew, does this sound like something I'd admit to if it weren't true?"

"I guess not. It's just hard to believe a lady would dare such a thing."

"This one did."

"How? Where? I mean, how did she get you off The General in order to steal him? Did she hold you up with a gun or a knife like a common highwayman?"

"No, of course not. Nothing that serious. She simply caught me unaware."

John briefly told him what had happened, ending with "When I helped her onto the saddle to walk her out of the park, she grabbed the leather from my hands and took off. You know how fast the General is. There's no way I could catch him."

"I'm surprised she could control him, and I daresay it was rather brazen of her."

"In one way, yes, but in another, no," John told him, unwilling to explain any better what happened between the two of them.

Andrew rubbed his chin and looked off into the distance as if he were studying something. "You say she was a lady?"

"Yes, and audacious to be sure. But her manner of dress and her speech were that of quality. She was no doxy from the streets."

"Was she young?" Andrew asked.

"Yes."

"Pretty?"

"Very. Why? What does any of this have to do with the fact that she took The General?"

"Nothing, other than the fact that you were, no doubt, paying more attention to how the lady looked than to what she was doing."

Yes, he had been too busy enjoying the way his hands felt around her small waist as he lifted her onto the saddle to notice what she was doing with her hands.

John started to protest but thought better of it. He couldn't fool Andrew. He'd known him too long.

He simply said, "Guilty."

Andrew threw back his head and laughed. "It serves you right that she took your horse."

"Because I noticed what a bright shade of blue her eyes were and how tempting her lips were and how small her waist was?"

"And I'm sure you were enchanted when she smiled at you and that you wanted to kiss her."

Andrew mocked him, but John couldn't find any anger inside himself against his friend, or what was more surprising, he didn't feel any anger toward the lady. It was more bemusement.

"No, you are wrong there."

Andrew's brow wrinkled in a frown. "You didn't want to kiss her?"

"Not the kiss. You bet your jacks I wanted to. But she didn't smile at me. Not once."

That was another thing that made this lady different from all the other ladies in his life. He'd never had a woman appear so self-confident in his presence before and that had impressed him. This was the first time he wasn't completely in control. That was new for him and he wasn't sure he liked it.

But it had left him eager to find out more about her.

"You lie," Andrew said, still not convinced.

"It's true. She didn't seem the least bit intrigued by my charm."

"Good Lord. What's this? Are you losing your touch with the ladies?"

"I hope to hell not."

"Well, she's cheeky to be sure, and I'd say she's one intelligent lady, and I'd like to meet her."

John gave Andrew a curious look. "Why?"

"She knows good horseflesh and she snubbed you."

John smiled and shook his head. "That she did, my friend."

"And?"

"And I'm not up for your verbal sparring right now, Andrew."

His friend grinned. "I understand. I suppose it was a big blow for you to lose your horse—to a pretty miss. Are you going to report her?"

"To whom? The Thames police? My uncle? I want to keep anyone from knowing about this if at all possible."

"It might be too late if Mallory has already seen her."

"That nod cock is probably already spreading it around the clubs."

"So now what do we do? Should we head to Bow Street and find a runner to search for her?"

"If we have to, we will." John reached his hand out to Andrew. "Give me a lift up behind you. The first thing we're going to do is scour the park and see if we can find my horse and the lady who rides him."

Three

"A horse! A horse! My kingdom for a horse!"
Is that quote from Shakespeare's work or from
our very own Lord Chatwin? It's been reported
that he was seen in Hyde Park on foot, brush-
ing dust from his clothing. While on the other
side of the park, a mysterious lady was seen
racing down Rotten Row on his horse. Hmm,
any guesses about what might have transpired
between the earl and the lady?

Lord Truefitt
Society's Daily Column

CATHERINE TWIRLED UNDER the arm of her dance partner as he led her through the first turn of the quadrille. The
tall, blond-haired man was not only handsome, he was a
skilled dancer, too. Lord Westerland's smoothness on his
feet easily made allowances for Catherine's lack of talent
on the dance floor.

The ballroom was on fire with hundreds of brightly
burning candles, lighting the magnificent room with a

grandeur Catherine had never seen in the small village where she grew up. There was a crush of handsome men dressed in elaborately adorned waistcoats of bright colors, expertly tied neckcloths, and fine coats with tails. Beautiful ladies gowned in silks, satins, jewels, and lace crowded the floor.

The room was lively with music, chatter, and laughter. The scent of candle wax, perfume, and liquor lingered in the air. Everything in the room seemed to glimmer and sparkle from the dazzling display of candle glow.

Catherine had spent the first hour of her first party trying to obey Victoria's strict rule that she not act as if this was the first time she'd attended so grand a party. But she was sure she'd failed miserably even though her dance card was full.

She had never even been in a room as large as the ballroom that must have held at least a hundred people. And she had certainly never seen such marvelous floral arrangements, brass candlesticks, and gilt-tipped columns decorating a room.

She'd read about the grand parties given by members of the *ton*. The articles didn't begin to do the events justice as far as she was concerned, especially this one. She had not been prepared for such a spectacular evening.

Catherine felt as if she had been promenaded around the room like she was a lady-in-waiting to the queen. So many gentlemen had begged introductions. Dukes, earls, and viscounts as well as barons and sirs had asked to be presented to Mrs. Goosetree's charge.

Victoria was doing her job as chaperone well, staying by Catherine's side the entire evening, making introduction after introduction until Catherine's head spun with so many names and titles that she couldn't possibly connect them to the right faces again.

Thankfully neither Mills nor her half sister had realized she had a strange horse tied to the back of the carriage when she arrived. After she had seen Mills and Victoria safely home, she and their footman went back out to look for the gentleman to return his horse. They were unable to find the stranger, but they had found her hired hack.

As the night wore on, Catherine kept hoping to see the man whose mount she'd borrowed in the park that morning, but there hadn't been a sign of him. His was one face she wouldn't soon forget. Nor would she forget the way he had made all her senses come alive and awakened those wonderful feelings she'd never experienced before.

He was far more handsome than most men, and he'd been a perfect gentleman right up to the time she left him. She hadn't turned back to look at him because she didn't want to see his reaction to her taking his horse without permission. But she was sure the man was not happy.

It was unbelievable to her that he would leave the park without his magnificent animal. She was left no choice but to have the footman stable the gelding at a private livery so there would be no questions about to whom the animal belonged.

Something had told her he wasn't the kind of man anyone would want to make angry, but Catherine was certain she had.

Over the hours she'd been at the party she'd danced until her feet hurt. All the young men were charming and lavished courtly compliments upon her, including the tall, blond gentleman who now led her around the crowded dance floor.

She had enjoyed herself immensely and was continuing to do so as she bowed and then turned under the arm of her partner.

With her father so ill, she hadn't been to a dance in over two years. Instead, she had spent her evenings with him reading and playing cards. After her first dance of the night, she realized she was much better at playing cards than she was at dancing.

Victoria said they had been invited to six different parties for the evening, but this soirée was the only one they would attend. Victoria had explained that this event would be the biggest party of the night, and any person of importance would find their way to the ballroom at some time during the course of the evening. It was best to stay put so they wouldn't miss anyone whom Victoria considered notable.

But what her sister didn't know was that Catherine was only interested in hearing the names of three men: Mr. William Walker Chatsworth, Mr. Robert Beechman, and Mr. George Wickenham-Thickenham-Fines. She kept thinking that surely someone from one of these families would be present tonight and she would be introduced to them. Once she made contact with someone from each of the families, she would go about finding out which one of the men was her real father.

It would have been so easy to have just told Victoria about her mother's journal and have Vickie make all the right introductions into the families, but she wasn't certain how Vickie would react if she suddenly learned that they were not half sisters after all.

Would Victoria tell her to throw away the journal and forget she'd ever discovered the truth about her parentage? Or would she throw Catherine out of the house and leave her destitute since they didn't have the same father?

Catherine didn't want either of those things to happen. She wanted to find her father and make him tell her why he abandoned her mother. Was he already promised to another? Was he going away to fight in the war, or was he just a cold-hearted man who didn't care about the woman he'd ruined?

Victoria was a widow with a home of her own, and to her nothing was more important than Catherine making a good match, preferably one with a titled gentleman, so she would collect the bonus that had been arranged for her by their father's will.

But the evening wore on and Catherine hadn't heard any of the names. It didn't help her cause that men with titles were usually introduced only by their title names and not their Christian or surnames.

It was quite possible that one or more of these men were from the peerage—a group of people Catherine knew very little about since she'd lived far from London all her life. Unless a titled man was a recluse, he spent at least some of the year in London, and since her county was not known for hunting, fishing, or racing, very few had made it to her hometown.

Maybe it wasn't rational to want to find her real father. She knew it would be a difficult task. But ever since she'd found out the truth, she'd felt as if a part of her was missing. She had lived a lie through no fault of her own.

Catherine wanted to know the truth. Who was her father and why hadn't he married her mother?

The quadrille had come to an end. Catherine faced her partner and he bowed. She smiled and curtsied, hoping he hadn't noticed that she had been distracted during the dance. Thankfully the tempo had been quite fast and there hadn't been much opportunity to talk.

"You are an excellent dancer, Miss Reynolds."

She first answered the Marquis with a smile and then said, "Your flattery of my skills is not warranted, my lord, but it is appreciated. Thank you."

"Perhaps you will favor me with another dance before the evening is over."

"It is already very late and I don't think we shall be staying much longer," she said, deliberately avoiding responding to his specific request.

Victoria had given her strict instructions not to spend too much time with any one gentleman her first evening and not to encourage any of them to ask for a second dance or to call on her tomorrow. Victoria had reminded her that men liked to stake a claim on a young lady's affections early in the Season, and when they did so, it limited the lady's options.

And Victoria would have none of that.

So it would be Victoria who would decide which gentleman was allowed to call on her.

"I'll see you back to Mrs. Goosetree," he said.

"Thank you, my lord."

Catherine allowed the Marquis to lead her off the dance floor and back to her sister, who was standing with a tall, buxom young lady who was introduced as Lady Lynette Knightington. The Duke of Knightington's daughter, Victoria emphasized, as Catherine forced herself not to stare at the dark red birthmark that covered most of the young lady's cheek.

Catherine had not seen it until Lady Lynette turned toward her. From one side it wasn't visible at all. She had large expressive green eyes and a deep voice. Even with the unsightly birthmark on her cheek, she was truly lovely, Catherine thought.

It was clear that the Marquis, Lady Lynette, and Victoria had known each other quite a long time as they chatted freely, engaging Catherine in conversation about the Northern Coast. Victoria complimented the Marquis on his knowledge of the area. A short time later the bell sounded for the next dance to begin, and the Marquis bowed and left the three ladies alone.

"Catherine, I must tell you that Lady Lynette is the perfect lady for you to talk to. She is always at the best parties and knows everyone in the *ton*. Not only that, but everyone adores her. You couldn't make a better friend in all of London."

"Enough of that kind of talk, Mrs. Goosetree, or I'll start blushing, and my face is already red enough."

Lady Lynette laughed at her own reference to her disfigurement, and Catherine marveled at what confidence the young lady must have to be able to make a joke about herself.

"In that case I will make my way to the buffet room and leave you two alone for a few minutes so you can get to know each other."

"I shall be delighted to entertain your sister for a few minutes. Take your time."

"Thank you, my lady. I'll make another pass around the rooms before I return to see if anyone has arrived to whom I might present Catherine."

After Victoria turned away, Lady Lynette looked directly into Catherine's eyes and said, "So tell me, are you enjoying your first party of the Season?"

"Very much, but I had no idea the event would be so crowded. London Society is very different from the village where I grew up."

"Is this your first trip to London?"

"Yes."

Lady Lynette's eyes took on a faraway quality and she said in a sighing voice, "Ah, there is nothing like a Season in London."

"From what little I've seen, I'm sure there's nothing to compare it to."

"Not even close. Each year I so look forward to the parties, the opera, the clothing, the people and"—suddenly she hesitated and the faraway look was replaced with a mischievous glimmer—"and the gossip."

Oh, yes, Catherine was getting acquainted with the gossip columns and how fast one little incident could get around Town.

"Do you stay in London the entire year?" Catherine asked, not wanting to be drawn into a subject she didn't care to discuss.

"No, we travel to our home in Kent by the end of June each year. I would love to return to Town during the winter. I miss the sights and sounds and even the smells of London, but my parents always have too many guests visiting us for house parties, and they won't let me travel back here with just a companion."

"Well, perhaps that will change one day and you will get your wish."

She smiled. "Perhaps." Lady Lynette bent closer to Catherine and said, "Has any young man caught your fancy since you've been here? If so, tell me and I will let you know all about him."

Catherine smiled. "I'm afraid I haven't been in London very long, and as the Season just started, this is my first party."

"But I've seen you dance with several gentlemen. Surely one of them has caught your eye."

The one who had caught her eye was not in attendance, and she had no idea what his name was.

"Not yet," she answered cautiously, "but the night is still young."

Lady Lynette bent closer to Catherine and asked, "How did you like the Marquis of Westerland? He's quite handsome, isn't he?"

"Yes. And he's charming, as have been all the gentlemen I've met and danced with this evening."

But the face of only one man had stayed in her mind.

"Hmm, I'm told that sometimes it only takes one look to fall in love."

"Is that right?" Catherine asked, wondering what had made Lady Lynette make such a comment.

"Oh, yes," Lady Lynette insisted. "You do believe in love, don't you?"

Catherine looked into Lynette's very pretty eyes, but it was the dark eyes of a stranger that filled her mind.

"One look to fall in love?" She questioned herself more than Lady Lynette. "I suppose I do. I've never had much reason to think about it."

The duke's daughter leaned closer to Catherine again. With a smile on her face she said, "Which can only mean you've never been in love. Am I right?"

Lady Lynette sounded wise beyond her years. Maybe from experience?

"You are right," Catherine admitted with a smile.

"Good. I was sure of it. Now, is there someone here you would like to meet?" She looked around the room. "I know everyone."

Catherine's heartbeat quickened. Yes, there was someone she wanted to be introduced to and it wasn't the handsome young man who kept invading her thoughts. This was her chance to find out a few things about Mr. William Walker Chatsworth, Mr. Robert Taylor Beechman, and Mr. George Wickenham-Thickenham-Fines.

"As a matter of fact, you can help me. I remember my father mentioning the names of some gentlemen he knew years ago when he frequented London. Perhaps you can tell me if any of them are here tonight. I'd like to meet them and say hello."

"Of course, what are the names?"

She took a deep breath, grateful for the opportunity to get some information about the men. "One is Mr. William Walker Chatsworth."

"Oh, yes, Mr. Chatsworth." A deep throaty laugh passed her lips. "You say your father knew him. I'm not surprised. He was all the rage a few years ago. One of those rare tall dark Englishmen. He was so handsome. In his day, he made all the young ladies swoon, but he's a bit dotty now."

Catherine pursed her lips in confusion. "Really? In what way?"

"He seldom leaves his house because he hates anything green."

"He what?" Catherine asked, taken aback.

"He has nothing the color green in his house. I've been inside, so I can attest to this fact. Nor will he eat anything green. And of course many things outside are green with all the beautiful shrubs, yews, and trees and such, so he seldom leaves his house. And when he does go out, he always walks with his head down."

How odd.

Could someone like that be her father? A dreadful thought. She knew her quest to find her father would be challenging, but she hadn't expected it to be alarming. What could have happened to make him hate the color green?

"But he loves visitors," Lady Lynette continued. "And he is an absolute champion at most card games. I'm told he enjoys it when someone will take the time to stop by and sit and play a game with him."

It was good to know he loved to play cards. Catherine was quite good at most games. Perhaps she could figure out a way to meet the peculiar Mr. Chatsworth and see what she could find out about his past.

But she found it most disturbing to think that a man who was that stricken by the color of green could be her father.

"What about a gentleman named Mr. Robert Beechman?" Catherine asked.

Lady Lynette screwed her face into a frown as she pondered. "Yes, Mr. Beechman. I have to say he's another peculiar person."

Dare she ask?

"In what way?"

"I don't know as much about him, but I do know that he walks everywhere he goes. He refuses to ride in a carriage or sit on a horse. He's rather dour most of the time, but he will attend parties maybe three or four times in a Season as long as it's not too far to walk."

"That is odd. Why won't he ride in a carriage or on a horse?"

"No one seems to know. I'm told he never goes to his estate in Kent anymore." Suddenly Lynette's eyes got bigger. "And I hear he has an exceptional display of snuff-boxes"—she bent close to Catherine's ear—"if you know what I mean."

Catherine wrinkled her brow, frustrated by the information she was getting on the men. "Ah, no, I don't believe I do."

"Some of them have nudes painted on them. Ladies and

gentlemen, and sometimes very close together on the same box."

"You mean—" Catherine stopped. What was Lynette trying to say about a man who could possibly be her father? Whatever it was, she wasn't sure she wanted to know.

Catherine continued with "Well, that really doesn't seem so strange. Most all of the famous painters like Michelangelo and Da Vinci painted nudes and sometime male and female very close together. Don't you think?" Catherine asked, not sure she really knew what Lynette was implying.

Lady Lynette's eyebrows raised a notch. She hesitated a moment before saying, "Yes, I believe they did."

Victoria wasn't off the mark when she said the duke's daughter knew everyone. Catherine was almost fearful to ask about the third man, but since her newfound friend was so full of knowledge, she had to. She had no doubt one of the men was her father and wanted to find him no matter his circumstances.

"How about—"

"Lady Lynette, what a dear you've been to keep my sister entertained for so long," Victoria said as she stopped beside Catherine.

What rotten luck!

Catherine knew there would be no more questions about the gentleman she sought. But with the stranger and the two eccentric men Lady Lynette told her about, she had enough to think about for now.

*J*OHN AND ANDREW took off their greatcoats, hats, and gloves and handed them to the servant at the entryway to the Grand Ballroom. They had made an appearance at every party in London that John knew about, and this was the only one left.

If he didn't find her here, he was calling it a night. He had been mocked and laughed at enough for one evening. He usually didn't mind the tittle-tattle of the gossip sheets so much. He'd thrived on them for years—the more that was said about him the better—but it seemed that everyone this evening wanted to talk about the lady who was seen riding his horse.

If he knew who wrote those damned gabble grinders, he could find her. They seemed to know everything and within minutes of it happening. Someone had left the park and went immediately to Lord Truefitt, whoever the hell he was, and told the gossip about the incident in the park.

John doubted it was Wilkins, though Phillips might have told the story over and over again. He wouldn't put it past Mallory and Westerland to spread the rumor to everyone they knew. No doubt they were all having a big laugh off the possibility of it. Several of his friends had questioned him about the writings that had appeared in the afternoon edition of "Society's Daily Column."

He had hoped to find the lovely horse thief before now, but so far the parties had yielded no more than the park had that morning. He and Andrew had ridden around the perimeter of the park, the paths, and around the Serpentine for most of the morning with no luck.

He was at a loss how to go about searching for her.

He'd told every man tonight the same thing: "You know I never listen to the gossip sheets, but The General is safe."

He only wished he knew for sure that was true.

"What are you going to do if you can't find her?" Andrew asked John.

"The hell if I know," John muttered, but then immediately said, "I have a man checking all the liveries in Town, but how can I possibly check all the private stables? I'll hire someone from Bow Street. It's like she disappeared into thin air."

"We both know that is impossible."

He turned and looked at Andrew as they headed toward the ballroom. "Of course. She simply rode out of the park, but to where?"

"And why? Why did she want The General? That's what we must find out. Surely she didn't want to try to sell him. The horse is too well known."

"No, I'm sure it's nothing like that. She said something about being on a mission and needing to borrow him."

Andrew gave him a wry look. "Are you sure you would recognize her? Maybe you've seen her tonight and you didn't know it. I mean, it was still rather dark in the park."

The lady's face flashed into John's mind. Blue eyes, full lips, saucy tongue, and more backbone than he'd ever seen.

"Oh, no, Andrew. I would know her anywhere. She's not the kind of lady you would soon forget."

"Hmm. That could be a problem, you know."

"Why?"

"When a lady stops being just another pretty face and becomes something more, you're in trouble."

"You think that's what I'm saying?"

"Aren't you?"

"Hell, no," John said with more irritation than he was feeling. "She stole my horse when I was trying to help her. I've been teased about it all night."

"And that pricked your pride."

"Andrew," John said tightly, knowing that was all he needed to say when his friend went too far.

They stopped at the entrance to the ballroom and looked out over the crowd. There were at least a hundred people in attendance. The *ton* were inveterate party goers and would stay and dance as long as there was music and drink.

"Looks like there will be a crush until the host runs us off," Andrew said. "There's no other party that I know about. We've made the rounds. If she's not here, we're not going to find her tonight."

"I am aware of that, Andrew."

John heard his name called and looked up to see one of the young bachelors he barely knew walking by with two other men.

"Chatwin, where's your horse?"

The young dandy waved to John, but thankfully he and his friends merely laughed and kept going.

"Don't pay them any mind," Andrew said.

"I'm not," John replied, knowing it was a lie. He did mind. He was becoming the laughingstock, all because of some blue-eyed horse thief.

"I don't believe she's here. Though I can't say I'd be hitting the parties if I had stolen an earl's horse."

"Why don't we head over to White's? No one will bother you there."

John shook his head. "I'm not going to give up until I've thoroughly looked over everyone in this place."

"After you have, why don't you go see Anne? She'll take your mind off the day."

"I'm in no mood for a mistress tonight. Besides, I've already given her a parting gift."

"Really? This is news. You didn't tell me. When did you find someone else?"

"I haven't. Not yet," John said as they started walking into the ballroom.

"Are you sure you want to leave her before you find someone else?"

He was sure.

"Anne was happy with the diamond-and-emerald necklace I picked out for her, and she told me her door was always open. But I've been ready for a change for a long time."

"You always give the same gift, diamonds and emeralds. Why?" Andrew asked.

"Ladies love them."

"They also love pearls."

John had always thought he'd give pearls to the lady he loved above all others. The problem was that he was certain he hadn't ever come close to truly being in love, though he had great appreciation for all women.

All of a sudden John tensed. His body grew rigid as his stomach knotted with an unfamiliar feeling that reminded him of jealousy. Surprise hit him in the chest with the force of a meaty fist.

"What is it?" Andrew asked. "Do you see her?"

"Yes," John said tightly, unused to the sudden angry feelings swirling around inside him. "She's walking off the dance floor, and look who she is with."

"Who? Damnation, John, everyone's walking off the dance floor because the music has stopped. Which one?"

"The lady with the Marquis of Westerland."

"No, no," Andrew said, shaking his head in disbelief. "Not the young lady with Westerland? That dandy! Is she the one?"

"That's her."

John's heart tripped.

"Damnation," Andrew muttered as he looked at John in outrage. "You were set up."

John jerked around to his friend. "What are you talking about?"

"That bastard Westerland. He knew the route you were taking in the race just as you knew his. I think he planned her to run out in front of you to keep you from winning the race."

John gave Andrew a quizzical glance before zeroing his gaze back on the lady. "The race was close. Once she stopped me for any amount of time, he would have won. Why would she run off with my horse?"

"You said she had a mission. Look at the ridicule you've taken throughout the day and tonight about an unknown lady riding your horse. John, taking The General was her mission."

Four

"*WESTERLAND'S A BASTARD,* but I can't believe he would stoop so low as to solicit a young lady's help to make me lose. It would have been too dangerous. We almost collided. She could have been killed. I'm certain it wasn't a setup."

"John, it's not like you to be gullible just because she's a beauty."

"I'm not being gullible or naïve about this," he said, unable to take his eyes off her.

"You said yourself that she must be an excellent horsewoman to be able to handle The General. She probably knew exactly how close to come to your horse without running into you."

"Trust me on this, Andrew. It doesn't feel right that he was in on this with her. I don't know how, but I know the two of them are not in this together."

John couldn't believe how beautiful she was in her low-cut beige gown with the wide satin bands circling the high waist and flowing skirt. Strips of ribbons and tiny white and pink flowers adorned her blond hair.

Westerland said something to her and she smiled at him. John's stomach twisted. She hadn't smiled at him, not even when he'd tried to charm her.

"I'd wager a handsome sum I'm right about this," Andrew insisted. "And I'd bet a few more pounds he's the one who leaked her taking The General to the gossips."

"That I agree with," John conceded.

"He wasn't satisfied with just winning the race; he wanted to make you look the fool, too."

Sometimes Andrew went over the top, and he was just about at that point with John right now, even though his friend made a good point. He couldn't put anything past the pompous Marquis.

"I'll soon find out."

John quickly sidestepped behind a column as the lady and Westerland left the dance floor. He didn't want her to see him while she was with Westerland.

When he talked to her, he wanted her to be alone.

"I'm going to stay out of sight for now, Andrew. Go and see what you can find out for me. I need to at least know her name and who her sponsor is before I approach her."

"Good idea. Leave it to me. I'll find out who she is and exactly what she is up to."

John reached out and grabbed Andrew's arm before he could walk away. "I'll find out what she's up to. You just get me her name."

His friend started to object but seemed to realize it wasn't his place to question John on this. Andrew simply nodded and walked away without further comment.

John was patient and stayed out of sight while Andrew

gathered information about the mysterious miss, and half an hour later he caught Miss Catherine Reynolds alone as she walked out of the ladies' retiring room.

She didn't see him at first and only looked over at him when he fell into step beside her midway down the corridor that led into the main party room. Her big, beautiful blue eyes rounded in surprise as she immediately recognized him.

She stopped in the dimly lit hallway and asked, "Sir, where have you been?"

Her instantaneous accusation stunned him for a moment. She was incredible. And beguiling.

"Where have *I* been?" he demanded. "Where do you think, Miss Reynolds?" He saw her lashes blink when he said her name. "Surprised? Yes, I now know who you are, and I've been looking for you since dawn."

She remained composed. "That's strange, because I've been looking for you as well."

"Obviously, not very hard."

He took a step toward her. He was clearly closer to her than good manners allowed, but she didn't back away and in no way appeared intimidated by him, nor was she flustered by him. For reasons he didn't understand, she was taking him to task.

"It would have helped had I known your name," she said.

"Would that have changed your actions this morning?"

"No," she said without hesitation or guilt.

Her truthfulness impressed him. She was apparently not a bit contrite about what she'd done.

"But," she added, "it would have helped me locate you when I tried to return your horse."

John tried to keep his frustration down and his voice low so as not to call attention to their conversation.

He said, "Then why did you run off like the hounds of Hades were after you before you knew my name?"

She lightly bit into her bottom lip and pulled it into her mouth as if she had to ponder what to say next. John had an instant urge to grab her and kiss her right there in the corridor where anyone could happen by and see him. Was she trying to seduce him?

"I was in a hurry," she finally said.

He looked straight into her eyes, bent his head close to hers, and said, "That I already know. Now where is my horse?"

She remained composed despite his nearness and his threatening stare. Usually his husky whisper was effective in intimidating. Any other lady and most men would have nervously backed away. She remained unaffected by his formidable approach.

"Stabled and well cared for, sir, not that you seemed to care a penny."

Again she astonished him. Maybe *incredible* wasn't a strong-enough word for her. She was beyond the pale. She was madness. And he was fascinated.

"You astound me, Miss Reynolds. How can you think I don't care about an animal that has won every race he's been in until this morning?"

She was unbelievable, exasperating, and for some strange reason he couldn't fathom, he was enjoying their banter.

"That's the way it appears to me."

"What are you talking about?" he asked, feeling more and more intrigued by her attitude and the way she stood up to him. "The General is a Thoroughbred, and if he is harmed in any way—"

"Harmed? By me?"

"By anyone."

She challenged him with her expression, with the way she refused to back away from him. If she'd been a man he would have already had her shackled at Newgate.

"Sir, if I had an animal like yours, I would have waited in the park for him to be returned to me."

She was acting as if this were his fault. She was bolder than any young lady he had ever met and far more forthright than any woman should be. He should be furious with her for taking his horse and trying to lay the blame on him.

But he wasn't. Instead, he was engrossed in her.

Had she really tried to find him? "Just how long did you think I was supposed to wait for you? I left and searched the park over for you."

"I told you I only needed to borrow him. You should have believed me."

He was trying not to look at the long dark lashes that hooded her vibrant blue eyes, or the natural pink color of her tempting lips. He was trying to remember that she had duped him and that his friends and foes alike were making fun of him about the lady who rode away on his horse.

But when he looked at her, he couldn't remember any of that. All he saw was a beautiful and tempting and exciting young lady.

"I don't know you. How was I to know you planned to return him? I think it's going a bit far to ask me to believe a horse thief."

Her chest rose with indignation as her eyes widened again. "Horse thief?"

"Yes," he said calmly.

"Sir, you have some nerve to suggest such a thing. I would never do that!"

"Oh, but you did. You took The General without my consent."

"Yes, but I didn't take him without your *knowledge*. I am not a horse thief. A horse borrower, yes, but never a thief. What kind of gentleman lays that kind of accusation on a defenseless lady?"

Defenseless? Was she mad?

He wanted to be enraged at her logic, but he wasn't. He was enchanted by the way she took him to task for something that was entirely her fault. Was she deliberately trying to seduce him in this way?

He didn't take his gaze from her face. Obviously she sensed he had no real resentment inside him about what she'd done, and he wasn't so sure that was a good thing. It allowed her too much control.

"Defenseless? You?" He laughed and shook his head. "Not even in your dreams would you be considered defenseless, Miss Reynolds. You are incredible."

And she was.

"And so are you, sir. Imagine leaving such a fine animal in the care of a stranger, but—" She paused and softly bit down on her lower lip as she looked up at him with those irresistible blue eyes.

Her voice had softened and her gaze swept up and down his face, sending a flash of heat scorching through him. She moistened her lips before sinking her teeth once again into her lower lip. John's lower body reacted swiftly, hotly, to the innocent yet provocative movement of her mouth.

He swallowed with difficulty. His throat wasn't the only thing that suddenly felt thick and tight.

It astounded him at how attracted he was to her after all she had put him through. He had to do something to counter it.

He managed to say, "Do you have any idea at the hell you—" Her eyebrows shot up. "Excuse me, the strife I've been through today because of you?"

Her eyes searched his as she said quite innocently, "Perhaps not."

"Everyone—and I mean everyone—I know has asked me about the mysterious lady who was seen riding my horse. Did it not cross your mind that if I were in the park that I might have friends with me who would want to know what happened to my mount?"

At last a contrite expression softened her face.

"I must admit that I acted so quickly that I failed to think about those things." A soft sigh passed her lips. "Perhaps I could have made my intentions on returning your horse clearer."

Finally a concession. A small one made on a sensual sigh.

His exasperation evaporated as quickly as a fine mist when struck by sunshine.

"Perhaps you could have let me help with whatever it was that made you so desperate that you took my property without my consent. That was a very dangerous thing for you to do."

She reached up and with a beautiful, delicate hand brushed a strand of hair from her face. "I couldn't allow you to help me. I'm truly sorry if I caused you concern. That was not my intention. Is there any way I can make amends?"

Well, yes . . .

He was quiet for a moment as he digested what she'd said. Did she really know what she was asking? Could he take advantage of her?

"You could start by returning my horse."

"Oh, but of course that goes without saying. I've had him stabled at a small private livery where he has received the best of care. Shall I have him returned to you first thing tomorrow morning?"

John felt a smile tugging on the corners of his lips as an idea formed in his mind. He hadn't come up with such an intriguing design in years.

"Yes, that would be appropriate," he told her.

"Splendid."

She smiled at him, and for the first time in his life John felt as if his heart fluttered. He didn't understand his reaction to her. He loved all women. He found them enthralling, desirable, and loved to be with them, but there was something different about what he was feeling for this lady, and it intrigued and worried him at the same time.

"When and where would you like me to have him delivered?" she asked.

John's smile widened.

A feeling of confident victory swept over him and he felt completely relaxed. There was a good reason he'd been one of the infamous Terrible Threesome for more than ten years. And a reason he was now one of the Terrible Twosome the gossips enjoyed slandering each evening in their broadsides.

"Where? Hyde Park. When? Tomorrow just before dawn."

It was her turn to give him an incredulous look. "You jest, sir."

"No, Miss Reynolds, I do not. Bring him to the same place where we met and you left me this morning. The same way. Alone."

Her eyes sparkled with outrage, and for the first time

she took a step away from him. At last she was showing some sign that he was affecting her.

"That would be madness; I don't even know your name."

He folded his arms across his chest, thinking that if he didn't do something to inhibit his hands he just might pull her to him and kiss those delectable lips that were so full of indignation.

He made a half bow and then smiled at her. "I'm Chatwin."

John watched as her eyes rounded in surprise.

"The earl?" she asked.

He may not know much about her, but it was clear she'd heard a few things about him. "Perhaps not the earl," he said, "but certainly an earl."

"You are one of the Terrible Threesome I've heard so much about."

He shrugged. "Yes, I do have the distinction of holding that dubious title. Though I believe that now most everyone in London is considering me one of a Terrible Twosome."

She huffed without any real indignation to her voice. "It sounds like you consider it a badge of honor to be so called."

"I might as well. It appears that I'm not going to lose the title anytime soon."

"And it sounds to me as if you don't want to."

He folded his arms across his chest. "I've no complaints about it. It has served me well."

Miss Reynolds took another step back. "Surely, my lord, you know that if I were caught alone with you in the park, my reputation would be in tatters."

"I agree—if you were caught."

Five

CATHERINE OPENED HER mouth to immediately decline, but for some irrational reason she went against her good common sense and hedged by saying, "You can't be serious that you want me to meet you alone at dawn?"

A slow delicious-looking smile eased across his full lips, and a mischievous twinkle appeared in his eyes. "Oh, but I am."

"Sir, you are no gentleman."

"Guilty again."

How could he look so charming while asking her to do something so forbidden?

"A true gentleman would not ask such a request of a lady."

"Of course he would. Assignations are arranged all the time. You just don't hear about them because they are secret."

"Well, that's not how we do things in the village where I'm from."

"Really? Might I point out that you were alone in the park this morning?"

"No." She shook her head once, then stopped. "I mean yes, I was when you saw me, but no, I wasn't alone in the park. My half sister, Mrs. Victoria Goosetree, was with me."

His brow wrinkled a bit as a doubtful expression eased across his handsome face. "I have met Mrs. Goosetree. I'm sure I would have noticed had she been there with you, Miss Reynolds. You were quite alone."

Catherine took a deep breath and looked up and down the corridor to see if their tête-à-tête had caught anyone's attention. For now it seemed no one was watching them, but she feared that at any moment Victoria would appear from around the corner and demand to know why she was talking with Lord Chatwin in the middle of a dimly lit hallway.

"Look, I know it must sound confusing. Vickie was not with me at the time I met you because our groom was injured and she had to stay with him. I was riding to get our carriage for them when you almost ran me over."

His expression turned from doubt to concern. "If you needed help, why did you not tell me and allow me to assist you?"

She took a deep breath and glanced down the corridor again. At last he understood.

"Victoria insisted I not stop and talk to anyone. I didn't want to cause any further distress by showing up with a stranger. Thankfully, we managed to get our groom into the carriage and home."

"But I could have helped you."

"I didn't want you to help me."

"But I did when your horse ran off; you stole mine."

Catherine gasped. She was trying to remain unflustered but finding the task more and more difficult.

"I borrowed your horse. Victoria is a stickler for obeying the rules, and she insisted I not stop for any reason. Besides, not only was I capable of handling the situation, I didn't want her to know that I'd talked to you."

"Surely she would have understood under the circumstances?"

"You say you have met Victoria Goosetree, but you obviously don't know her."

"Is she your sponsor for the Season?"

"Yes."

"Your parents are deceased?"

She nodded. "Even now, I know Vickie would be appalled if she knew I was speaking to you when I haven't been properly presented to you. She's extremely strict about Society's rules."

His gaze swept down her face and lingered on her lips before darting back up to her eyes again. His bold assessment caused a curl of anticipation low in her stomach and sent a shiver of awareness spiking from her breasts to her toes.

Good heavens. She'd never had such a wonderful feeling before. What was it about him that made her react so differently from all other men she had met?

"I believe we are past formal introductions by now, aren't we, Miss Reynolds?"

Immensely so.

Her gaze held fast to his. "Yes, without a doubt we are," she answered.

"So, does that mean you will meet me in the morning and return my horse?"

As Catherine looked into Lord Chatwin's handsome face, she saw laughter, high spirits, and confidence. And she was drawn to all those things. She hadn't been around a lot of men since she came of age because her father had been so ill, but surely of the gentlemen she had met, none of them had affected her like the entrancing, flirtatious man before her.

He was compelling, self-assured, and captivating. No wonder his attention was so sought after by all the young ladies.

She could admit to herself that she found the idea of meeting him in secret thrilling, tempting even. She would absolutely love to see him riding astride his magnificent horse with his hair blowing away from his face and the ends of his neckcloth flapping softly in the wind.

Most gentlemen looked uncomfortable and rigid sitting on a horse, not knowing how to move with the animal. Somehow Catherine knew that this man would sit tall but comfortable in the saddle, his body moving easily with each stride of his mount.

Yes, she had no doubt that he would look simply dashing sitting in the saddle atop the horse he called The General.

"Might I think your hesitancy means you are considering my request?" he asked.

She cleared her throat and her wayward thoughts and lifted her shoulders and her chin defiantly. "Absolutely not, sir. I will not meet you. If I were caught in the park alone with you, I'd be banned from every respectable household in Town."

Catherine knew she couldn't allow that to happen no matter how tempting his offer. She had every intention of gaining introductions to the three men she sought. Once she made contact with someone from each of the families, she needed to be accepted into their homes. That was the only way she could start trying to discover her real father.

Lord Chatwin moved a step closer to her. "No one will see us. I promise."

She felt his breath flutter past her ear and her chest tightened. For reasons she really didn't understand, she hedged again.

"How can you promise such a thing? Someone saw me riding your horse just this morning and now everyone is talking about it."

For the first time that evening she saw displeasure ease across his face.

"I know. I've heard about nothing else all evening. You certainly know how to start gossip."

"I can assure you that was not my intention."

"I'm beginning to believe you. No one knows you are that lady, do they?"

She considered what he said. "Not that I know about, and I desire that it stay that way."

"I don't intend to tell. Do you?"

"Certainly not."

"Good. There's no reason to think your luck won't hold for tomorrow morning as well."

"But, my lord, it would be folly to tempt fate twice."

He smiled. "I think there is every reason to tempt fate more than once. I do it every day."

"I am not that bold."

"You don't give yourself enough credit. I think you are."

A twinkle shone in his eyes and his gaze stayed steadily on hers. For a moment she could believe he spoke the truth. Was she truly the way he saw her?

"Catherine, there you are. I've been looking everywhere for you. You must not wander away from me again."

Catherine turned at the sound of her sister's voice. Victoria hurried toward her so swiftly that her light brown skirts billowed behind her long legs.

Lord Chatwin took a short step away from Catherine as Victoria almost hurled herself between the two of them. Catherine had to step back in order to make room for her.

"It's so nice to see you, my lord. It looks as if you are doing well," Victoria said to the earl.

"Quite fine, Mrs. Goosetree. And might I say you are looking lovely this evening."

Victoria gave him a tight smile, but she couldn't keep her brown eyes from sparkling at his flattery. "Thank you, my lord. How nice of you to notice me when there are so many beautiful ladies in attendance tonight." She cleared her throat and lifted her chin slightly while letting her lips relax from the strained smile. "I see you have made the acquaintance of my half sister, Miss Catherine Reynolds."

"We were just getting better acquainted," he said as calmly as if they had been talking about the weather.

"Yes, I saw how *closely* you were getting acquainted," she said rather stiffly and turned from Lord Chatwin and centered her pointed gaze on Catherine. "I wasn't aware you two had met. Who presented you to the earl, Catherine?"

Merciful goodness.

"Oh, well it was . . ."

Her mind raced. What was she going to say? She didn't want to lie to Victoria, but how could she tell her no one had introduced them? Should she own up to having met Lord Chatwin in the park earlier that morning when she was riding?

No.

She had to think of something. Fast.

"Why are you hesitating?" Victoria asked.

"Perhaps because she can't immediately remember the name of the person who did the honors," Lord Chatwin said.

Catherine almost gasped out loud. He dare speak for her? And to say something that was so out of character. She had a very good memory.

"Miss Reynolds was just telling me how this was her first party, and that she was having trouble remembering the names of all the people she's met."

Victoria turned back to the earl with a confused expression on her face. "It's true I've kept her busy tonight meeting everyone in attendance. But what does surprise me is that Catherine is usually so very good with names and faces." Vickie paused. "So tell me who presented her to you so that I might thank them."

Lord Chatwin cleared his throat. "It was his grace the Duke of Beaumont. You do know him, don't you, Mrs. Goosetree?"

Her lashes fluttered. She was clearly impressed.

"Oh, my, yes, yes, of course. We were first introduced years ago. I didn't realize His Grace was here tonight, nor did I know Catherine had been presented to him either. I haven't seen him this evening." She looked around the room smiling as she touched her hand to her hair. "I don't know how I could have missed, but how splendid of him to do the honors."

"I believe he was on his way out when he left us," Lord Chatwin said.

Victoria turned a slightly disapproving face to Catherine. "You must remember the names of all the dukes, my dear. Forgetting any name is unacceptable, but forgetting a duke is an outrage."

Catherine bristled and forced herself not to look at Lord Chatwin. He hadn't managed to help her at all. She knew enough to know that forgetting the name of any titled gentleman was just as big a faux pas as conversing with a man to whom she hadn't been properly introduced.

"I know it's unforgivable, Vickie." She threw Lord Chatwin a "thank you for nothing" look, but to her half sister she smiled and said, "It won't happen again. I promise."

"Good." Victoria returned her focus to Lord Chatwin. "Now, my lord, was there a particular reason the duke made introductions to my sister tonight?"

Catherine was surprised at Victoria's impudence.

Lord Chatwin cleared his throat again and said, "Yes. Absolutely. With your permission, of course, I'd like to call on Miss Reynolds tomorrow afternoon and take her for a ride in Hyde Park."

Victoria shook open her fan as she smiled sweetly at him. She pretended to ponder a moment or two before she said, "How lovely that would be, but alas, Catherine isn't available. Unfortunately I've already agreed to other plans for her for tomorrow afternoon. You understand that we couldn't possibly change them at this late hour, don't you?"

"Of course, Mrs. Goosetree."

"And you will ask her for another time, won't you, my lord?"

"I'll consider it an honor."

"Splendid."

Catherine wondered if the earl had changed his mind and decided he wanted her to go for a proper ride in the park with him or if he was just using that as a cover for Victoria's benefit. She didn't know what plans Victoria had for her tomorrow, but she knew they wouldn't be as interesting as riding in the park with the handsome and intriguing earl, and not nearly so stirring as meeting him in secret at dawn.

"Thank you, Lord Chatwin. We shall look forward to another time. Now, come along, Catherine. I can see that you are dead on your feet. I will take you home. Good night, my lord."

"Mrs. Goosetree. Miss Reynolds."

Victoria turned away and Lord Chatwin quickly stepped up to Catherine and softly whispered where only she could hear, "Before dawn in the park. I'll be waiting."

His voice so close to her ear sent shivers up her arms and down the back of her neck. She couldn't believe Lord Chatwin still wanted her to meet him.

Alone.

And she couldn't believe how much she wanted to deny her common sense and do just that, but of course, she couldn't.

Could she?

Catherine and Victoria immediately collected their wraps and called for their coach. As soon as they were comfortably seated inside the warm compartment and headed toward home, Victoria clasped her hands under her chin and started laughing.

Hazy yellow light filtered inside the cabin of the landau from lanterns that were positioned outside the coach. Catherine saw self-satisfaction in Victoria's face. That seemed strange to her. She thought she'd get a stern rebuke from Victoria as soon as they made it to the carriage for failing to remember a duke's name.

Catherine found the rocking motion of the carriage and the clipping of the horses' hooves on the hard-packed road soothing. Her heart rate slowed, her breathing calmed.

After a few moments she turned to Victoria and asked, "What has you feeling so jovial?"

Victoria looked at Catherine. "The Marquis of Westerland and Lord Chatwin, of course. I can't believe you have caught the eye of the Marquis and one of the Terrible Twosome Earls."

Catherine was puzzled. "It pleases you that I've caught Lord Chatwin's attention?"

"Did I not say as much?"

"Yes, but why?"

"Because it's wonderful to be sought after by an earl!" Victoria sighed contentedly as she relaxed against the seat cushion.

"But he's considered a rogue."

"Oh, yes, he's a rogue of the highest order," Victoria agreed gleefully.

"An unredeemable one I might add, if all I've heard about him is true," Catherine said, still wondering why Victoria would want her to be pursued by a gentleman with a blemished reputation.

"I'm sure every morsel you have heard is true, but he's also an earl! And everything worked out perfectly tonight."

Catherine didn't understand her half sister at all. From the moment she'd arrived in London, Victoria had preached that she must find an acceptable young man to marry before her first Season was over.

How could a rogue, no matter his title, be acceptable?

"What exactly worked perfectly?"

"My plan, of course," Victoria said with a satisfied smile. "Lord Westerland was captivated by you tonight. I observed the way he couldn't take his eyes off you while you were dancing with him. And when I saw Lord Chatwin come in earlier tonight with the Earl of Dugdale, I remember that Lord Chatwin saw you right away and watched your every move."

I bet he did.

"He couldn't stop looking at you even when he talked to Lord Dugdale. I knew immediately that he was interested in you."

Oh, yes, I'm sure of it.

Victoria flipped open her fan again and continued talking as the carriage bumped along the road leading into Mayfair.

"But I decided I wouldn't introduce you right away. And it was the right decision. When I didn't proceed at once to present you to him, he found someone to make the introductions for him. And to ask the Duke of Beaumont— well, that's almost like asking the Prince himself to do the honors."

Catherine couldn't keep a smile off her face. If only Victoria knew the real reason he'd come looking for her was not because he'd been enchanted with her but because she had his horse.

"The Marquis would be the better catch for you, no doubt about that, but for the past ten years I've watched that earl outfox cagy fathers, escape irate dukes and guardians, and bring pushy mamas to tears. It's time he was caught."

Victoria stopped talking and laughed again. Catherine couldn't believe how excited her half sister was about Lord Chatwin.

"What a challenge—what an achievement it would be to snare him. Mark my words, dear Catherine, Lord Chatwin will be asking for your hand before this Season's over."

The smile withered from Catherine's lips. "Vickie, you can't be serious. Surely you don't want me to marry a man with such a questionable reputation?"

Victoria's stern gaze landed on Catherine's eyes. "Of

course I do. I can see I have much to teach you about Society. Our father left you in the country far too long. He should have sent you to me years ago."

"I couldn't have left him while he was ill."

"I know and I'm glad you were there with him. But because of that you are two years late on your coming out. Now, the first thing you must remember is that it's *your* reputation that matters in this Town, dear Catherine, not his. It would be very difficult for an earl to do anything that would tarnish his name beyond repair. You, on the other hand, are a very different matter."

Catherine was aware of that. That was why she had continued to reject the earl's tempting invitation to meet him at dawn.

"Besides, remember my allowance from our father will increase if you marry a titled man," Victoria said. "As a widow, I'm aware of my finances and desire to keep my standard of living."

How could I forget?

Catherine asked her sister, "If you are happy about his desire to take me for a ride in the park, why did you tell him I wasn't available tomorrow afternoon?"

"Because, my dear, that, too, is part of my plan. It will make you far more appealing and intriguing to all of them if I keep you at a distance."

"But from what I've heard about Lord Chatwin and the Terrible Twosome, I don't believe he is interested in marriage at all, only a bit of sport."

"Merciful goodness, Catherine, you're not supposed to think that way. And every titled man is interested in marriage. It's just that some take longer than others to make up their minds."

"I didn't think he was the kind of gentleman you wanted me to be interested in."

"His being an earl makes all the difference. My dear Catherine, there is a reason our father left you in my care. I will not fail him. I will see to it that you make a perfect match, and I would prefer it with the earl who couldn't be caught. Now, sit back and relax and trust me to handle everything." She laughed again. "I think I'll have a spot of sherry when I get home. I'm so pleased with myself, I deserve it."

Catherine turned her head and looked out the small windowpane and watched the street lamps pass by.

How could she relax now?

Victoria seemed to have made up her mind that the earl was the man she wanted to snare for Catherine. He was certainly far more appealing than the Marquis of Westerland.

She could only hope Victoria wouldn't be too disappointed when Lord Chatwin dropped her like a hot poker once she returned his horse.

Finding a husband was not what Catherine wanted to do right now. Yes, the earl was the most handsome man she'd ever seen, and she would enjoy the opportunity to explore the wonderful feelings that stirred inside her whenever she was near him, but finding her real father had to come first. She wanted to know if his eyes were blue like hers. Did she have his smile or the color of his hair? She had to fill in that part of her past that was missing.

Six

MISS CATHERINE REYNOLDS was fascinating, John thought as she and her half sister disappeared from his view.

He'd always been good at reading women. It was as if he could see inside their minds and know what they were thinking. He'd always known ahead of time which lady would agree to a rendezvous with him and which one would decline.

Until Miss Reynolds.

He hadn't been able to read her. And not being sure about her decision made her all the more intriguing. Would she meet him tomorrow morning or would she just send him word where he could pick up The General?

A few more moments in her presence and she would have had him forgetting he even had a horse.

She'd had no trouble looking him in the eyes when she spoke to him. He liked that. He also liked the fact that she found it difficult to lie to her sister about their lack of a proper introduction, while it hadn't bothered him at all to do it.

It wouldn't matter if Mrs. Goosetree asked the Duke of Beaumont about presenting Miss Reynolds to him. Everyone knew the old duke couldn't remember much of anything anymore.

John knew that Mrs. Goosetree was playing him, and that didn't bother him, either. Other guardians had used the hard-to-get ploy with him in the past. It was amusing that she didn't know he was on to her.

He loved a good game—as long as he won.

And he would.

The lovely Miss Reynolds's explanation of why she ran off with his horse seemed reasonable and plausible, but that didn't take away the rub of the teasing he was getting.

"Fines, did you find your horse?" someone called to him from across the room.

John looked up and saw one of the old bachelors looking at him and grinning. He smiled and waved to the dandy, hoping like hell the old curmudgeon wouldn't join him.

He was amazed at the commotion that the lady riding his horse had caused.

Miss Reynolds was a menace.

Did she know what she'd started?

The furor over this could be bigger than the time when he was twenty and was caught trying to crawl in the bedroom window of Miss Penelope Hardgraves. Thankfully his uncle Bentley had appeared on the scene and kept him from being leg-shackled.

The gossips had always written about him. That was nothing new, but this story seemed to swell with a life of its own.

"I saw Miss Reynolds leaving with her sister just a moment ago," Andrew said as he walked up beside John. "What did you find out?"

John turned to his friend and said, "That she is more intriguing than ever."

Andrew shook his head in exasperation. "Damnation, John."

"What is it?"

"I fear you are in more trouble than you know."

John harrumphed. "Why do you say that?"

"I wasn't asking about the lady. I was inquiring about what you found out regarding the whereabouts of your horse. The prizewinning Thoroughbred for which you paid an enormous amount of money. The General, do you even remember him?"

John took a deep breath and groaned inside. Bloody hell. Maybe Andrew was right. It wasn't like him to forget about his horse.

He had always enjoyed all women, but no lady had ever been that important to him.

Ignoring Andrew's jibe, John said, "She told me right away that The General is safe and stabled privately. She'll return him tomorrow."

A knowing grin eased slowly across Andrew's face and a sound very much like a laugh flew past his lips and was quickly lost in the crowded room.

"You let her outfox you again, didn't you?"

"What the bloody hell do you think? Of course not." John tried to look and sound outraged but wasn't sure he succeeded on either account.

"Oh, really?" Andrew mocked him with a friendly snicker under his breath. "Tell me, my friend, do you know where your horse is?"

John groused to himself. "I just told you he's stabled privately."

"Do you know where?" Andrew asked again, remaining firm on his point.

"No," John finally admitted and hated doing it, but he was only confirming what his friend had already figured out. Andrew knew if anyone else had possession of The General, John would have insisted on *immediately* going to get his horse.

"Tsk, tsk."

"Go to hell," John swore under his breath but loud enough for Andrew to hear.

"My, my, but we are in a state," Andrew said with no real offense in his tone or expression.

"I'm not in a temper, or anything else. She offered to return him tomorrow, and I agreed, so there was no need to ask her where the devil he is at this very moment."

"So, she's going to have him delivered to your stables first thing tomorrow morning."

John hesitated, not knowing how much more he wanted Andrew to know. His boyhood friend already thought him a complete fool.

"Well? I'm waiting," Andrew said.

John shrugged. "Not exactly."

For the first time Andrew's brow furrowed with real concern. "John?"

"All right, if you must know, I asked her to bring him to the park."

Shock flashed in Andrew's eyes. "What's this? You want half the *ton* to see her returning your horse?"

"Of course not."

"I can't believe you even want to see her again knowing she's probably in on this with Westerland."

Another mistake.

John was making far too many of them where Miss Reynolds was concerned. He had been so enchanted by her, he'd forgotten to even question her about the dance with the Marquis.

He had to get his head out of his trousers and back on his shoulders where it belonged.

"I told you I don't think she and Westerland were in this together. In fact I'm sure of it. He simply saw she was beautiful and asked her for a dance the way I'm sure a dozen or so other men have done tonight."

"You're smitten," Andrew said without fanfare or accusation.

"I'm patient."

"You're enchanted."

"I'm interested." John paused. "With the same interest I have for every new lady at the start of the Season."

Andrew chuckled with no amusement in his voice. "You're all head of ears for her. Admit it."

"No. You know me better than that."

"Do I?"

"I adore all women equally. She hasn't changed that."

"I don't think so. I believe she has knocked your feet right out from under you."

John frowned. His friend was going too far, but John was reluctant to call him on it.

"You're too deep in your cups to know what you're saying. I can still look around this room and see at least six or seven ladies I'd like to ask to meet me under the arbor for a few passionate kisses."

To prove his point, John glanced around the crowded room, but to his astonishment he realized that which was true only yesterday was no longer the case. He scanned the room quickly and then again more slowly, letting his gaze sweep from one beautiful face to another. He didn't see any lady he wanted to meet under the arbor for a few quick kisses.

Damnation! What had happened to him? If he didn't know better he'd think he was the one who had fallen off the horse. Through the years he had been amused by beautiful young ladies, but surely this was the first time he had ever been bewitched by one.

"If you can, it's only because Miss Reynolds is not in the room right now," Andrew said. "And mark my words, time will tell which one of us is correct about her and her relationship to Westerland."

"He doesn't have anything to do with this, and she'll return The General tomorrow," he said with more confidence than he was suddenly feeling.

Andrew shook his head. "I still don't think it is wise to have her bring The General to the park. It's not a good idea for anyone to see her with your horse again. This has already caused a scandal that's made you a laughingstock and it's growing by the hour."

John didn't need to be reminded of that. "No one will see us. I've asked her to come at dawn."

Surprise lit in Andrew's eyes for the second time and a low chuckle rumbled in his chest. "You blasted devil. You scoundrel. You plan to ruin her for stealing your horse, don't you?"

"Of course not," he exclaimed as softly as he could.

"Why not? It's a dastardly thing to do, but look what she's put you through."

John glanced around the room to see if anyone took notice of their vigorous conversation. He caught sight of

Westerland looking at him from across the dance floor. The Marquis gave him a sneering smile and with his hands made the motion of riding a horse.

John's insides burned.

"Damnation, Andrew. You know I would never intentionally ruin a young lady's reputation. What do you take me for?"

"Perhaps a man who needs to get his dignity back. And at the expense of the lady who caused him to lose it seems the way to do it, as far as I'm concerned."

"Well, I won't. That never entered my mind. I just wanted to have a—"

John was interrupted by a friendly slap on the back and he turned around.

"Fines, did you find your horse?" Wilkins asked as he joined the two friends.

"Yes, I did," John said, barely holding on to his temper. "All's well."

"Glad to hear it. Everyone's talking about it, you know. I can't believe how word's gotten around, but apparently Mallory wasn't the only one to say he saw a lady riding The General."

That wasn't what John needed to hear.

"No doubt the gossip about that will have passed by tomorrow morning and the wagging tongues will be on to something or someone new."

"Yes, I would think the bigger story would be Westerland's stallion beating your gelding, not some ghost of a lady riding your horse."

"Right," Andrew said. "Every betting man knows how fast John's gelding is. He hasn't been beaten all year until this morning and that a mere technicality. John would have

won had he not almost run into that lady—bird—I mean—
a lazy bat." Andrew swore under his breath. "That is if a
bat hadn't spooked his horse."

Andrew finished somewhat frustrated, and Wilkins
looked at him as if he thought he was ready to be commit-
ted to Bedlam.

John wanted the subject dropped.

Now.

"Look, ol' chaps, the best thing you can do for me is to
let the matter die."

"John," asked a new arrival, "what is this I keep hearing
about a lady riding your horse in the park today?"

John didn't know how, but he managed to hold his
tongue as he turned and looked into the eyes of his favorite
uncle.

Not him, too!

How did one little incident become such a nightmare?

The very distinguished-looking Bentley Hastings stood
just an inch or two shorter than his nephew but with the
same broad shoulders, narrow hips, and self-confident carriage. His full, thick hair and closely cropped beard were
brushed with a silvery shade of gray, and his eyes always
seemed to have a mischievous twinkle.

Bentley was his mother's brother, but he and John's father had been closer than most blood brothers.

"It's just the usual gossipmongers," John muttered
tightly.

Miss Reynolds and her little stunt had caused him a lot
of unwelcome grief. It would serve her right if he followed Andrew's school of thought and found a way to dis-
credit her.

"Everyone here at the party seems to be talking about it."

I know.

"Laughing about it is more like it," Wilkins said and chuckled.

John threw him a "you're not helping me" look, and the young man mumbled his good-byes and hurried away.

"It's nothing but a silly rumor, Uncle," John insisted.

"We think the Marquis of Westerland started it after a race this morning," Andrew added.

"Yes, I heard about that, too, and find it rather odd that he would." Bentley's thick eyebrows twitched. "No reason for him to start something like that when he was the winner."

"Well, sir," Andrew countered, "you know that the entire family has been easily offended since John turned down the duke's offer to marry his daughter."

Both Bentley and John looked at Andrew.

As if realizing that he had spoken out of turn, Andrew took a step back and cleared his throat. "Well, I think I'll go get myself a drink and let the two of you talk about this in private. I'll see you tomorrow, right, John?"

He nodded and Andrew said his good-byes, leaving as quickly as Wilkins.

John turned back to his uncle and simply said, "I agree it would be odd for Westerland and his friends to make up a story like that. But queerer things have happened."

"Indeed. I suppose this whole thing could be his doing. Andrew was right about Westerland's entire family still being snappish over your not marrying Lady Christine last year."

"Could be."

"Well, I suggest that you be seen riding The General in the park for the better part of the day tomorrow. It will soon put to rest such fanciful notions as a lady riding your horse."

John had always had great respect for his uncle. He occasionally gave John advice, but he never meddled. John appreciated his concern and his discretion over the years.

"I'll do that."

"Good. I think I will ride with you. Should we go early?"

"No," he said almost too quickly. "I think the afternoon would be better for me, and there'll be more people out in the park later in the day. If that will not inconvenience you?"

"Not at all. I'll meet you at the usual place in the park at four."

"I'll be there."

His uncle walked away and John wondered what he would do if she didn't show with his horse?

Miss Reynolds had given him no indication that she would meet him. In fact, she stressed that she would not. But surely if she didn't come to the park, she would have his horse delivered to him now that she knew who he was, or at least send word early in the day where he could reclaim The General.

Andrew was right. She had outfoxed him again and once again his anger was not what it should be considering the predicament she had put him in.

He should have insisted that she immediately tell him where the horse was so he could go and retrieve him tonight.

She was still in control. Was she playing a game with him or was she as pure and innocent as she appeared to be?

Miss Catherine Reynolds had made havoc of his day, and for some reason he didn't understand, that didn't bother him nearly as much as it should.

Seven

IT WAS COLD, dark, and misty, but Catherine was warm and light of heart as she rode with purpose into the park leading the big horse called The General. Over her hastily donned riding habit, she wore a black hooded cape which she pulled low over her face.

Even if anyone saw her, there was no way she would be recognized without the hood being ripped from her head.

She planned to make sure that didn't happen. Catherine was an excellent rider, and with the spirited mare beneath her she had no fear that anyone could catch them if she were given chase.

What she was doing was madness, but she hadn't been able to stop herself. She'd wanted to accept Lord Chatwin's challenge and meet him in the park to return his horse. She knew if she was caught, her mission in London would be in serious jeopardy and Victoria would probably lock her in her room.

She knew she couldn't become caught up in her infatuation for John. But she'd never been able to pass on a challenge or a dare.

She rode the same mare she'd ridden yesterday. The big gelding behind her didn't like being led. He made it known by constantly throwing his head up in the air and snorting. He pulled on the reins as if trying to get away, but Catherine kept him on a short rein and didn't allow him to intimidate her even when he pawed the earth with impatience and retaliation.

Catherine had secretly slipped out of Victoria's house and run to the stable. The young groom who slept in the barn loft had been shocked and a bit confused to see a young lady alone at the door. At first he'd been reluctant to let her have the horses. But his scruples vanished when she dropped a few shillings into his hands and assured him she was the lady who left The General at the establishment the day before.

He had asked if she wanted him to ride with her, but she declined. She only wanted to get to her destination and back home again without being accosted by anyone who would want to know why a lady was riding the streets alone at night.

Since she'd returned home from the ball, she'd divided her time between thinking about the handsome Lord Chatwin and the two gentlemen Lady Lynette had described to her during their conversation at the party. One obviously afraid of horses and the other afraid of the color green.

Catherine shivered. She wasn't sure she liked the idea of either of these men siring her, but she needed to know the truth of her parentage. She had the right to know who fathered her, so she would pursue both men, no matter how strange they were.

She would make a point of getting to know Lady Lynette a little better, so she could ask her to make the proper introductions.

As Catherine entered the park, it felt eerily empty. Gray mist hung in tree branches and puddled around the ground.

Her heartbeat seemed to keep time with the plopping of the horses' hooves on the hard-packed ground. She kept up a steady, brisk pace, and even through the drifting, early-morning fog, as best as she could tell, she rode directly back to the place where she had almost collided with Lord Chatwin the morning before.

When she halted the horses and dismounted, it was suddenly very quiet except for the rapid heaviness of her breathing, and the snorting and prancing of The General behind her. Her own horse nickered.

Catherine looked all around her, but with the enveloping fog, seeing farther than a few feet was impossible.

For a moment she wondered if Lord Chatwin would show, since she had really never agreed to meet him. Suddenly out of the quietness came the rustling of leaves and the cracking of twigs.

The earl, cloaked in a black cape that fell behind his shoulders, proudly rode out of the gray mist. The rhythm of Catherine's pulse quickened. For a heartbeat, Catherine's stomach fluttered deliciously.

Even in the semidarkness she could see that he had taken great care with his appearance. He was immaculate with a fashionable waistcoat and his neckcloth simply tied. Suddenly Catherine wished she hadn't been so lax in her dress, but she'd been thinking more of not getting caught than how she looked.

He jumped down from the saddle and started toward her. Everything about him, from the way he arrogantly carried himself, to his easy stride appealed to her. The masculine boldness with which he took every step was hard to ignore. He filled out his black cape with broad shoulders that tapered to a flat stomach and narrow hips. His long legs looked powerful in his shiny riding boots as he walked toward her.

He was devastatingly handsome, displaying self-confidence in every purposeful step. He wasn't close enough for her to know if he looked at her or his horse, but she noticed that he held something in his hand. As he came closer, she saw that it was a bright red apple.

The General nickered and shuddered. Catherine gave the big animal enough leather to walk to his master as she jumped down from her own horse.

She watched in the shadowy light as Lord Chatwin ran his gloved hand down his gelding's long, wide nose before letting him munch on the apple from the palm of his hand. He patted the animal's strong neck and whispered something to him.

Catherine was mesmerized by the relationship Lord Chatwin had with his mount. She liked the way he touched his horse and talked to him in a calming whisper that made the animal's ears twitch. The General tossed his head as if he were agreeing with every word.

She was impressed that the earl had thought to bring a treat for the animal.

Finally Lord Chatwin looked over at Catherine. Even through the misty grayness she could see that his dark eyes had a polished sparkle in them that shone with pleasure and appreciation.

Without taking her gaze from his face, Catherine pushed the hood from her head and let it fall to her back. She'd left her hair unbound, not wanting to take the time to put it up, and it now pooled around her shoulders. She lifted the weight of it from her cloak and shook it free of the hood.

The chilling air kissed her cheeks and nose as she extended the reins to him. He took them, making sure his gloved fingers briefly closed over hers before drawing the leather away from her grasp.

He smiled at her and said, "I wasn't sure you would come."

Catherine cleared her throat, giving herself time to recover from the thrill of his unexpected touch. "Neither was I, but sometime during the night I convinced myself that I needed to return him myself, since you so kindly let me borrow him yesterday."

Lord Chatwin laughed gently as he moved to stand closer to her. It was a wonderful-sounding chuckle that echoed all around her but somehow managed not to disturb the quietness of the night.

"You do have your own enchanting way of remembering things, Miss Reynolds."

"Is that not the way you remember our encounter yesterday morn?" she asked, suspecting he wouldn't agree, but knowing she would never admit to having stolen the horse.

"No, fair lady, it is not."

"Well, I suppose we all do have different ways to remember."

He nodded. "Did anyone see you riding into the park this morning?" he asked.

"I don't believe so, but then I didn't think anyone had seen me riding yesterday, and I was very mistaken about that."

The earl's horse nudged his back restlessly, but Lord Chatwin didn't seem to notice. "Indeed you were. You have caused quite a stir among my friends and foes alike."

"I hope you believe me when I say that was not my intention."

"I do and I'm hoping this"—he turned and patted the bridge of his horse's nose again—"will put a stop to all the gossip."

From the look on his face he didn't seem too worried about the gossip, but she said, "I hope so, too. No doubt you were not happy to be the brunt of jokes about a lady riding your horse."

"Well put, Miss Reynolds. I've had my name linked with countesses, princesses, and even Josephine a couple of years back when I traveled through Paris, but this is the first time I've been associated with a mysterious lady who rides my gelding as if he were her own."

She smiled her appreciation at his compliment.

Catherine found Lord Chatwin's disposition comfortable, and it was easy to flirt with him even though she'd had very few opportunities to develop the skill.

"Perhaps we both have reason to worry about our meeting this morning as well. It would have been easier for us had you simply allowed me to have your horse delivered to your stable."

"Easy, yes, but what excitement would there have been in doing something as simple as that?"

Excitement. That wasn't a word that she had used a lot or knew much about.

Could it be that is why she had decided to go against her better judgment and meet him? After living so long in the somber Northern Coast, was it excitement she wanted? Was that part of the reason she wanted to find her real father and confront him and ask him why he deserted her mother when she was carrying his child twenty years ago?

No. She was far too sensible for that. She wanted answers. She wanted to know what made her father deny his responsibilities and not marry her mother. How could she go through life not knowing the answer if there was any possibility that she could find out?

She knew if it became known that she was looking for her real father, she would be branded a bastard, but not even that fear would stop her. And finding that man is what she must concentrate on. Not the thrilling way this attractive man standing before her could make her feel.

"Not excitement to be sure," she answered with assurance as their gaze met and held once more, "but certainly it would have been much safer for both of us."

"I've never played it safe, Miss Reynolds."

Catherine's breaths shortened. "Perhaps that is what attracts me to you, my lord."

He moved still closer to her. She felt warmth from his body even though he didn't touch her. His gaze searched hers. His lips were parted and moist, and she found herself wondering what it would feel like to be kissed by him.

"You admit you are attracted to me?"

There was an awareness of him that she hadn't felt with any other man. When he was near, her heart skipped beats, her chest tightened, and her strong legs suddenly seemed as weak and trembly as a newborn foal.

"Yes," she said, seeing no reason to deny what he must already know.

"You are brave to do so when your sister acts as if you have no interest in me whatsoever."

"I can afford to be because that attraction has nothing to do with why I am here. I came only to return your horse."

A slow, handsome smile eased across his face.

"Whichever brought you here, I'm glad you came. I wanted to spend some time with you without the watchful eyes of Mrs. Goosetree and half the *ton*. I'm glad you felt safe enough with me to come."

Lord Chatwin's horse stomped and pawed the ground restlessly, reminding Catherine that she needed to go. She knew she could spend the entire morning talking with him, but she'd already stayed longer than she should have.

Every moment she was with him she was taking a chance of being caught; still she was reluctant.

"But I have no time to converse with you. I must go back before someone in the house realizes I'm gone."

"What are you doing this afternoon?"

"Why do you ask? Victoria has already explained I'm not free to see you."

"It's natural to want to know the name of my competition, don't you think?"

Catherine's smile turned into a soft laugh.

"Why does that amuse you?"

"Because, my lord, I have heard all about you."

"And what exactly does that mean?"

"That I'm afraid your reputation precedes you. You don't consider that you ever have any competition. From what I've heard you have never had any doubts of winning the heart of any lady you so desired."

"Ah—you heard that about me? Am I really that much of a rogue?"

"Well, perhaps not in those exact words, but that is the impression I was left with. Because you are one of the Terrible Twosome, I have heard many things about you, not the least of which is that you are not interested in making a match."

"And you are."

"Of course. It's what young ladies do."

"But just because I'm not interested in being leg-shackled at this time does not mean that I'm not attracted to you."

"I would never believe you have eyes for no one but me. I've heard the stories of how many young ladies have thought so in the past only to have their quivering hearts torn from their chests when you gave your attention to another."

Lord Chatwin gave her a lighthearted shrug. "I've enjoyed the attentions of many ladies, but I've never made a promise to any of them."

"And from what I hear, you are not likely to make one any time soon."

"I suppose your sister would like to see you make a match before the Season is out."

"She would like that, yes."

"And what about you?"

"It is what our father wanted—an acceptable match for me, but I don't see that it necessarily has to happen this year. I'm in no hurry to marry and quite willing to wait another year. Vickie is not."

"She seems to be doing a good job of watching over you."

"She has good reason."

"Because she's so devoted to you?"

"That, too, but—" Catherine laughed. "But mostly because it benefits her. My—*our* father decided to make it well worth her while to see to it that she did her best by me."

"In what way?"

"She receives a generous amount of money once I've wed."

His eyes sparkled mischievously. "That makes it nice for her."

"Yes, especially because she gets an extra bonus if I marry a titled gentleman and still more if I marry the first year."

He laughed. "Are you sincere?"

"Quite. Are you worried?"

"Should I be?"

"Perhaps."

"I'm not."

"Maybe you should be. It depends on how serious your interest is, but I think Vickie has decided you would make me a fine husband, and she's determined to match wits with you over the possibilities."

"I thought as much. I'm up to the challenge and welcome it, but tell me, don't you have a choice in who you marry?"

"Oh, yes, my father made it clear I have to be in agreement."

"So she can't marry you off to someone like the Duke of Wellsgarten, who is near eighty if he is a day."

"Not unless I agree." Catherine looked behind her. "Now I really must go." She turned to leave, but Lord Chatwin touched her arm and she glanced back to him.

Their eyes met and held.

"Before you go, I want to—"

He quickly bent down and touched his lips to hers softly, briefly. It was over much too fast. She didn't have time to savor the exhilarating feel of his warm lips pressed lightly against hers before they were gone and she was looking into his dark eyes once again.

A soft gasp passed her lips and a tingling thrill shot across her breasts and spiraled downward to her stomach.

"Did my kiss frighten you?"

"No, it surprised me."

"Good. I don't want to frighten you."

Without really knowing why she did it, she ran her tongue over her lips and then laughed softly.

"What is it?" he asked, looking confused by her laughter.

"Nothing bad. It's just that your lips left the taste of apple on mine."

He grinned. "You caught me. I brought two apples for my horse, but I ended up eating one while I waited for you."

"I'm sure The General will forgive you."

"And what about you?" He reached out and softly let her hair glide through his fingers. "Will you forgive me for wanting to kiss you again?"

"I have no fear that you are romantically interested in a lady who would borrow your horse without permission."

"You assume too much, Miss Reynolds."

Catherine stared at him, unable to move or even breathe as his hand played with her hair. Was he asking for permission or making a statement? She wasn't sure, but she found herself giving him a slight nod.

Lord Chatwin let his hand drop to her waist and he slid his arms inside her cape, moving them all the way around her to the small of her back. She allowed him to pull her up close. She had never felt such warmth as the heat that came from his body.

She had been kissed once before much like Lord Chatwin's first kiss, but she had never been held so protectively in the strong arms of a man. It felt wonderful.

It was exciting.

Yes, this was what excitement meant. That giddy and breathless feeling. This was that feeling of which the poets spoke. And it was heavenly. Amazement at its best, she thought as she leaned into his strong chest and settled her breast against him.

She watched as he bent his head and his face came
closer and closer until his lips touched hers again. Warmth
slid all the way down her. She savored the sweet taste of
apple on his lips. Catherine's legs went weak again, and
she seemed to melt closer to him as his lips moved
smoothly, confidently, effortlessly over hers.

This time the kiss lasted longer. He didn't pull his
mouth away from hers. His lips were tender, his teeth occasionally nibbling softly at her lips. She opened her mouth
and his tongue darted inside and teased hers.

She felt liquid and limp as he pressed her closer to him.
The kiss deepened. Was this what passion felt like? If so,
no wonder the poets wrote about it, exploring the subject in
great detail. She had never been kissed like this, but it
didn't take long for her to learn how to participate.

Catherine was swept along with the new sensations
curling and twirling inside her.

Catherine knew she was taking a risk allowing him this
freedom, and as much as she hated to, she pushed away
from him. He let her slip from his grasp.

"Did I hurt you?" he asked, his breath ragged.

"No, again I'm surprised. I didn't expect to find your
kisses so pleasurable."

He smiled softly. "I'm glad I please you."

"Did you enjoy my kisses?" she asked with some hesitancy.

"Very much so."

She returned his smile. "I really must go. If I delay
longer, the sun will be bright and I will surely get caught
slipping back into the house. I can't let that happen."

"You're right. But first, my uncle is having a dinner
party tonight. I'll have an invitation sent over. Do you think
you and your sister can come?"

"I believe our schedule is full."

"Try?"

He picked up her hood and placed it back on her head, pulling it low over her face and stuffing her hair to the back of her shoulders.

Lord Chatwin cupped his hands for her foot so he could lift her onto the saddle. Without looking back at him, she took off, intending to let the mare have her head and gallop out of the park, but she very quickly realized Lord Chatwin was following her at a distance. He rode his gelding and was leading the other horse.

She stopped and turned around and rode back to meet him.

"Why are you following me? Is something wrong?"

"No."

"Then go some other way. Someone might see you following me."

Lord Chatwin smiled. "Miss Reynolds, I've been following you ever since you left your aunt's house an hour ago."

She gasped. "Surely not."

He smiled. "Of course I have."

"I would have noticed."

"I'm very good at what I do."

That I can't argue with.

"If you chose to meet me, I wasn't going to have you riding the streets alone with no protection. What kind of gentleman would I be if I did something like that?"

"The kind I *thought* you were. But I see now that is not true."

"I always try to be a gentleman whether or not I succeed."

"Why did you wait until I got to the park to make yourself known? I could have turned over your horse at any time along the way."

"Yes, but we wouldn't have had our kiss, and I don't know about you, but I am most happy I didn't miss that."

Catherine gave him a guilty smile. "You are a charmer, my lord."

"And you are a beautiful temptress, Miss Reynolds. Now ride fast. You are chasing daylight and you don't have much time."

That exciting, thrilling feeling whipped through Catherine again. She smiled at him before turning her horse around and racing out of the park.

Eight

"*Up, dear girl,* up! See what a beautiful day it is outside. Spring is here and the birds are singing. Life is beautiful. Up, up."

Her lids were heavy, but Catherine tried to open her eyes against the glaring streak of sunshine streaming through the window dressings Victoria had just flung open. She didn't want to wake up. She wanted to think about a handsome man, a warm, strong embrace, and moist kisses that sent shivers of delight from her head to her toes.

Suddenly her eyes popped open.

"I couldn't let you sleep a moment longer, as we have much to do today."

Catherine squinted against the strong glare of the sun. "Have I overslept?" she asked groggily, remembering she hadn't gotten any sleep last night because of her secret, wonderful rendezvous with Lord Chatwin.

"No, no. It's not late. Now, put your pillows behind you

and I'll get your tray. I have chocolate and toast ready. Madame Parachou is already on her way over to fit you for another gown."

More gowns? Surely not.

"Sweet mercies, Vickie," she mumbled, touching her fingertips to her lips as she remembered Lord Chatwin's kisses and how they made her feel all delicious inside. "I have a room full of gowns I haven't even worn yet."

"Oh, you do like to exaggerate. You can't possibly have more than four or five, maybe six that you haven't worn."

That was six more gowns than she needed as far as she was concerned, and she had more than enough day dresses, carriage dresses, walking dresses, not to mention all the gloves, bonnets, and wraps to match.

Victoria stood before her and smiled down at her with her brown eyes sparkling like the finest of gemstones.

"You don't have plenty. Not anymore. I sent word for Madame Parachou to come at once, and I told her there would be an extra payment for her if she made it here within the hour."

Catherine had realized when she first arrived in London months ago that there was no point in quarreling with Victoria about clothing. That was one argument Catherine wouldn't win.

She pulled her nightcap off her head and shook out her long hair, letting it spill over her shoulders. She remembered how her breath had come rapid and deep when Lord Chatwin had cupped her hair in his hands and let its length thread through his fingers as if he were caressing the finest silk.

Still looking quite pleased with herself, Victoria waved

a sheet of vellum before Catherine and said, "Guess what arrived very early this morning?"

"I have no idea," she mumbled as her thoughts drifted back to her meeting with Lord Chatwin a few hours ago. Their kisses, and the pleasure they created inside her, still lingered with her.

She could still feel his strong arms around her. It was unbelievable to her at how warm his body had been and how strong his arms and firm his chest. His lips had been soft and tasted of apple. She moistened her lips, hoping to find the fruity taste still there, but it was gone.

Vickie placed a tray across Catherine's lap and laid the sheet of vellum on the tray. She looked down at Catherine with a very pleased smile on her face and said, "This is an invitation for us to attend a dinner party at Lord Chatwin's uncle's house this evening. Isn't that wonderful!"

Yes, because she wanted to see Lord Chatwin again. What was she doing thinking about the earl? She needed to concentrate on finding her father.

"I'm glad if you are pleased," she said, keeping her eyes on the tray of hot chocolate, toast, and cooked figs. She wasn't sure she should sound interested in Lord Chatwin.

"Of course I'm pleased. I'm ecstatic! I can't believe how well your first week is going." Victoria walked away from the bed and over to Catherine's dressing table and sat down on the stool.

She looked at Catherine in the looking glass. "I always suspected I had very good matchmaking skills and this proves it. And it's quite enjoyable. I might hire myself out to make matches for other young ladies."

"Would you really want to do that, Vickie?"

"Yes. For a fee, of course, you understand. And I would

let it be known I'm available only after I have you safely betrothed to Lord Westerland or Lord Chatwin, which shouldn't take too much longer. One of them is bound to make an offer very soon. Everything seems to be falling right into my plan."

Catherine knew Victoria well enough to know that if she spoke in favor of something, Vickie would talk against it.

With that in mind Catherine said, "Vickie, I'm not as old or as wise as you, but from all I've heard, Lord Chatwin is not a good choice for me. I understand he will give a lady attention for a few days and suddenly start paying court to another without so much as a good-bye."

"You cannot believe everything you've heard about the earl. It can't all be true."

Catherine smiled to herself. Victoria had said just the opposite last night. Obviously it didn't take much to sway her.

"Lord Westerland is not nearly as handsome, or charming or friendly as the earl."

"Friendly?" Victoria screwed up her face into a frown. "That has nothing to do with which man will be the better husband for you. I must admit that Lord Chatwin presents the bigger challenge, so naturally he would be the better choice. And I find matching wits with him quite stimulating."

Sometimes Catherine didn't understand Victoria's reasoning.

Catherine sipped her chocolate and pondered her half sister's words. Yes, Lord Chatwin was a challenge.

"Other ladies have not known how to make Lord Chatwin seek their daughters. I do. We will not fail, dear Catherine. I know what I'm doing."

"I'm not sure I want a husband," she said as thoughts

about her real reason for being in London swept through her mind once again.

Vickie's brown eyes rounded in horror as her lips formed an O. "That's blasphemous! Of course you want a husband! All young ladies do."

Catherine had to smile because Victoria looked so stricken. "I meant right now. I would like to have time to get to know more people here in London."

"Lord Chatwin is young, handsome, and titled. He will provide well for you and give you many children. What else could you want?"

"How about love?" she asked, remembering her conversation with Lady Lynette, remembering how Lord Chatwin's kisses had made her feel passion for the first time in her life.

"Love? You don't know what it is and neither do I. Perhaps there really isn't such a thing as love. Those kinds of fanciful notions only exist in poetry and daydreams, and it seems only to affect young ladies like you."

Lord Chatwin certainly had all her senses on alert, but could she ever love him?

"I don't know anything about love," she admitted, "but I think I should look for a man who will love only me. Not someone who will give me attention for a few days and then move on to another lady."

"Don't worry about anything like that. It's not important right now. All that will work out once you are married." Victoria rose from the stool and turned back to Catherine. "Finish your chocolate. The only thing we need to do is get him, or Lord Westerland, to offer for your hand, and I'm working on ideas about how to accomplish that."

And Catherine had her own plan she was going to be working on tonight. And she'd start with seeking out Lady Lynette.

JOHN DIDN'T KNOW what was wrong with him. He must have eaten something that hadn't agreed with him. He felt restless, which was unusual for him.

Not only that but he kept watching the front door with the anticipation of a youth waiting to look at his first nude. He wanted the next person to walk through the front door of his uncle's home to be Miss Reynolds.

The party had started well over two hours ago. Champagne flowed, flowers graced corners and tables, and hundreds of candles burned throughout the house. His uncle's dinner parties were always well attended, and the one tonight was no exception.

The music had remained lively and John had already danced with three young ladies who had just been presented at court. But right now he couldn't even remember what they looked like. He had no one on his mind but Miss Reynolds.

He knew the two sisters had other events to attend. Miss Reynolds had said as much, but he'd been hoping Mrs. Goosetree would decide to pass on the other parties and come directly to his uncle's house.

It didn't appear they had done that. And he was beginning to think they might not show at all.

He couldn't help but wonder whether Mrs. Goosetree sincerely didn't want him pursuing Miss Reynolds or if the older sister was just trying to make him appear eager? She wouldn't be the first to have tried it. The odd thing was that it had never worked before, and he kept telling himself that he couldn't let it this time.

Still, he kept watching the door.

For some reason, he had the feeling that Mrs. Goosetree fancied herself smarter than he, and it was clear that she was trying to outmaneuver him where Miss Reynolds was concerned.

But John could play that game, too. Maybe after tonight he should appear to have no interest whatsoever in Miss Reynolds. That should set the formidable Mrs. Goosetree on her heels and send her scurrying to do his bidding.

But he also had to be careful. After all, Miss Reynolds had stolen his horse. There was always the possibility she had something else up her sleeve, although John had seen no evidence of that.

He couldn't ignore her, so he would pursue her, but he would do it on his own terms and he would be wary.

As soon as that last thought sifted through his mind, Miss Catherine Reynolds walked through the door and into the room. John felt as if his heart leaped from his chest into his throat. His breathing grew shallow and fast as his heartbeat accelerated.

She was a lovely young lady like so many others he'd taken note of over the years. But Miss Reynolds was stronger in determination and more capable of holding her own with him than most of the ladies he'd known.

She wore a beautiful gown in the color of aged pearls. A wispy layer of delicate lace covered her skirt and the short sleeves were sheer lace, making her look even more feminine. The simple round neckline plunged just enough to make him want to see more of her creamy white breasts that were hidden beneath the bodice of her gown.

His lower body swelled in anticipation of the possibility.

Her hair was swept up in a light chignon with little white blossoms woven through it. Small golden curls delicately framed her face. She smiled at the servant when she handed over her cloak.

He watched as her blue eyes quickly scanned the packed room. Anticipation raced through him. Was she looking for him?

His breath caught in his throat for a moment. He felt different whenever he looked at her, and that was something he'd never experienced with any other lady.

She'd admitted she was attracted to him, and she had been receptive to his kisses earlier that morning, but then most ladies were amenable to his overtures, so what made her special?

John knew she couldn't see him from where he stood on the third stair because he was hidden behind a column. But he could see her clearly.

For a fleeting moment he wanted to race down the stairs, greet her, and monopolize her time. He wanted to stake his claim on her before another man dared. But his mind told him to be sensible.

He was no longer an uncontrollable youth even if his lower body and his heart were suddenly feeling that way. John knew the danger of showing any one young lady too much attention. That was a good way to become legshackled. If he wasn't careful, the Society pages would have him all but married to her.

That she had come to his uncle's party was enough— for now.

It was his turn to make Mrs. Goosetree wait. He'd seek Miss Reynolds's attention soon enough.

In the meantime, he'd make sure he said hello to every young lady at the party and have another dance or two before approaching Miss Reynolds.

John folded his arms across his chest and leaned back against the column. He chuckled to himself. He'd been caught with his own game. He was usually the seducer, but not this time. He didn't know quite how she had done it, but Miss Reynolds had seduced him.

Nine

"Behold a pale horse: but what is the name that sat on him?" There is no doubt that Lord Chatwin rode atop his horse in Hyde Park today, but who rode him yesterday? Who is the mysterious lady who was seen riding his mount? More than one person bears witness of her. Lord Chatwin is staying quiet on the subject, while the other member of The Terrible Twosome, Lord Dugdale, defends his friend so vigorously one can't help but wonder why the gentleman protests so much.

Lord Truefitt
Society's Daily Column

OVERHEAD CANDLELIGHT BATHED the room with a soft golden glow as lively music, chattering, and laughing drifted from corner to corner of the room. Beautiful ladies clothed in satin, silk, and lace danced with fine-looking gentlemen dressed in elaborately tied neckcloths and coats with tails in the crowded drawing room where furniture had been shoved to the walls to make room for all the guests.

Catherine watched as Lord Chatwin danced, twirled, and bowed to yet another young lady as the four-piece orchestra struck up another familiar tune. She was glad she hadn't set her sights on the handsome gentleman, for surely he was living up to his reputation of being a man for all the ladies.

He didn't seem to favor one with more attention than another. He danced with them all: young, old, tall, short, and every lady between.

Victoria took a glass of champagne from a server who was passing with a tray and patted her foot on the floor with determination.

"Imagine!" She huffed in an irritated voice. "I can't believe that Lord Chatwin invited us to this lavish affair and has not been gracious enough to even show his face to us for the entire evening!"

Catherine hid a smile behind her gloved hand before saying, "Vickie, how can you stretch the truth so far? The entire evening indeed. We haven't even been here an hour yet, and the night is still young."

"With the way he has treated us, it feels as if we've been here days."

Catherine shook her head in amusement. "You are too impatient in all that you do. For a small dinner party there are a great many people here. Lord Chatwin probably hasn't even seen us yet and we were too late for the receiving line."

Victoria sipped the champagne, then fanned herself vigorously with her intricately hand-painted fan. "Oh, botheration, Catherine! He's seen us all right. I'm sure of it."

"I thought it was his uncle who invited us to this party. I should think he is the one we need to make sure we speak to."

"Yes, yes, of course, the invitation came from Mr. Hastings and we will speak to him. But I'm just as certain that it was Lord Chatwin who put him up to sending it. In my day, a gentleman would have never treated a young lady so shabbily as to invite her to a party and then completely ignore her. Not even the rogues of years ago were this bad."

"How can you say we've been ignored? We could have made a point of going up to the earl and saying hello to him."

"No, no, my dear, that is not how this works. Lord Chatwin must seek us first. He's no doubt playing the same game I'm playing, but he will not win."

Catherine didn't mind the cat-and-mouse game Victoria was playing with Lord Chatwin or the Marquis. It was her hope that it would keep her sister occupied and her mind off any young man who might be a serious contender for Catherine's hand. As long as games were being played Catherine had the time she needed to find her father.

"And what game is that, Vickie?" Catherine asked, trying to keep her gaze and her thoughts off Lord Chatwin.

"Hard to get, but worth the wait. Most men want the thrill of the hunt. They don't want to catch their wives too easily."

Catherine laughed again, though she had been wondering, too, why the earl seemed to be talking and dancing with every young lady but her. Perhaps now that she had let him kiss her, he had already grown tired of her and was in pursuit of another lady?

For some reason that thought caused an empty feeling in her stomach, but she refused to let it consume her.

"From all I've heard in the short time I've been in London, Lord Chatwin seldom behaves as a proper gentleman should."

"Yes, that is true, but things are different now. You are in my care, and I intend to see that he doesn't treat you this way. This is an outrage."

"Perhaps you are being overly sensitive. I think he was just giving us time to avail ourselves of the buffet and get something to drink."

"Perhaps, perhaps. But just maybe he is trying my patience on purpose. Well, I will not allow him to fluster me. I can wait him out. Watch me. If we must, we will give our regards to his uncle and leave the party without having said a hello to him."

"But, Vickie, that would be impolite," Catherine said, realizing she didn't want to leave the party without speaking to the earl and asking if there had been any problems with his horse.

"As if he would notice." Victoria took another large sip of her champagne. "Do not let this cause you one moment of chagrin, my dear. I have everything under control and I know what I'm doing. He is not the only titled bachelor in Town. The Marquis of Westerland would suit you nicely. You do *remember* him, don't you?"

"Of course. I danced with him. We've discussed him." Catherine wished Lord Chatwin had never indicated to Victoria that she did not have a good memory even if it had gotten her out of trouble at the moment.

"No doubt he has attended other parties this evening, which is what we should have done. This one is not up to the nines." Victoria fanned herself. "Now that I think about it, I don't believe their two families get along very well."

"Why is that?"

"The *on dit* is that the Duke wanted Lord Chatwin to marry his youngest daughter, the Marquis's sister, and Lord Chatwin declined even after a handsome dowry was announced. No matter, we will see the Marquis again. Perhaps later tonight or tomorrow evening for sure."

Catherine didn't want Victoria setting her sights on the Marquis, or any gentleman who was seeking a bride. The Marquis was tall and handsome, but she had felt nothing of the excitement she felt whenever she was near Lord Chatwin.

Since Lord Chatwin didn't want to make a match, he was the perfect man for Victoria to be after. If Catherine could keep the earl's interest, it would give her the entire Season to meet Mr. Beechman, Mr. Chatsworth, and Mr. Wickenham-Thickenham-Fines and find out which of the three was her real father.

And the lady who could help her find out more about the man she sought just walked into the buffet room.

"Vickie, I think I will go and speak to Lady Lynette, if you don't mind."

"Not at all. I think you should. She's the Duke of Knightington's daughter. You must not forget that."

"I haven't forgotten, nor shall I," Catherine said, trying hard not to sound irritated at Victoria's continued reference to Catherine's lack of memory.

"The poor girl has few if any prospects of marriage with that dreadful birthmark, but you couldn't make a better friend. Now run along and be sure to give her my regards."

Lady Lynette was drinking a cup of punch when Catherine walked up to her and said hello.

"How lovely to see you again," Lady Lynette said with a smile on her face, "And please, let's don't be so formal. I consider us friends after our long conversation last evening. You must drop the lady and address me only as Lynette. May I call you Catherine?"

"Yes, of course. Thank you, Lynette."

"That sounds so much better. Are you enjoying your evening?"

"Very much."

"I thought so. I've noticed that you've been watching Lord Chatwin."

Lady Lynette was either very perceptive or she had the eyes of a hawk. She didn't seem to miss a thing. There was nothing to do but admit to the truth.

"I'm sure you did," Catherine answered honestly. "He is very handsome. It would be difficult not to notice him no matter how big the crowd."

"He's very charming, too. He's one of the few gentlemen who will dance with every young lady no matter her age, beauty, or rank, and he makes every one of us feel as if he could fall in love with us when he looks in our eyes." She sighed. "But alas, he never does."

"I'm sure that must be true. He's been dancing ever since I arrived tonight."

"That's not unusual. And don't worry. He will get around to asking you."

As much as Catherine wouldn't mind talking about the intriguing earl, there were three other gentlemen she wanted to discuss.

"Oh, if he does, he does. If not, I think I shall live."

Lady Lynette laughed. "And so you shall. I see so many young ladies who think they will die if they don't get offers from certain gentlemen."

"I've heard enough about him from Victoria to know there is nothing to be gained by giving your heart to Lord Chatwin."

"I used to think that Lord Chatwin couldn't be caught, but ever since the first of the Terrible Threesome, Lord

Dunraven, married last Season, I've changed my mind. However, I had always thought Lord Dugdale would be the first to marry."

"Why is that?"

"It's no secret that his lands are encumbered, so I've just always assumed he would consider his duty to his family and make an advantageous match." Lynette smiled. "Maybe I'm wrong and he'll hold out for love."

"For love? Truly? A man?"

Lady Lynette's eyebrows twitched. "Why not?"

"While I'm quite willing to accept that most women believe in love and long for it, I wasn't sure any man would admit to such a fanciful notion."

"I think they have such feelings. A gentleman can become just as smitten over a lady as a lady over a handsome face and physique."

Catherine smiled. "I'll consider that encouraging."

"Did you hear anything more on the gossip about a mysterious lady who was seen riding Lord Chatwin's horse yesterday?"

"I'm sure everyone has either heard it or read about it by now, but no, nothing new," she said, hoping to avoid being downright untruthful about the incident.

"I have no idea who she might be, but I'm simply dying to find out. Do you know?"

Catherine hesitated and cleared her throat to cover it. "I came to Town only a few months ago. I really don't know many ladies at all."

"I won't stop looking until I find out who she is. Everyone wants to know. You will tell me immediately if you hear, won't you?"

"I'm certain I will be the last to hear anything about that, but should the occasion arise I will come to you," she answered, wondering why it was so important that Lady Lynette know who rode the horse.

"There was talk today that it was really a ghost who rode his horse."

"You can't be serious."

"Oh, yes it's quite possible. According to the people I've talked to, the whole incident was really rather queer. It seems something mystifying and shadowy spooked his horse. It threw him and ran off. The next time the animal was seen a lady whom no one recognized was riding him. I'm beginning to think there might be some truth to this ghost story."

"Surely, you don't mean that."

"Of course I do. It's well known that there is a phantom lady who rides the hills looking for Lord Pinkwater's ghost."

They thought her a ghost! How did that happen?

"My goodness. I don't believe I've heard that story before."

"She's Lady Veronica. It's believed that at one time she was his lover."

Catherine shook her head. What was she doing talking about ghosts and lovers? She needed to be asking more questions about her father.

"There are certainly a lot more intriguing people here in London than where I grew up. For instance, the gentlemen we were discussing last evening."

"Oh, yes, I remember. Mr. Chatsworth and Mr. Beechman. They are odd, but harmless old gentlemen."

"I'm sure of that. But there was one other man that I wanted to ask you a—"

"Good evening, ladies, how lovely to see both of you this evening."

Catherine felt her heartbeat speed up the minute she

heard his voice. It was amazing how her stomach contracted and how her pulse raced whenever he was near. She turned around and faced him. Her eyes went straight to his tempting lips. She kept remembering how delicious they had felt against hers.

Greetings were exchanged and Catherine could have sworn that Lord Chatwin's gaze lingered on her own before he said, "Miss Reynolds, this dance is promised to Lady Lynette, but perhaps you will allow me a turn with you later in the evening."

"If I'm still here when your dance card is empty, my lord, I would be happy to stand up with you."

He gave her a "touché" smile and led Lady Lynette away.

How could Catherine be upset that he was dancing with Lady Lynette? Especially if what Victoria said was true and she had little chance of making a match.

Catherine turned to visit the buffet room to get something to drink and think about Lord Chatwin and about how she could go about meeting the two men she'd discussed with Lady Lynette when she saw Victoria striding purposefully toward her.

"I can't believe this. This is an outrage. He dances with Lady Lynette and not you. Come, Catherine, we'll leave immediately."

"Calm down, Vickie. Lord Chatwin asked me for a dance later in the evening."

"It's about time, but it's too late. We shan't be here for you to have it. We shall leave. But before we do, come, I want to present you to Lord Chatwin's best friend, Lord Dugdale. If we can't have one earl, we'll try for another."

"Is he the one who is light in the pockets?"

Victoria frowned. "Nothing to worry about."

"Are you sure?"

"Of course. He's an earl. An eligible earl and there aren't that many of them. I believe his financial disabilities are probably just rumor. If it were true, he would have made a match with a duke's daughter—someone like Lady Lynette—if he were as financially embarrassed as the rumors say. No, no, dear, there is nothing wrong with Lord Dugdale that your dowry wouldn't cure."

Catherine shook her head in disbelief as she followed Victoria to the other side of the room. She was beginning to wish her father had never promised Victoria a bonus if she married a titled gentleman her first Season. It made Victoria at times seem mercenary and without feelings for Catherine.

They stopped beside a man who was only an inch or two shorter than Lord Chatwin but just as handsome in a more roguish sort of way. He was impeccably dressed in evening attire and he had the same dark hair as Lord Chatwin, but Catherine knew the minute his golden-brown eyes landed on her that he would not be nearly as friendly.

"Lord Dugdale, may I present my half sister, Miss Catherine Reynolds. Catherine, the Earl of Dugdale."

"How do you do, Miss Reynolds?"

Catherine could have sworn he was decidedly cold toward her as he spoke. There was no warmth in his gaze and that was definitely not a welcoming smile he had on his face. She answered him and curtsied appropriately, but he made only the stiffest of bows.

Another lady arrived and claimed Victoria's attention for the moment. Lord Dugdale immediately situated himself between Vickie and Catherine, turning his broad shoulders so that they hid Catherine from Victoria's view.

In a low voice he said, "Why are you here at this party, Miss Reynolds?"

His voice was as cold as the look he gave her, and his question sounded much like an accusation. His manner shocked and intrigued her at the same time. What had she done to incur such a strong, adverse reaction from him?

Surely he knew she would have been invited to attend.

"I beg your pardon, my lord."

"And so you should," he whispered only loud enough for her to hear. "You made Lord Chatwin the laughingstock of all of London by stealing his horse and riding it out of the park."

So he knew.

But that didn't keep Catherine's spine from stiffening at his allegation. "I did not steal his horse, sir. I borrowed it."

"Without permission, which is the same thing as stealing no matter how you try to twist what you did with words and make him believe otherwise."

His anger was real and harsh.

"I really don't see how any of this is your concern."

"John is my friend."

Catherine realized that was the first time she had heard Lord Chatwin's name.

"I'm aware of that, but your friend and I have already settled the matter between us. Civilly, I might add, so your intervention is not necessary."

He cut his gaze around to make sure that Victoria was still engrossed with the talkative lady who was demanding her attention.

"I hardly call it settled when your stunt is still making the scandal sheets and still the subject of conversation in half the clubs in Town."

"I can assure you I have no control over what gentlemen say to each other."

"You would do well to stay away from Lord Chatwin. You've caused him enough trouble."

"Are you threatening me, sir?"

"Take it however you wish, but understand that I intend for you to heed me."

"How dare you be so boorish?"

"I dare because I don't know what you are up to and I intend to protect my friend."

Catherine didn't know how she remained so calm and collected as she said, "I don't know Lord Chatwin very well, but this I do know: He does not need his friends to threaten ladies on his behalf. If he wants me to stay away from him, he is quite capable of speaking for himself. I have no doubt now which one of you the word *terrible* was directed at when the term *Terrible Threesome* was coined."

"What was that you said?" Victoria asked, turning back to the two with a questioning expression on her face.

Catherine realized the other lady was gone. She could only hope she didn't look as angry as she felt.

She cleared her throat and tried to speak calmly as she said, "I was just telling Lord Dugdale that I was sorry he must leave so soon."

"Yes, please excuse me, Miss Reynolds, Mrs. Goose-tree," Lord Dugdale said and walked away.

"Well, Catherine," Victoria said, "he certainly left in a hurry. I don't think you charmed him."

What an understatement!

"Not in the least."

"You weren't impolite to him, were you? He is an earl, you know. I thought I detected a note of annoyance in your voice."

It was more like outrage.

"Ill-mannered? Me? No, no. I think we caught him at a

bad moment," Catherine said, almost holding her teeth together as she said it.

"Well, we'll see him again another time. I do believe I'm ready to quit this party. We'll go to Lady Windham's. No doubt the Marquis of Westerland will be there, and I'm sure he will be more receptive than either earl has been tonight. I must pay a visit to the retiring room first and then we shall leave."

Catherine nodded and said, "I think I'll have something to drink while I wait for you. I'll be near the buffet table."

Catherine walked into the dining room and asked for a glass of champagne. She took a sip of the bubbly liquid and let it fizzle down her throat. She had never been spoken to in such a manner as she had just now with Lord Dugdale.

In a way she admired him for wanting to help, or was it to protect his friend? Loyalty was no small matter. Friends couldn't survive without it, but even giving him credit where it was due, Lord Dugdale went beyond the line in speaking to her about John's horse and suggesting she stay away from him.

And she would bet her next quarter's allowance that Lord Chatwin had no idea what his good friend had just said to her.

Catherine took another sip of her champagne and turned away from the table and right into Lord Chatwin.

They just stood there looking at each other for a few moments, neither of them saying a word. All thoughts of Lord Dugdale's rude behavior faded from her mind. She was sorry that by taking his horse she had caused Lord Chatwin so much trouble, but she wasn't sorry that incident had created an unusual bond between the two of them. She hoped nothing his friend could say would change that.

"Will you walk with me?"

She should resist him. Victoria was right; he had ignored her all evening. His friend had threatened her. Finding her real father was supposed to be uppermost in her thoughts, and she was allowing this man and her unexpected feelings for him to overshadow that.

She opened her mouth to decline but couldn't. How could she not talk to him?

Just for a moment.

She said, "I have only a few minutes. I'll be leaving when Victoria returns."

His gaze stayed on hers, and for a moment she thought she saw disappointment in them. "We haven't had our dance yet."

"That is because you are too much in demand, sir. Besides, I believe there is one other party my sister wants us to attend this evening."

"Why? Anyone she should want you to see tonight is right here."

"You would think so, but Victoria would not agree with you. She believes the Marquis of Westerland will be at Lady Windham's, while she's fairly certain he will not be at this party."

"That's for sure," he said dryly.

Catherine couldn't believe she'd told him that Victoria wanted her to see the Marquis tonight. Was she trying to make the earl jealous?

Surely not.

"Victoria insists that we need to make an appearance at Lady Windham's."

"You do not need to spend any time with Westerland," he said with no hint of a smile on his face. "He is not a likable chap."

"That almost sounds like a jealous remark."

"Maybe," he added with a twinkle shining in his eyes. "I'm not sure that term has ever been accurately applied to me before."

"And it's probably not now," she admitted with a gentle laugh. "So tell me about you, Lord Chatwin. I just found out tonight that your first name is John."

"That's right and I think it's time you called me John and not Lord Chatwin. And I will call you Catherine."

She nodded. "All right, John, I think Vickie would approve of that. Tell me, how is your horse? Did you find him to be in good condition?"

"Yes. I never had any doubt that you would take excellent care of The General. Did I ever mention how impressed I was with how well you handled him."

Pleasure filled her at his compliment and she smiled at him again. "I love horses and my favorite time to ride is in the quietness of early morning when dawn first breaks the sky."

"We'll have to do that sometime—ride in the early morning while others slumber."

"And tempt fate yet again?"

"Yes."

The way he looked at her reminded Catherine of how he looked that morning just before he kissed her. A sense of longing surged inside her, and with all her heart she wanted him to kiss her again. She knew that was impossible in a room that was filled with people, but that didn't keep her from aching for his touch.

She needed to break the spell he had cast on her, so she said, "Your Christian name is John, but I do not recall hearing your family name."

"A circumstance easily remedied," he said.

He stopped in front of a large portrait of an older, handsome man dressed in a stunning red coat adorned with shining gold buttons. His black waistcoat was quilted with gold thread and he wore fawn-colored pantaloons. He looked like an older Lord Chatwin.

"Here is a portrait of my father before he inherited the title." Bowing he said, "Miss Reynolds, may I present the honorable George Wickenham-Thickenham-Fines.

It took a moment for it to register on Catherine what he'd said, and suddenly she gasped and jerked her head toward John.

She suddenly felt hot and cold at the same time and weak.

"You can't be serious? This—this is your father? Your real father?"

"Unless someone has been fooling me for thirty years."

This was no time for jokes.

"His name was George Wickenham-Thickenham-Fines?" Her breathing was so constricted she could hardly get the words past her lips.

He smiled at her, that devastatingly handsome smile that made her chest tighten with all those warm mysterious feelings he invoked in her. Obviously he didn't see in her face the distress she was feeling.

"Yes, although my father has been dead for many years now."

Catherine just looked at John, not wanting to believe what she'd just heard. What could she say? What was she going to do? She turned away from him and squeezed her eyes tightly.

The man who stirred her senses like no other man ever had could be her brother.

Ten

John left the buffet room by way of the servants' corridor and took the back stairs to his uncle's book room. He didn't bother to go over to his desk and light a lamp but instead went straight to the handsome mahogany side table and poured a large splash of brandy into a glass.

He took a swallow and let the strong liquor settle on his tongue for a moment or two before letting it wash down his throat. He breathed in deeply and took another quick sip.

He knew the room well. Floor-to-ceiling bookshelves covered two walls, a fireplace and old paintings of Bentley's deceased family members hung on a third wall. Twin chairs upholstered in the finest English fabrics stood on a hand-woven carpet. The room smelled of musty leather, stale pipe smoke, and melted wax. It was odd how he'd never noticed those scents when his uncle was present. They were always too busy talking about whatever might have brought John to the house.

John knew he'd bungled tonight as if he'd been a callow youth. No, he thought as he sipped the drink again and walked over to his uncle's dark wood desk and sat down behind it.

It was worse than that.

He'd allowed himself to be drawn into a game he was beginning to believe he didn't want to play. In his hopes of besting Mrs. Goosetree and remaining aloof he'd offended Catherine. Like a common scoundrel, he'd danced with first one lady and then another after Miss Reynolds had arrived, and all the time she was the only one he really wanted to dance with.

What was he thinking?

Was he trying to make Catherine jealous or was he trying to make Mrs. Goostree think he wasn't interested in her sister?

He'd played this same game many times before. For years.

So why did it feel so wrong tonight?

Why was he left feeling bereft when Mrs. Goosetree suddenly appeared in the doorway telling Miss Reynolds they had to leave immediately? He'd tried to forestall her leaving, but she'd hurriedly brushed past him with a barely audible good-bye.

John stared at the dark liquid in his glass. He'd wanted to dance with her, so why was he playing the young and foolish games of the past?

He didn't really know why yet, but he knew he no longer wanted to play those games with Catherine. He realized now that she was too important to him, and he didn't want to treat her that way.

He didn't understand his feelings for her.

She was beautiful, but beauty had never been a priority

for him when he sought a woman. Each lady had her own kind of loveliness. He had always accepted that and enjoyed the differences in them.

Catherine was intelligent, but he'd been attracted to many women who knew how to talk to him about politics, arts, or history. She could verbally spar with him, and he'd met a few, perhaps one or two who could hold his interest that way.

So what made her different? There was no doubt that she was. He felt it in the way he wanted to spend time with her, the way he felt good whenever he saw her walk in a room.

She was definitely more of a challenge than any other woman had ever been. What other lady would steal his horse and later risk her reputation to return it? Her courageous spirit was appealing.

Catherine had said her sister wanted them to go to Lady Windham's to see Westerland. John didn't want her dancing with the Marquis. It was strange, but John knew he wanted her to be interested only in him. That was a big change for him.

"Is your uncle conserving oil?"

John looked up from the brandy in his glass and saw Andrew leaning against the doorjamb, one foot carelessly crossed over the other.

"With hundreds of candles and every lamp in the house lit, I doubt it."

"Then why sit in the dark?"

I think better in the dark.

Until a few days ago Andrew could say anything to John and it didn't bother him. In fact, he used to enjoy a good row with his friend, but recently he hadn't been in the mood for Andrew's mockery and especially not tonight.

"I assumed it would be obvious that I was hoping no one would see me in here."

"Why?"

"Do you suppose it could be because I wanted to be alone?"

"No." Andrew strode into the library and folded his arms across his chest. "How can you be alone in a house full of people?"

"There was no one in this room until you stopped at the doorway."

"And it's a good thing I did. Is that your uncle's favorite brandy you're drinking?"

"Bloody hell, Andrew, I'm not in the mood for your sarcasm tonight." John put his glass to his lips and downed the rest of his drink.

"Then get up and let's head to White's and have a port there. It's not like you to sit around brooding."

"I'm not brooding." John rose. "I was just thinking I might head over to Lady Windham's soirée."

"All right. Let's go there."

John hadn't planned on Andrew going with him. He walked over to the side table and placed the empty glass by the brandy decanter.

"Did I tell you I met Miss Reynolds tonight?" Andrew asked.

Thankful it was dark, John turned toward his friend and tried to sound disinterested as he said, "No."

"Yes. Fascinating lady. Quite fiery. I bet she would be a hot tumble under the covers for you."

Without thinking, John grabbed Andrew by his coat and shoved him up against the wall.

"Don't ever say anything like that about her again."

John's angry gaze locked with Andrew's in the darkened room.

"I won't," Andrew said calmly. "I don't have to now that I know where you stand concerning her."

John saw there was no malice or resentment in Andrew. His friend hadn't put up a fight or any kind of resistance when John grabbed him and pushed him against the wall.

He let go of Andrew's coat and turned away from him. He swallowed hard. If Andrew had made that comment about any other lady, John would have probably agreed with him, but hearing it said about Catherine enraged him. He took a steadying breath.

"You said that about her on purpose, didn't you? You wanted to know if it would rile me."

Andrew straightened his coat. "Yes. I thought I knew where you're headed with her. I wanted to make sure you knew."

"I know," he said, even though he wasn't sure that he did. She had him all twisted up inside. His loss of self-control disturbed him.

"And now so do I."

"You could have just asked," John said.

"I don't think you knew the truth until just now. I'll be at White's if you decide to come in for a drink or a game of cards later," Andrew said, then turned and walked out.

John took a deep breath and poured himself another brandy. He knew the truth now. For the first time in his life he'd met a lady who was more important to him than any one else. He didn't want to believe that he could be close to falling in love.

*P*OSSIBLY HER BROTHER.

What was Catherine going to do? The feelings she was having for John were anything but brotherly!

After having spent a restless night and a miserable morning, Catherine walked into the discreetly accommodating parlor of Victoria's home carrying her favorite book of poetry. She hoped to use it as a foil. She could pretend to be reading when she was really trying to come to terms with the possibility that she and John might have the same father.

Aside from her bedroom with its dark lilac colors, this room was her favorite. The walls were papered a pale yellow with hand-painted flowers. The velvet draperies were a light shade of amethyst adorned with fancy stitched embroidery of ferns and elaborate fringe cording.

The matching Hepplewhite settees were upholstered in a busy flower pattern that coordinated with the walls and the window dressings. Over the fireplace hung a stately portrait of Victoria's dearly departed husband, flanked by silver-sheathed swords.

Catherine pushed aside the heavy velvet drapery panel and looked out onto the garden below. An unusual amount of sunshine for the past several days had many new flowers in bloom.

It knotted her stomach and caused heaviness in her chest to even think about the possibility of Lord Chatwin being her brother. She had enjoyed his kisses that chilly morning in the park. She'd welcomed the funny fluttering in her breast and low in her abdomen whenever he was near.

Catherine lifted her shoulders a little higher. She was strong, intelligent, and capable. She could do it. She had known it would not be an easy task when she set out to undertake this mission.

She had to know now more than ever.

She awoke that morning with the feeling that she was more determined than ever to find out which man was her father, and if that meant he was also Lord Chatwin's father, she would find a way to live with it.

But how difficult would it be to discover if her father was dead? She had no choice but to solicit Lady Lynette's help.

"It is just going to take some time." She sighed heavily. "Maybe a lot of time."

"Catherine, whom are you talking to?"

Surprised to hear Victoria's voice, Catherine turned around from the window and laid her book on the side table that stood against the far wall. "I must have been mumbling to myself," she answered.

"You looked so deep in thought. I didn't think you saw me come in. What are you mumbling about on a beautiful day like today?"

"I was just wondering how much time I have before the Marquis arrives."

"Half an hour. Now turn around and let me look at you. Your dress must look as pretty from the back as it does in the front. Is your hair pinned straight?"

Catherine slowly turned around, waiting for Victoria's approval. Catherine was not used to having someone fuss so over her day in and day out. All Victoria seemed to be interested in was how Catherine looked.

She wished she could confide in Victoria about her mother's diary, but not knowing how she would react made that impossible.

"I really don't think you should have agreed that Lord Westerland could come for refreshments without consulting me, Victoria. I'm not at all certain I'm interested in the man."

"Nonsense, of course you are interested." Victoria fiddled with the lace trim around the neckline of Catherine's dress. "He's a Marquis. I shall not be derelict in my duty to find you a suitable husband."

"But I must approve the man I marry, too."

"He has a title and he's handsome. How can you not approve of him? He's perfect for you."

Catherine had to smile at Victoria's words. "Wasn't it just two nights ago that you thought Lord Chatwin was perfect for me?"

"Yes, and I still do." Vickie smiled, too. "However, I reserve the right to change my mind when I need to in order to benefit you. Lord Chatwin is playing with us. So now I'm thinking the Marquis might be a better choice. He's younger than the earl and one day he will be a duke." Victoria's smile widened. "Imagine yourself a duchess."

"Right now I'd rather imagine myself unwed. I don't want to be hurried into making a decision about with whom I shall spend the rest of my life."

"Who's hurrying you? There's no hurry. The Season just started. You have at least six weeks to decide."

Victoria laughed softly as she retied a bow on one of Catherine's sleeves. Catherine realized Victoria was very pretty when she smiled. Her brown eyes sparkled with happiness, and for a moment Catherine wondered why her sister had not married again.

Catherine had known from the moment she landed on Victoria's doorstep in London that her sister would relish every second of being her guardian, and Victoria had not disappointed her. She had forsaken all her social duties to be constantly by Catherine's side.

Victoria paused in her fussing over Catherine's dress. "Did you hear that?"

"Yes. It sounded like a knock on the front door. Do you suppose the Marquis is early?"

"By half an hour?" Victoria exclaimed. "He would not be so lacking in manners. No, most likely it's someone delivering another invitation for us. You have been quite popular, I'm happy to say."

"Even if it is the Marquis, it's not a problem. I'm ready."

Catherine was eager to get the afternoon over with. She was no more interested in spending time with the Marquis this afternoon than she was in dancing with him last night after she'd left Lord Chatwin. The only thing she was eager to do was to find out more about the earl's father and the other two men. And she was hoping to see Lady Lynette tonight and solicit her help.

What a dreadful task she had before her. One man was dotty about the color green, one wouldn't ride a horse or carriage, and the other was the father of the only man who had ever stirred her womanly senses. Her stomach knotted again at the thought.

"We don't want the Marquis to know you are ready. If it's him, we'll just have him wait."

A young, rotund maid appeared at the doorway of the parlor and said, "Lord Chatwin is here to pay a call on Miss Reynolds. He wants to know if she is receiving visitors."

Catherine's heart started hammering in her chest. Lord Chatwin? He had come to see her.

Did she want to see him? Yes, of course, she had to see him.

She had to determine if he was her brother. She turned to Victoria, who looked shocked that the earl would defy her.

"What audacity he has calling on you without asking for my permission. That is unheard of."

Catherine said the first thing that came to her mind. "Not in the village where I grew up."

"But you are not in the Northern part of the country anymore. You are in London. There are rules and he must obey them. I told him we had no time for a visit from him today."

"You mean yesterday. You didn't speak to him about this last evening. It was the evening before."

Victoria started pacing. "What day it was we spoke about this is beside the point." She stopped and looked at the maid and said, "Lizzie, please take Lord Chatwin's card and tell him Miss Reynolds is not receiving guests this afternoon."

The maid nodded. "Yes, Madam."

"Wait," Catherine said to the maid, and Lizzie halted mid-turn. "Tell him I'll see him."

Victoria put her hands on her slim hips. "You are not serious. The Marquis is due here."

Catherine remained calm, though it was quite clear that Victoria was in a dither. "But not for half an hour. We can give the earl five minutes."

"But he didn't even dance with you last evening after inviting you to the party," Victoria said, clearly exasperated and unforgiving.

"But he did ask. It was not his fault we had to leave before my turn came around. Don't be so stuffy, Vickie."

Victoria tapped her foot on the floor as she seemed to ponder Catherine's words.

"All right, we'll allow him to see you. And if he by chance sees the Marquis here it might do both of them good to see the other here."

"Vickie, I don't think that would be a good idea at all."

"Of course it is. I've been married, my dear, and you have not. I know how a man's mind works. Let me handle this. I know what I'm doing." She turned to the maid again. "Ask him to come into the parlor."

Catherine wasn't happy about the idea of the two titled gentlemen seeing each other, but she was very sure she wanted to see Lord Chatwin.

John walked in and his eyes immediately found Catherine, but he quickly sought out Victoria first and said, "Good afternoon, Mrs. Goosetree." He bowed and kissed her hand.

"This is a surprise, my lord," Victoria said in the tight voice she reserved for when she wasn't in control.

Not responding to Victoria's reprimand, he turned to Catherine. He smiled, bowed, and took her hand and kissed it, squeezing her fingers ever so lightly. "Miss Reynolds, you are beautiful this afternoon."

Catherine's breath became shallow and a fluttering started in her chest. His gaze never left hers.

"Thank you, my lord."

Somehow she knew this man could not be her brother. She didn't know how or why, but she felt it deep inside herself. Now all she had to do was find some way to prove it.

And she needed John's help to do that.

"I see you don't play by the rules, Lord Chatwin," Victoria said, forcing John to step farther away from Catherine.

He gave Victoria an exaggeratedly curious expression and said, "I've been accused of that before, Mrs. Goosetree. What rule have I failed to follow this time?"

"You should have asked my permission before calling on my sister today."

"I merely stopped by and asked if she were available to see me. There is nothing wrong with that. Had it not been convenient, I assume you would have declined and sent me on my way."

Victoria cleared her throat rather loudly and said, "Yes, I'm afraid I will have to do just that shortly, as we do have another gentleman caller expected in a matter of minutes."

"Then I thank you for giving me the few you have."

"I do so only because I assume you want to apologize to Catherine for ignoring her last evening. And with that in mind, I'm going to sit over here by the window and give you a few minutes to speak to her alone."

He bowed to her again. "Thank you."

Victoria walked over to a flower-printed armchair on the back wall of the parlor and took a seat. She picked up the book of poetry Catherine had placed on the table and opened it.

Catherine looked up at John and realized he was smiling down at her with his eyes, his lips, and his whole expression.

She so wanted to be captivated by him but couldn't allow herself to be knowing he might be her brother.

"You do have quite a nerve to come here, my lord."

"My nerve is second only to a lady who has the cheekiness to steal an earl's horse."

"Borrowed, Lord Chatwin," she said softly as she walked closer to the doorway, and farther away from Victoria's hearing.

"It's John, remember, and it is as you wish on what happened in the park," he said, keeping his voice low and easing farther away from Victoria. "However, your sister is right. I should have spent more time with you last evening. I should have danced with you before you had to leave."

"You were busy dancing with all the other ladies in attendance. And I hear that is a nice habit you have."

His gaze stayed steady on her face as he said, "You are the only one I wanted to dance with."

That fluttering feeling started in her chest again. He sounded so sincere, her heart melted.

"Don't say that."

"It's true. I was wrong to ignore you last night. I want to know what parties you are attending tonight so I can find you."

Catherine looked down at her folded hands. She desperately wanted that, too, but she had to say, "That wouldn't be a good idea."

"Why? Because of my behavior?"

She shook her head but didn't speak. Dare she tell him the truth? What would he say? Would he believe her?

"Is it because I've said I have no thoughts on getting married?"

She looked back into his eyes. "No, it's not that."

"Then why?"

She glanced over at Victoria and was quite certain she was straining to hear everything they said. Catherine positioned herself so that Lord Chatwin was between her and Victoria.

Softly she said, "I'm privy to some information that I don't think you are aware of."

He gave her a quizzical look. "What kind of information?"

She took a deep breath and said, "I think you might be my brother."

"What?" he asked loudly, his dark eyes glittering with shock.

Victoria cleared her throat.

"Shh," Catherine warned him. "You must not speak where she can hear you."

She peeked around him and looked over at Victoria who was looking up at them. She smiled at her sister, and then turned back to John and said, "Please keep your voice down."

"That's asking a lot when you say something like I might be your brother. What in the devil's name are you talking about?"

"It's true. There is a possibility that you might be. I came to London to find my real father. I don't have much to go on, but I do have three names, and I just discovered last night that your father's name is one of those."

She watched the shock in his eyes turn to anger. "What kind of game are you playing now?"

Catherine put her finger to her lips to remind him to keep his voice low before she answered, "This is no game, sir."

"I think it is. First you steal my horse and cause me grief with my friends, my enemies, and the scandal sheets. Now you come up with this scheme, this wild story about us being related."

"There is the possibility that's true."

"If you thought it was true, why did you let me kiss you in the park?"

"I told you I only found out your father's name last night when you pointed out his portrait and said it. I've known you only by your title name, Lord Chatwin, which is the name you go by. No one ever told me your family name until you did."

"So you didn't come to London for a husband? You came here looking for trouble."

"That's not true. I came looking for my father." She glanced around him again to see if Victoria was watching them. She seemed engrossed in the book.

Catherine knew she was taking a chance telling him her

predicament, but she desperately needed to know if he was her brother and he could help her discover that.

"Victoria thinks I came to London only to make a match, and I will need a husband one day, but I'm more interested in finding the man who deserted my mother and refused to marry her after he got her with child."

His expression turned grim. "And you think my father did this?"

She let her eyes implore him. "I don't know. His name is listed in my mother's diary as one of the three men she was considering marrying. There are very few readable pages. It's been badly damaged over the years. In the last entry she mentions that she is very much in love with the man whose child she carries and that she plans to tell him that very evening. She doesn't refer to him by name on that page."

"So your father could be anyone?"

"No, only one of three," she said indignantly. "I feel certain he is one of the three men she mentioned who were courting her because no other gentlemen's names are listed."

"This sounds preposterous to me. I don't know that I can believe you on this."

"The story is unbelievable to me, too, but I believe my mother. Do you think I like knowing that the man I always thought was my father isn't? I lie awake at night and wonder who fathered me. What does he look like? Is he tall or short, heavy or thin? Is he a kind man or harsh? I feel like a piece of me is missing and I have to find it. I have to know who my real father is. And I refuse to give up until I do."

His head shook with skepticism. "If this is another one of your ploys, I'll see to it you are never welcomed in anyone's home in London again."

She believed him and it caused her to shiver. "I don't

know what I can say to make you believe me, but I desperately need your help to find out if my mother and your father were ever together. I'll be twenty-one soon. Was your father married twenty-two years ago?"

"No, I'm sure not. My mother died when I was two and my father never remarried."

Catherine was glad of that. At least if he was her half brother, that meant her mother was not mistress to a married man. But she didn't know that it made her feel any better thinking her mother had just been a foolish young girl who'd given her heart away to an undeserving man.

His expression remained serious. "Tell me when exactly this liaison between my father and your mother would have happened if—if it did."

"The best I can figure from my birth date, it would have been late in the summer of seventeen ninety-eight."

"All right, that gives me somewhere to start. I'll go directly to my uncle's house and see what he remembers from that year."

Unaccustomed fear welled up inside her. "You won't tell him about what I'm doing, will you?"

"No. I just want an answer. Today if possible."

"Thank you for your help with this."

"Which parties will you be at tonight?"

"Well, I know the first ball we are attending will be at Lady Waverly's."

"I'll find you there."

"Excuse me, Madam. The Marquis of Westerland has arrived."

Victoria rose with a satisfied cat grin on her face and put her book aside. "Tell him he'll have to wait a few minutes."

"Not on my account, Mrs. Goosetree," John said. "I

must be on my way. Would you prefer that I take the back stairs?"

"Not at all. Lizzie will show you out through the front as usual."

He gave Catherine a grim look before he turned and walked away.

A seed of hope planted itself in Catherine's stomach.

*J*OHN WAS IN no mood to see the pompous Marquis standing like a piece of statuary in the foyer as he descended the stairs. He was dressed in a bright red and black striped waistcoat, and he was holding a rather large and obnoxious bouquet of flowers. But John felt somewhat better when he saw the shock on Westerland's face at seeing him.

"You get around quickly," Westerland said as John reached the bottom of the stairs.

"I do like to get to know all the new young ladies as soon as possible."

"I don't know why since you never intend to marry any of them."

"You just never know when I might change my mind."

"I saw that you found your horse."

"He was never missing. I knew where he was." John lied without guilt.

"Really?"

"Yes."

"That's not what the scandal sheets say."

"I'm not surprised you believe what's written in them."

Westerland sneered at John. "What I believe is that your horse threw you and ran off. Obviously there was a maid in the park, and she found your horse and rode away on him. I know you were searching all the stables trying to find him, so don't try to tell me you knew where your horse was."

"I knew where my horse was," he said again and with more conviction in his voice. He was not going to be bested by this fop.

Westerland laughed. "Let's just see what gets printed in the papers about it tomorrow."

"I have no doubt they will say whatever it is you and your friends want them to say."

"Well, they haven't failed me so far where you are concerned. Now that you have your horse back, I assume you are ready for a rematch."

"Any time you are ready."

"Good. I'll let you know the time and place. I want to see if White's is interested in upping the stakes for a rematch."

John's eyes narrowed. "I believe Miss Reynolds is waiting for you."

John opened the door and walked out.

Eleven
❧

CATHERINE SAT ON the opposite end of the floral-printed settee from the Marquis. Victoria sat opposite them on a matching piece while they all enjoyed refreshments of tea and spiced-apple preserves on scones.

Catherine didn't know how the Marquis could sit so straight and still for so long without hurting his back. He was much too formal for her taste. She kept contrasting Lord Westerland with John and found the Marquis lacking.

She could also see where the starch and the tightness of his collar and cravat had chafed his neck. She was trying not to look at it, but the redness seemed to stand out against his pale skin, and her eyes were drawn to the irritation.

She had discovered that the Marquis of Westerland's name was Christopher Corey, though most everyone referred to him as the Marquis. Victoria kept the conversation steady by asking about his family and recent travels he'd made to Spain, but few words had been said between Catherine and their guest.

She felt as if she had been sitting on a cushion of pins ever since John left. She was eager for the visit to be over so she could go to her room or take a walk in the garden and be alone with her thoughts.

John had been quite shocked by her pronouncement that she might be his half sister. At first he had looked at her as if she were mad. She'd taken a big chance in telling him her plight, but thankfully, like her, he wanted to get to the bottom of this and find out if there was any possibility they could be related.

Catherine took a bite of the scone topped with spiced apples and realized it was so quiet she could hear herself chewing. She was never at a loss for words when she was in John's presence. In fact, she never had time to say all that she wanted to. But she couldn't think of anything to say to the Marquis.

Apparently Victoria realized Catherine had been too quiet, because she made a big production of setting her empty cup and saucer on the round table that stood between them and said, "I think I'll sit over by the window and continue reading. That will give the two of you a few minutes alone."

"No, don't," Catherine said and caught herself in time to finish by saying, "You don't have to do that, Vickie."

"A chaperone must always be seen, but she doesn't always have to be heard."

"But we enjoy chatting with you, isn't that right, my lord?" she asked, smiling at the Marquis.

"By all means, Mrs. Goosetree, please feel free to stay in our company," he said as stiffly as he sat.

"You are so kind, Marquis, but I have a few pages I want to finish before the afternoon is over. If you'll excuse me."

The Marquis stood and waited until Victoria moved her post to the far back wall before he sat down again. Why did she find John, who broke more rules than he should, immensely more appealing than the perfect gentleman before her?

"Let me replenish your cup," she said to him.

"Thank you."

Catherine couldn't really see anything wrong with the Marquis. He was just as tall and almost as handsome as John, though they were different in looks. John had dark hair and eyes while Lord Westerland had thin blond hair that he pulled back in a queue and tied with a short black ribbon. Both men were self-confident to a fault.

John's confidence showed in a seasoned inner-strength while the Marquis tended to be arrogant in a priggish sort of way.

But the main difference between the two had nothing to do with the way they looked or acted. It had to do with the difference in the way they made her feel. Just thinking about John could make her heartbeat speed up, her breath grow short, and her insides tighten. Sitting near the Marquis, she felt nothing but impatience for him to leave.

"I hope you've had no trouble making friends, Miss Reynolds."

"No, not at all. The parties have been grand and everyone has been pleasant." She handed him a dainty cup. "Lady Lynette Knightington has been especially helpful in my getting to know people," she said and then asked, "Would you care for another scone?"

"No, thank you." He chuckled lightly. "Lady Lynette

makes it her business to meet everyone new to the *ton*, be they a young lady like yourself or a long-lost cousin of a duke or earl. It's to be expected. Everyone feels sorry for her, and I think that is why she is so well accepted in every circle. No one has the heart to rebuff her, the poor dear."

The fine hairs on the back of Catherine's neck rose. She certainly didn't feel sorry for Lady Lynette; she genuinely liked her. Furthermore, Catherine hadn't picked up even a hint of anyone feeling sorry for the duke's daughter including Lady Lynette herself. Even John had seemed quite fond of her when he'd asked her to dance and Lynette had said as much about him.

"I found her to be capable, intelligent, and confident. She's an enjoyable person. As far as I'm concerned, there is no reason to feel sorry for her."

The Marquis gave Catherine a skeptical look and then placed his cup on the table. Somehow he managed to do it without moving any part of his body but his arms. "That's not very benevolent of you, Miss Reynolds, considering her circumstances."

"What circumstances would those be?"

"Surely you can see she has very little chance of making a match because she's been marked. That's got to be difficult for the duke."

"That's ridiculous. Nonsense," she said, a little more than annoyed at the Lord Westerland's haughtiness. "The fact that Lynette was blessed with a little more color to her cheeks than some of us have should not keep any gentleman from calling on her. She's a lovely person."

The Marquis cleared his throat and sniffed, all the while keeping a smile on his lips. "I don't disagree with you on the kind of person she is, but most men would rather have a beautiful young lady like you beside them than someone who has Lady Lynette's disfigurement. Now tell me, have you had the opportunity to meet my sister, the Viscountess Dunhillington?"

Catherine didn't like the way he dropped Lynette from the conversation in favor of his sister. That showed another big difference between John and the Marquis. John had no problem at all in having Lady Lynette by his side.

"No, I don't believe I have met her," Catherine said tightly and wondered how much longer it would be before he rose and excused himself.

*J*OHN MANEUVERED HIS curricle through the streets of Mayfair at a much faster clip than he should have been driving in the residential area, but he was eager to get to his uncle's house. He just hoped Bentley was home. He needed to question him about Catherine's startling possibility.

What was she going to come up with next?

Stealing his horse was nothing compared to this outrageous claim that his father might also be her father.

Just the thought of her being his sister twisted his insides. He didn't want it to be true. He had to prove it wasn't.

He slapped the ribbons against the horses' rumps to speed them up so he could pass a landau and a hack that were traveling much slower than he wanted to go. The driver of the landau shouted something to him as he passed, but John paid him no mind and kept the horses running at a fast clip.

Catherine was too important to him not to seek answers immediately.

John's life had been charmingly happy until his run-in

with Catherine Reynolds. Now he felt as if he was losing control of his life all because of one lady. A lady he had met only a few days ago.

How had that happened? He'd never cared enough before to let anyone upset his life so dramatically. Andrew had been keen enough to sense his involvement that first morning.

John had never been the kind to take matters of the heart too seriously, but last night he realized that Catherine had changed all that. He wished he could just dismiss her from his thoughts as he had every other woman in his past, but he couldn't. She meant too much to him.

John drew rein and pulled the horses to a jarring halt outside his uncle's town home. He set the brake and jumped down, and a footman ran out to grab the reins. As he walked toward the door, the landau he'd passed drove by and the driver yelled at him to stay off the roads before he killed someone.

John paid him no mind.

After being announced, he strode into his uncle's book room just as he had the night before, but this time his uncle was sitting behind the desk.

"Sit down, John," his uncle Bentley said. "It's not often you stop by in the middle of the afternoon. To what do I owe the pleasure of this visit?"

John was restless. He would rather just stand up and blurt out what he wanted to know, but he knew it would be much wiser to proceed cautiously. He took a seat in the comfortable wing chair that stood in front of his uncle's desk and tried to look relaxed.

He wasn't sure Bentley Hastings would be able to help him, but his mother's brother seemed the best place to start looking for answers since he was John's father's best friend. John wasn't sure he would like Bentley's answers, but he had to know the truth.

"Would you like something to drink?" his uncle asked.

It wasn't that he couldn't use a drink. It would probably help calm him, but his stomach felt as if it had been turned inside out, and he couldn't bear the thought of putting anything in it. He truly could not bear the thought Catherine might be his sister.

"No, I stopped by because I'm hoping you can help me with a bit of family history."

His uncle seemed surprised. "Well, indeed I will if I can. It's about time you took interest in your heritage."

It wasn't his heritage he was looking for. It was Miss Catherine Reynolds's heritage that held his interest right now.

Bentley's chair creaked as he sat back in it, a smile on his face. "How far back would you like to start? One or two hundred years or maybe further?"

John shifted in his seat and cleared his throat. "Ah, no, not that far back. Only about twenty years for now. Do you know if my father ever kept a journal or record book of any kind?"

"Well, there's the family journal that follows the title. You should have that among your father's books. Are they still at the house in Kent?"

John nodded, suddenly wishing he'd looked over his father's volumes. But he'd only been fifteen when his father died, and after finishing his education John had never wanted to take the time away from his busy life in London to spend it reading books at his country estate.

"That has recordings of births, marriages, and deaths. Things like that if that's what you had in mind. I don't ever recall him keeping a day-to-day personal journal as I've always done." Bentley's expression turned pensive. "Can you be more specific about what exactly it is you are looking for?"

"For reasons I'd rather not get into I'm particularly interested in the year seventeen ninety-eight."

His uncle put a finger to his lips and seemed to ponder. "Something about that year sounds familiar. Let's see, that would have been about twenty-two years ago and that would have made you eight or nine. Your mother had already died."

"Yes. Did my father do anything unusual or did anything out of the ordinary happen that year?"

"Unusual? Nothing that immediately leaps to my mind. Let me see if I have anything in my own journal."

Bentley rose from his desk and walked over to one of the bookshelves. He studied the rows, and after putting a finger on several books, he pulled one out and walked back over to his desk and sat down behind it again.

A musty smell drifted past John. He tried to stay quiet and patient as his uncle flipped through page after page of the aged yet handsome leather-bound book. John was not good at the waiting game.

"Well, it's certain that Napoleon was on the rampage that year with quite a few successes."

"But my father wasn't in the military during that time, so he wouldn't have been away on any of the campaigns, right?"

"Well, no, let's see, here we go—oh, yes. Wait, I remember now. How could I have forgotten?"

"What?" John asked, moving to the edge of his seat in anticipation with fear and hope.

"That's the year we took you and spent the summer touring Scotland."

John's heart rate increased. "Scotland. Yes, I vaguely remember being there, and you say it was seventeen ninety-eight? Are you sure of the date?"

He rapped on the book with his knuckles. "I have it recorded right here."

"How long were we gone?"

He thumbed through the yellowed pages more quickly, scanning the top portion of each page. "It appears we left as soon as the Season had ended and didn't return until just before Christmastime."

John's breathing was laborious with excitement. "And my father was with us all the time?"

"Yes, I just said so. There is no doubt about this." He closed the book and pushed it toward John. "Take it with you and read it all for yourself. It tells all the places we visited and mentions you and your father. I'm not so old that I've forgotten everything. I would have remembered if your father had left the trip early."

If they were gone from summer through the end of that year, Catherine couldn't possibly be his sister. Relief drenched John.

Some other man was her father.

John rose and picked up the book from the desk. "I'll get this back to you."

His uncle looked up into his eyes. "No hurry. What is this about, John?"

"I would confide in you if I could, but there are other people's feelings to consider. Suffice it to say I was made aware of something that happened a long time ago and there was a possibility—" He paused and drew a heady breath. "A slight possibility that my father had been involved in something, but since you are certain he was in Scotland with us, then there is no way he could have been involved."

"That's good to hear. I'd hate for anything to tarnish your father's good name."

"It won't."

"While you are here, John, I'll mention something I've been reluctant to bring up lately, but maybe with this incident and the one with the horse I should."

"What's that?"

"You need to think seriously about your responsibilities and duty to the title. And I don't say that because I have an interest in it. You know I don't. But your father has been gone a long time now and you are past thirty."

John nodded. "You needn't say more on the subject. I've been recently thinking about the same thing myself."

"Good. I won't say any more."

"Thank you for understanding, Uncle. I've always appreciated that you've let me be my own man."

Bentley sat back in his chair and smiled. "How could I do it any differently? You are the earl even if I am the elder."

"And far wiser than I."

John walked out with the book under his arm, anxious to read for himself what the journal said.

Twelve

❦

"A racehorse needs only a touch of the whip; a clever man needs only a hint." But what does Lord Chatwin need to tell us who rode his horse? Bets are on the rise as to the identity of the mysterious lady rider. More than twenty pounds was recently placed on Lady Veronica, the lovely phantom who prowls the darkened hillsides searching for Lord Pinkwater's ghost.

Lord Truefitt
Society's Daily Column

"*DID ANY OF* you see Lord Truefitt's column this afternoon?" Rachel Dawson asked the group of five ladies who were standing with her at Lady Waverly's soirée.

"No, what did it say?" The bright-eyed Beverly Moorehouse responded first.

"They now think it was a lady ghost riding Lord Chatwin's horse in the park."

A collective gasp came from all the ladies, but none of

them was as loud as Catherine's. All that nonsense about a lady ghost was printed in the scandal sheets? How outrageous.

"A ghost?" Margaret Anderson exclaimed, her dark eyes wide with disbelief. "You must be teasing us."

"I'm not. It's true. Gentlemen are already placing bets that she's the lady rider. You've heard of the phantom Lord Truefitt referred to, I'm sure. It's Lady Veronica. Some say she was once Lord Pinkwater's lover. She now roams the hillsides at night looking for him. She wants their souls to be united."

Catherine remained amazed as she stood among the young ladies and listened to them converse. Candles glistened, music played, and people chatted and laughed throughout the large home in Mayfair. Everything was perfectly normal except this unfortunate spreading of the story of the ghost and John's horse.

Where on earth could such a bizarre idea have come from? The story of who rode John's horse should be old news by now, but it seemed to be growing bigger and more preposterous every day instead of fading away.

This latest addition was lunacy.

"Did you see the article?" Rachel turned to Catherine and asked.

"Ah—no, I didn't," she answered, trying not to sound as astonished as she was.

And she could only hope John hadn't seen it. She'd thought he was just beginning to forget about her taking his horse that morning, but he never would if the gossips wouldn't stop. How could something so utterly unbelievable have gotten started?

And to think men were placing bets on it.

"I don't believe it because I don't believe in ghosts,"

Margaret said disdainfully and sniffed into her lace hand-kerchief.

"I don't know whether or not there are ghosts, but if there are, can they ride a horse?" Beverly asked as she looked from one lady to another.

"Of course," Rachel said with conviction. "A ghost can do anything it wants to do. And, for your information, Margaret, the sightings of Lord Pinkwater's and Lady Veronica's ghosts are well documented."

"Maybe in poetry and horrid novels," she responded and followed with a short laugh.

Rachel's brows shot together in a deep frown, and she pursed her lips for a moment before saying, "Many people have reported seeing Lord Pinkwater's ghost in their homes and gardens, and remember he was once accused of stealing art objects from members of the *ton*."

"Yes, I remember something about that a couple of years ago," Beverly said.

"I remember the Mad *ton* Thief, too," Margaret said. "And as I recall, it was discovered that a member of the *ton* was the thief, not a member of the spirit world."

"I've never seen Lord Pinkwater's ghost or any other specter," Beverly said. "Do you personally know anyone who has ever seen one?"

"It so happens I do," Rachel answered. "My maid told me that one night she saw a ghost in her bedroom in a house where she worked. She left her employment and that house the very next morning and never went back."

"It's my guess that she left her employment because it was the master of the house who'd slipped into her bedroom, not a ghost."

"Margaret!" Rachel exclaimed, her pale face turning a bright shade of pink.

All the young ladies laughed except Catherine, and she managed a smile big enough to make the ladies think she was enjoying their conversation as much as they were, but she wasn't.

She was responsible for this tittle-tattle.

Had she known that such ridiculous gossip would have swept through Society like a practical joke gone awry, she would never have borrowed John's horse. But no way could she have foreseen something like this a few mornings ago. Her only desire had been to get help for the groom.

"All of you are wrong," Evelyn Wintergarden said, speaking up for the first time. "I don't think she was a ghost at all, but a flesh-and-blood woman. It's my thought that she was Lord Chatwin's latest lover, not Lord Pinkwater's mistress."

A couple of the ladies giggled again while Margaret nodded her head in agreement and said, "I believe you are right."

Catherine didn't like the sinking feeling in her stomach when Lord Chatwin's lover was mentioned. Perhaps the best thing for her to do was to excuse herself from the group. It was amazing to her how freely the young ladies talked to each other about lovers.

"I've heard that Lord Chatwin has many lovers, but I don't think he would give his horse to any of them for any reason."

Catherine winced inside but tried not to let it show. She must get away from these ladies before they decided to bring her into the conversation and ask her something she didn't want to answer.

She looked around the room to see who else might be available for her to talk to when she noticed John standing by a doorway watching her. Her heart felt as if it dropped to her knees.

Did he have news? Her gaze held on his. She couldn't tell from his expression if he had information about whether she was his sister or not.

He motioned with his head and eyes that he wanted her to follow him through the doorway, and then he disappeared.

Should she follow him?

How could she not?

Even if he had news she didn't want to hear, she had to know. She swallowed her trepidation of hearing the truth and took a deep breath.

Catherine glanced around and saw that Victoria was deep in conversation with a group of matrons on the other side of the room. The coast was clear.

Catherine excused herself and slowly made her way to the spot where she'd seen John. She had to slip out of the room without her sister or anyone seeing her.

As she leisurely made her way to where John had just exited, she smiled at a gentleman who waved to her, then she nodded to a Countess she had met the night before. When she stepped through the doorway, it took her into another room that was just as crowded as the one she left.

Unobtrusively she looked around the room in a manner so as not to bring attention to herself. Finally she saw John standing by another doorway.

When he was sure she had seen him, he went through it. Her pulse rate shot up. She glanced around and it didn't appear that anyone watched her, so she followed and slipped through the doorway that led her directly into another large room.

There was the clatter of silverware on plates, lively

chatter from guests who were enjoying the food and the now distant sound of music. An older gentleman had cornered John and was talking to him, so Catherine eased over to the table that held the punch. She asked the servant for a cup and then strolled along the food-laden tables while she waited for John's next move.

She helped herself to a sugary fig pudding. When she looked at John again, he had extracted himself from the man and was standing near yet another opening. When their glances met, he disappeared through the doorway again.

Catherine's heart pounded in her chest. The stealth with which they were maneuvering through the rooms in the house left her breathless. Excitement unfurled low in her stomach, filling her with anticipation. Was she really playing this "follow me" game with John and right under the watchful eyes of half the *ton*?

Another glance around the room told her yes. Fortunately, no one was paying attention to her.

She handed her cup of punch to a passing servant and followed John through an archway that this time led into a long, narrow, dimly lit hallway.

The passageway was empty. She didn't see John or anyone else.

Had she lost him? She glanced down the corridor behind her. He was nowhere in sight. The seconds ticked by. Maybe she'd missed him. She peeked back into the buffet room, but he wasn't there, either, so taking a deep breath, she cautiously started tiptoeing down the corridor.

Suddenly John grabbed her hand and pulled her into a small, dark room and closed the door behind them.

There was very little space, and she found herself squeezed between John and something hard and uncomfortable pressed against her back. At first it was too dark for her to see him even though he stood only inches from her. She heard his breathing; she felt the seductive heat from his body wrapping around her.

"Where are we?" she whispered.

"In a closet filled with furniture."

As her eyes adjusted to the darkness, she looked behind her and saw a small window that wasn't much bigger than a single pane of glass. If not for it, the room would have been totally black. Shadowed moonlight filtered inside, and she could see that chairs, small tables, and lamp stands had been stacked on top of each other.

"I should have guessed. I think I have a chair leg sticking in my back."

"Come here," he said and pressed her up close to him and away from the furniture. His arms sailed around her waist, and he turned her so that the furniture was to his back and she was against the door.

He settled himself against a chair and pulled her to his chest, closing her in his embrace. The lower part of Catherine's arms rested on his chest, keeping her from falling flat against him.

"Is that better?" he asked.

"Mmm, yes," she said, knowing she was talking about the way she felt with his arms around her, and his hands moving up and down her back. "But why didn't you just ask me to dance or to take a walk with you on the terrace?" she whispered.

"There was too much of a chance of someone overhearing us or Mrs. Goosetree following us. I've noticed she seldom lets you out of her sight. Besides, if I had done that—I couldn't do this."

Suddenly his head dipped low and he kissed her

soundly, briefly on the lips, and then he lifted his head and said, "You are not my sister."

Relief and happiness mixed with a little doubt flooded her. She needed to be convinced. "Are you sure?"

"Very," he answered as his open hands continued to move up and down her back, keeping her warm and feeling protected.

"How? Tell me what you found out that makes you so positive."

"I went to see my uncle—my mother's brother."

Her body went rigid under his touch. "You didn't tell him what I told you about my search, did you?"

His hands tightened on her. "No. I promised I wouldn't. I only mentioned to him that I needed his assistance with my father's whereabouts for the year in question. I couldn't believe it either when he told me that he had it written in a journal that he, my father, and I spent the last six months of seventeen ninety-eight touring Scotland. My father was nowhere near London that fall and could not have fathered you."

She wanted to believe him so much she squeezed her eyes shut for a moment. "Is he sure of the dates?"

Keeping his voice low, he said, "Yes. And I'm sure. I took the journal home and read it for myself. I found out things about my father I never knew, some things I didn't remember from our tour because it was so long ago, but most important it told me that he never left Scotland while we were there and that means there is no way that you and I could be related."

She smiled, almost feeling giddy with relief. "I'm so happy about this, John. I don't know how, but deep inside here"—she put her hand on her heart—"I knew you were not my brother, yet it had to be verified since your father's name was in my mother's diary."

"And now I've made certain."

She paused. "Thank you for doing this for me."

"You're welcome."

It also meant she could now mark Mr. George Wickenham-Thickenham-Fines off her list, leaving only two. But she didn't want to think about those men right now. She only wanted to think about being in John's arms.

She could see him smiling down at her. She smelled the scent of his shaving soap and felt the worsted wool of his coat beneath her thinly gloved fingers.

His hands moved to her upper arms, that small area of exposed skin between the capped sleeves of her gown and her long white gloves. His touch warmed her cool skin, and his fingers lightly caressed her.

"Are you cold?" he asked.

"Not anymore. In fact, I'm beginning to feel quite flushed."

With confidence his hands slid across her shoulders all the way up her neck to cup each side of her face. She remained very still as first one thumb and then the other caressed her lips once, twice, three times.

"Catherine, you set me on fire," he whispered as he reached down and tenderly kissed her cheek, then inhaled her scent. "You have from the first moment when I held you in my arms and you started kicking me and demanding that I set you down."

"I hope I didn't hurt you."

"Not at all."

Suddenly she reached up and grabbed one of his wrists

and guided his hand to her lips. She planted a soft, moist kiss in his palm.

She heard his breathing change tempo to choppy gasps and it thrilled her.

"What was that for?" he asked huskily.

"To thank you for helping me. I'm one man closer to finding out who my real father is."

"That wasn't my reason for doing it, but if it helps you in your quest, that's all the better."

She smiled up at him, wishing she could see his eyes more clearly. "It helps me more than you could know."

"And you tempt me more than you know." He placed the palm of his hand to her lips and she kissed it again. "If you only knew what your kisses did to me, you would run out of this closet screaming for help."

All of a sudden she reached up and kissed him on the side of his mouth. She didn't know how or why such a simple kiss should send a thrill of desire shooting through her, but it did.

She said, "I'm not afraid of you, John."

He pulled her closer, and held her tighter. "You should be. You know if we are caught in here like this your reputation will be ruined forever."

A small confident laugh passed her lips. "I also know you would be forced to marry me, so I'm confident you have made sure no one will find us alone together in here."

He chuckled lightly, too. "You are right, beautiful, and ever so tempting."

John bent his head and his lips touched hers. The kiss was warm, pleasing, and brief.

"And you are reckless, sir."

"I know. I've had a few close calls over the years, but none more worth the risk than what I'm doing right now."

His fingers played with her earlobes, the soft skin at the back of her ear, and down her neck. She loved the tightening low in her abdomen at his touch.

"Then perhaps you are just brave."

"I'll agree to that, and to trusting myself to protect you. I wanted a place where I could talk to you alone. I checked every door down the hallway while I waited for you to follow me. This room is perfect. It's at the rear of the house, and only servants pass by this way. They all know furniture is in here and will have no reason to open the door."

"You did well. I feel very safe here with you, but I really should be going before Victoria comes looking for me."

"Not yet. A few moments more?"

"Just a little longer."

It was so easy to give in to his wishes when her body was feeling as it did right now. Expectant.

"I like the way the moonlight plays on your lips." He rubbed his thumb over her mouth again. "It makes them very seductive. So enticing that I'm going to put aside my good sense and instead of letting you go, I'm going to kiss you again, but this time longer."

John dipped his head and captured her lips in a harder, more passionate kiss than before. Her lips parted and his tongue slid inside and he tasted her. She gasped at the pleasure that filled her. His invasion was tender yet commanding. A wave of desire floated low in her stomach, and she moaned softly against his lips.

Her arms rested on his chest, forming a barrier between them, keeping them apart. She needed to be closer to him. There was an ache in her breasts, and she wanted to feel them against his chest, so she lifted her arms and circled his neck.

John took advantage of her movement and pulled her

tightly against his body as his lips and mouth plundered hers, softly, deftly. He must have loved her touching the back of his neck, his shoulders, and his back, because his breathing grew faster. His lips moved down her cheek, over the line of her jaw, and rained kisses down her chest to the low neckline of her gown.

She loved the feel of being completely caught up in his arms. She knew she'd been waiting for this to happen between them ever since their first kiss in the park. On that early morning, she had her first taste of passion, and she had been longing to experience it again.

He lifted his head and said, "That kiss was much better but still not long enough."

"I don't know why, but I feel breathless when your lips are pressed against mine."

"That's the way you are supposed to feel. Breathless and hungry."

He kissed her again and again and she loved it. A fluttering filled her chest. His mouth and tongue ravaged hers in a slow savoring kiss meant to seduce and be victorious.

Catherine had no desire to stop him, but she did mumble against his lips, "I really should go. I don't want to get caught."

"We won't. I'm listening for footsteps and voices in the hallway," he answered as his lips left hers and he kissed his way down her neck and back up again to her mouth.

"It sounds as if you have been in a situation like this before."

"Once or twice," he admitted with a soft chuckle.

"You are a rogue, Lord Chatwin," she whispered.

"I know." He kissed the tip of her nose.

"I expect you ask for, and receive, kisses from all the

young ladies you corner in closets. That is part of your charm."

"Is it? I don't even remember the other ladies I've kissed anymore," he said softly.

"You lie, my lord."

He looked down into her eyes, and she noticed that he looked serious when he said, "Not this time. Not with you."

He reached up and kissed her eyelids, letting his lips linger. He slowly kissed his way down her nose and across first one cheek and then the other, teasing her. His lips slid over her jaw and down her slender neck. She threw her head back to give him greater access to the places he wanted to go.

Catherine loved the feel of his lips moist against her skin. She trembled with a need and a wanting she didn't understand.

His hands moved to her waist and rested there for a moment before moving on to outline the flare of her hips, over to her stomach, and then around to the rise of her buttocks. She gasped excitedly with each new place he stroked. No one had ever touched her in these intimate areas before.

"You are a beautifully shaped woman, Catherine," he whispered to her.

"And you are big and strong," she answered as her hands roamed over his broad back and shoulders.

She had no idea it would feel so wonderful, so satisfying, yet leaving her with a feeling that she wanted so much more.

But more of what she didn't know.

His hands slid up her arms to her neck, and once again his fingers caressed her earlobes and that soft skin behind them. He played with the long dangle of her sapphires that fell from the lobes of her ears and farther down to the heavy jeweled necklace around her neck.

Slowly his hands slid down to her breasts and he fondled them both at the same time, softly caressing them with the confidence of a man who had no fear he'd be spurned.

Catherine gasped at his boldness, but had no desire to stop him.

His hands stilled, but he didn't move them away from her breasts. He lifted his head and looked down into her eyes.

"How does my touch make you feel?"

"I've never been touched so intimately before. It's—it's wonderful, exciting."

He smiled and resumed his firm yet gentle caressing of her breasts. "That's very good. And just so you know, it wouldn't necessarily feel this way with every man."

"It wouldn't?" she asked, barely able to speak coherently for the delicious thrills racking her body from his masterful ministrations.

"No, you have to be attracted to a man to feel this way."

"Does the same hold true for a man? Does he have to be attracted to a woman to feel such pleasure?"

He raised his head and looked down into her eyes as he smiled. "No. Not always. Men are different."

"What makes them different?"

He laughed lightly. "Nature and that is all I'm going to say on the subject."

"But do you touch me because you are attracted to me?"

The smile faded from his lips and his eyes, and a serious expression masked his face.

"Oh, yes," he whispered huskily. "Have no fear or doubt, Catherine. I touch you because I desire you like I have no other woman."

He bent his head and captured her lips in a fierce kiss of passion. Catherine didn't know if she believed him, but right at that moment she didn't care. All that was important was that he was receiving as much pleasure from her as she was from him.

John's hands moved from her breasts to her buttocks, and he fit her lower body up against his. Catherine felt a hard bulge beneath his trousers, and it quickened her breath. She had never felt anything like it before, but knew she didn't want it to go away.

She raised her hips up to meet his demand, and she felt him shudder with passion and a soft moan of pleasure passed his lips. He dipped his tongue in her mouth, deeper, farther. Slower and then faster. They couldn't kiss or touch or press fast enough to sate the passion raging out of control.

Catherine glowed red hot. A longing ache started between her legs and rose up to spread throughout her abdomen, stomach, and breasts. Everything she was feeling was so new to her. She didn't have time to wonder if what she was feeling was simply passion or something akin to the love she had read about in her poetry books.

Finally John lifted his head. His breathing was fast and erratic as he said, "You are so lovely, so tempting. You feel so good in my arms, I ache to take you right now and make you mine."

"Can you do that?" she asked and didn't know why she had except that she didn't want the thrilling feelings inside her to stop. Somehow she knew they had not finished what they had started, and she wanted him to continue.

She reached out to him, but he stepped back as far as he could without tumbling the furniture. Her heart constricted.

He took a deep steadying breath before lowering his

voice to a husky whisper, "No, I must not touch you again. I can't do this to you. Not here. Not like this."

Without giving her time to respond, he reached over and took her gently by the shoulders and eased her away from the door.

"I'll go out first and make sure the hallway is clear. If you hear me talking to anyone, do not come out. Understand?"

She blinked rapidly, trying to clear her thoughts. "Yes, but I'm wondering how you can sound so coherent when I'm still reeling from your touch," she said feeling a bit rebuffed.

His eyes held on hers. "I have to get away from you now—before it's too late for you, or me." He took another long breath. "Besides, I've kept you away from the party much too long. I'm sure Mrs. Goosetree is looking for you."

"Probably," Catherine said, but what she wanted to say was "I don't care. I want to be in your arms again."

"When you walk back into the buffet room, if anyone asks where you have been, tell them that you became lost in the house."

"I know how to handle myself in a delicate situation, sir. I shall be fine and need no tutoring from you."

He nodded. "I have no doubt of that. I'm going to find Mrs. Goosetree and tell her I'm coming to take you for a ride in the park tomorrow afternoon."

What a confusing man he was. He pushed her away and now he was telling her he intended to see her again. She didn't know whether to be angry or relieved.

"You can try, but, John, you know Vickie. She could very well say I'm not available."

"I won't take no for an answer. We need some time to talk about what you are doing."

"You mean by allowing you so much freedom to touch

me when we kiss? I want to do that. You are not forcing me against my will."

"I know that, Catherine. What I want to talk to you about is your ill-fated search for your father."

He opened the door and stepped out, closing it behind him.

Just like that he was gone.

Catherine couldn't have been more surprised if he had thrown cold water in her face. Her search for her father was not ill-fated.

How dare he? Did he think she could stop her search now?

Suddenly the man who she wanted to continue kissing and caressing her just moments before, she now wanted to strangle.

Thirteen

"*How dare you*, Lord Chatwin?" Catherine whispered to the closed door. "Ill-fated, indeed." She huffed. "We'll see about that. Not only am I not going to stop searching, I will find a way to convince you to help me."

How could she stop looking for her father? Especially now that she had whittled her list of possibilities down to two? She was making progress, and neither Lord Chatwin nor the fact that the two remaining men were odd was going to stop her.

One of them was her father, and she was more determined than ever to find out which one was.

She folded her arms across her chest and softly tapped her foot on the floor until she realized what she was doing. She would not let John frustrate her or pressure her to give up her quest.

She had to admit that the men she sought were a bit different with their unusual quirks: one hating the color green and the other walking everywhere he went. But none of that mattered. How could she go through the rest of her life not knowing what her real father looked like, not knowing why he never married her mother?

Catherine deserved to know.

It wasn't that she wanted either one of these peculiar men to have fathered her. She had been quite happy with the father she'd known all her life. But her mother had loved one of these two men enough to lie with him before marriage.

Catherine wouldn't be content until she knew which one. She wanted to talk to him and find out what happened all those years ago. She needed to know what her mother's diary didn't tell her.

And her task would be so much easier if John helped her. As an earl he could make the introductions to the two men, which would give her the opportunity to talk to them, get to know them, and question them about their past.

She leaned back against the furniture and pondered. Yes, she really needed John's help. Even though she found him immensely charming, and it was truly unbelievable how much she enjoyed his kisses, he was not to be a serious contender for her husband no matter what Victoria thought. He'd proven that the night he invited her to his uncle's party and then danced with everyone but her.

And it wasn't just John's kisses that made her light of heart when she thought about him. She liked the fact that he never told anyone she took his horse that day. She liked the way he favored Lynette and other young ladies who weren't beautiful with dances and compliments. When she told him she might be his sister, he immediately went about finding the answer without hesitating and without telling his uncle about her plight.

He was trustworthy and that made him all the more desirable.

But his reputation was undeniable. She fully expected him to enjoy her kisses and caresses for a few days and then move on to the next young lady to catch his fancy. She wanted him to show her attention and the thought of him going to another woman made her heart ache.

Catherine took a deep breath. Tomorrow she would ask him if he would help her discover which man was her father.

The problem was in deciding what she could offer John in return for his help. She'd always heard that everything had a price.

What would tempt John to agree?

Suddenly she gasped. She tempted John. When they'd kissed so passionately, he'd told her she tempted him like no other woman.

She had no reason to doubt what he said was true. He certainly acted as if he were enjoying himself when they kissed. What would he say if she offered him her kisses in exchange for helping her?

Would he agree?

"I'll soon find out," she said aloud. "I will ask for his help and repay him with kisses."

That settled Catherine realized she'd stayed in the closet far longer than John had told her to. She touched her hair, then opened the door and stepped out right in front of a young maid who was walking down the hallway with a tray filled with tinkling glasses.

Catherine kept her composure and never blinked an eye. Lifting her chin and her shoulders, she smiled at the wide-eyed servant in a gray dress and white apron and said, "Excuse me, but I seem to have lost my way. Is the buffet room through there?"

The young maid's eyes grew wide. "Yes, miss," she said, looking at Catherine as if she'd seen a ghost.

"Oh, perfect. Thank you."

Catherine tried not to hurry as she walked past the maid and down the corridor. Meeting the servant was too close for comfort. It could just as easily have been the lady of the house or the butler who saw her coming out of the closet. Neither of whom would have hesitated to take her directly to Victoria.

Taking a calming breath, Catherine strolled into the buffet room as unobtrusively as possible and made her way over to the champagne table and asked for a glass. She was trying her best not to look or act as if she had just been in a dark closet passionately kissing the most handsome man.

She took her first sip of champagne, and the cool bubbly liquid was almost as satisfying as water to her dry throat. She had to force herself to remain calm and not look or act as guilty as she suddenly felt. No one was paying any attention to her and she wanted to keep it that way.

When she lifted the glass for her second sip, she saw Victoria enter the room and spot her immediately. Obviously she'd made it into the buffet room just in time.

"There you are," Victoria said, walking up to her with a worried expression on her face. "I've been looking everywhere for you."

"Have you? I've been in the house all evening," Catherine answered in all truthfulness.

"I suppose you were going into one room while I was coming out of another. Lady Waverly is fortunate to have one of the largest houses in Mayfair, but it does make it difficult to find anyone when you need them. No matter, I wanted you to know that I have finalized your plans for tomorrow."

Oh, no, that meant she would not get to see John. She took another sip of the champagne and it went down fast. Kissing surely made one thirsty.

"What plans have you made for me?" she managed to ask.

"I have just moments ago finished talking with Lord Chatwin, and I agreed that he could take you for a ride in Hyde Park tomorrow afternoon." Victoria fanned herself. "It will be lovely. Everyone will see you."

Catherine's stomach jumped in anticipation. She was thrilled. John had kept his word and wasted no time finding Victoria. Tomorrow she could proceed with her proposition to the earl, but tonight she couldn't sound too eager.

"I'm surprised you are allowing me to accompany him, Vickie."

"Why so?"

"I thought you had changed your mind about the Terrible Twosome earl and had decided that the Marquis was the gentleman for me."

"Nonsense. I'm for whichever gentleman seems most interested in you. I was very clever and told Lord Chatwin I would rearrange your schedule for him and that it would make some other gentlemen very unhappy." She smiled and her brown eyes sparkled mischievously. "He seemed quite pleased by that."

"I'm sure he was," Catherine murmured.

She was going to see him so that she could convince him to help her find her father.

"Finish your champagne quickly and meet me by the front door. I'm ready to go to the next party. Perhaps we'll see the Marquis there so that I can plan your afternoon for the day after tomorrow." She paused and suddenly an expression of concern hooded her eyes once more. "Your lips look a little red and slightly swollen."

"They are?" she whispered.

Catherine's fingers flew to her lips and she covered them. She was caught. Victoria knew she'd been kissed.

What was she going to do?

"Yes," Victoria continued. "I've noticed that you have a habit of sinking your teeth into your bottom lip and sucking it into your mouth."

Did she?

"I do?"

"Yes, and you must not do that anymore, Catherine."

"Right. No more," she managed to say coherently.

"It makes your lips too . . . too—"

"Too what?" Catherine asked, remembering how passionately John's lips had ravaged hers over and over again.

"Well, they look too kissable."

"Too kissable?" Catherine choked out between pretend coughs, which she hoped covered her shock at how close Victoria was to knowing exactly what went on in that closet.

"Yes, and they might tempt some brave young gentleman to try and kiss you. Especially a rogue like that dashing Lord Chatwin. We wouldn't want that, would we?"

"N-no, we wouldn't."

Victoria smiled, again seeming quite pleased with herself. "Splendid. So no more teeth on your lips."

"I'll be more conscious of that, Vickie. Thank you for pointing it out to me."

"Now finish your champagne and meet me by the door." With that Victoria whirled and left in a puff of brown satin skirts.

When Victoria was out of sight, Catherine handed her

glass to a servant and walked over to a dark corner where a large urn filled with flowers stood and hid behind the arrangement. She put her hand over her mouth and laughed softly. She was weak with relief that she hadn't been caught and giddy with happiness.

She couldn't believe she had passed another close call. Obviously a guardian angel had been watching over her tonight.

She was grateful Victoria didn't know that her lips had already been kissed. She leaned against the wall and smiled. She felt wonderful. She would be seeing Lord Chatwin tomorrow. And while it was very important she convince him to help her find her real father, she realized that it was even more important to her that she just spend time with him. She knew that all too soon he would want to leave her for another.

Catherine heard voices and laughter very close to her, and that reminded her she needed to meet her sister. She started to push away from the wall when she heard Lord Chatwin's name mentioned. It wasn't her intention to eavesdrop, but her curiosity got the better of her, and she found herself moving closer to the flowers so she could hear what the group of young men were saying.

"Poor Lord Chatwin, what an unlucky fellow. I wouldn't want to be in his boots."

"Me either. Not for his title and all the land that comes with it."

"Imagine, having all of London thinking that a lady ghost spooked your horse and then rode off on it."

She heard laughter. And at John's expense.

A protective feeling unlike anything she'd ever felt before rose up inside her. She wanted to tell them to stop.

"And it's not only the phantom lady he has to worry

about. Imagine the whole of London knowing he was thrown from the gelding when he's supposed to be one of the best riders of the old bachelors."

Old bachelor? Catherine wasn't sure she was hearing this correctly. Was Lord Chatwin now considered one of the old bachelors? Surely not? John was maybe a year past thirty. She remembered how hard his chest was and how firm and muscular his back and shoulders were. Even now she could close her eyes and feel the strength of his embrace as he held her close.

Old? John?

She peeked through the flowers and recognized the three gentlemen as young men in their early twenties. Perhaps they did consider John old, but Catherine didn't.

"Damnation, do you think he's losing his skills with the ladies?"

There was more laughter.

"Do you think he really believes it was a ghost who knocked him off his horse?"

"I heard the Marquis say that he looked as if he had seen a ghost that morning."

"All I can say is I'm glad I'm not the one who fell off my horse."

Anger built inside Catherine. They were not talking about the Lord Chatwin she knew. Catherine had a strong desire to bound from behind the urn and tell the young men that she was the lady on the horse.

"Bloody, yes."

"Some of us have decided to meet in the park at dawn tomorrow morning to see if we can find Lord Chatwin's lady ghost. Do you want to come along?"

"I'll be there. If there is a specter haunting the park, I want to be one of the first to see her."

There was more laughter and then the shuffling of feet as they walked away.

Why wouldn't this story go away?

She wished she'd never taken his horse that morning. It was her fault that he was being ridiculed like this. First with the young ladies earlier in the evening and now with the men. Even his best friend Lord Dugdale had been outrageously angry with her about what this story had done to John's reputation. And now she understood Lord Dugdale's feelings.

She couldn't let this go on.

She had to do something.

But what?

She looked around the room as if some inspiration would hit her out of the blue. And it did. There in a flowing gown of a faded plum color was Lady Lynette standing by the buffet table eating an apple tart.

Lynette had once boasted she knew everyone in the *ton*, and others had told Catherine that, too. Catherine was going to give her the chance to prove it. What she was about to do would make Victoria very unhappy, but it was time for Catherine to step up and take responsibility for what she had done and suffer the consequences whatever they may be.

Shoring up her courage, she walked over to Lynette, who had just taken the last bite of her tart, and said, "Lynette, do you mind if I have a moment of your time?"

"Of course not," she said, daintily dabbing at the corners of her mouth with a napkin.

"Good. I need you to help me with something."

Clearly she was taken aback by Catherine's comment. "Me? Oh, I'd love to. I don't think I've ever had anyone ask for my assistance before."

Catherine smiled, glad that she had flattered Lynette, although that wasn't her intention.

"I'm sure that's not true. You seem very levelheaded to me."

"Thank you. What can I do for you?" she asked eagerly.

Catherine sucked in her breath and said, "You indicated to me a few nights ago that if I knew something about Lord Chatwin and who rode his horse in the park that I should talk to you."

Lynette's eyes lit with intrigue and Catherine watched as her gaze scanned the room as if to see if anyone were watching or listening to them.

Then she said, "Yes, by all means if you know something, you can surely tell me."

"The person I really need to talk to is Lord Truefitt, and I was hoping you could help me find him."

Her eyes widened. "Oh, but you can't talk to him. No one knows who he is."

"Piffle. I don't believe that. How does he get the information that he writes each day in his column? Someone must know how to get in touch with him to give him the information he writes about."

Lynette remained quiet, studying Catherine.

"Would you know how I could get some information to Lord Truefitt?"

Lynette laid her napkin on a table and touched Catherine's arm and indicated for her to move to the far side of the room with her.

Catherine followed.

Lynette bent close to her and in a low voice said, "I might. I'm not promising anything or admitting to anything, but I may know how to accomplish getting information to him."

"I would really appreciate your help."

"If I do this for you, you must promise never to tell anyone I helped you. My name must never be mentioned in connection with Lord Truefitt."

"Oh, never would I tell anyone."

"Promise not to tell and hope to die if you do."

Catherine was a little stunned at the juvenile oath from a lady who had to be in her late twenties, but she immediately agreed. "Yes, I promise."

Lynette smiled and relaxed. "All right, I believe you. Now tell me what you know."

Catherine took a steadying breath. "I have proof Lord Chatwin was not thrown from his magnificent horse, and it was not a ghost riding the animal in the park. The woman was flesh and blood."

Her eyes rounded. "You know who she is?"

"Yes. I was the lady riding his horse."

Doubt showed in Lynette's face and her eyes. "You? Are you sure?"

Exasperated Catherine said, "Of course I'm sure. I was there." Catherine stopped. Saying that made her sound as silly as Lynette.

"I wouldn't admit to this if it wasn't true."

"Perhaps you are trying to get your name mentioned in the column."

"No, that's not true. In fact, I was hoping Lord Truefitt would find a way to get the straight story without using my name. I have no desire to show up in his column."

Lynette nodded. "All right, go on."

"I only want Lord Truefitt to know I was the one riding the horse so he will stop writing about it in his column so everyone will stop teasing Lord Chatwin about a ghost."

Lynette's lovely green eyes widened even further with surprise. "You are in love with him, aren't you?"

Catherine gasped. "What? No. Of course not. How absurd. I know he is unattainable."

"Good. He has broken many young ladies' hearts. All of them were sure they could win his."

"I understand that." Catherine wasn't prepared for how empty she felt when she admitted that. "I simply feel guilty that his fine reputation is being ridiculed when all he did was help me when I needed it."

Lynette didn't look convinced and the truth of it was Catherine wasn't convinced herself, but she didn't have time to argue the point with Lynette or search her inner feelings.

"So tell me, how did you come to be riding on his horse?"

"It's rather a long story."

"I've got time and I want to hear it all."

"But I don't have that much time," Catherine said, glancing at the door. "Vickie is waiting for me so we can go to another party."

"Then quickly tell me what happened."

Suddenly Catherine wished she had something to drink. Her throat was dry again. She felt desperate to clear John's name no matter the cost to her own. She had no intention of telling Lynette exactly what happened, only as much as she wanted her to know.

Catherine told the story, making John out the hero who assisted her and let her borrow his horse.

"My goodness!" Lynette exclaimed. "Your horse almost collided with Lord Chatwin's. How dangerous. Were you harmed?"

"No, but it was frightful. If not for both of our riding skills, the horses would have smashed together and been injured or killed, not to mention what would have happened to us. As it was, my mare, who was not as well-schooled as Lord Chatwin's, panicked and tossed me off, then ran away."

"Leaving you there alone with Lord Chatwin."

Catherine cleared her throat. "Yes. And he was a perfect gentleman. I told Lord Chatwin that I needed his horse so that I could get help for our groom." She tried not to worry about not telling the story the exact way it happened.

"What did he do?" Lynette urged her when she had stopped for a moment's breath.

"Lord Chatwin of course offered to do the proper thing and ride for help, but he didn't want to leave me alone in the park, so we decided that I should ride his horse and get help as quickly as possible."

"That is a fascinating story. Why didn't you want anyone to know?"

"Lord Chatwin suggested we not tell anyone about it because he didn't want it to in any way blemish my reputation as this is my first Season and the incident was truly innocent."

Lynette's face softened and she smiled wistfully. "He is a true gentleman."

"Yes, that is why I can no longer allow this outlandish story of a ghost to continue. There is no ghost. But having only been in London a few weeks, I have no idea how to get the story to Lord Truefitt so that he might write about it. Lord Chatwin would never speak up and tell the truth of what happened, so I must even if it damages my reputation."

Lynette smiled the most satisfied smile Catherine had ever seen anyone wear, and suddenly she knew that she had done the right thing. The true story needed to come out.

"Do not worry, Catherine. I will see to it that the real story comes out and that your name will not be listed. And I will make sure that both you and Lord Chatwin are considered heroes."

"Both of us? But I did nothing but take his horse. That is, when he offered it."

"And help your groom."

"Oh, yes, right. Thank you for doing this," Catherine said.

"No, my dear Catherine, thank you, and remember our deal that you tell no one you spoke to me about this."

"I won't forget."

Lynette reached out and took hold of Catherine's hand. "Thank you for trusting me with this. I have one other very dear friend who once trusted me like this. Her name is Millicent. She's the wife of Lord Dunraven. He's the married one of the Terrible Threesome. Have you met Millicent?"

"No, I don't believe I have."

Lynette smiled. "I'll see that you do. I think you two will become good friends."

Fourteen

I T WAS THE warmest day of the year so far, and John felt every degree of temperature, but his hotness had nothing to do with the hat on his head, the gloves on his hands, or his intricately tied neckcloth. It was all about Catherine Reynolds.

He'd been in a perpetual state of heat since he first glimpsed Miss Catherine Reynolds's blue eyes, and it had only gotten worse when he'd tasted her passion. He took hold of Catherine's hand and helped her step up and into his phaeton. She sat on the seat cushion and arranged the skirts of her French blue carriage dress as he climbed up beside her.

It was the first time he'd seen her wear the color blue, and it made her eyes all the more startling and gorgeous. She seemed to match everything including the clear blue sky that for the first time in months didn't have a white or gray cloud anywhere in sight.

He was going to have a hell of a time keeping his hands to himself. Already he wanted to touch her soft cheek and feel the firmness of her breasts again.

She looked delicious enough to eat with a spoon. His lower body stirred with an awakening that he knew he was going to have trouble keeping under control the entire afternoon.

Catherine popped open the lace-trimmed parasol that matched her dress before waving good-bye to Mrs. Goosetree who stood in the doorway of her home watching them. John picked up the ribbons and then pulled the brake handle. He was eager to be away from the watchful gaze of Catherine's domineering sister.

As they drove down the street, he realized he liked the fact that of all the young ladies in London Catherine was the one sitting beside him on this glorious spring day. He was looking forward to spending a couple of hours alone with her.

"Did you see the Marquis last night?"

John didn't know why that question was the first one out of his mouth except that it had been on his mind since she'd told him she planned to see Westerland at a party last night.

"Yes."

That was all she was going to say?

"Did you dance with him?"

"As a matter of fact I did."

John's stomach knotted with that same feeling he'd experienced before whenever he thought of Catherine with Westerland. He didn't want Westerland even touching her when dancing.

"Did you take a walk with him on the terrace or somewhere else?"

Like to a private room somewhere in the house.

He looked over at her. She was staring at him, surprise showing clearly in her lovely face and eyes.

"Yes. How did you know?"

I'm a man.

The only answer he gave her was a shrug. How could he admit that he knew every man wanted to steal a few kisses from a woman as beautiful and as charming as she. The problem was that because of Society's strict rules concerning proper behavior, most of them didn't have the courage to do it.

Did Westerland?

John didn't know.

"Did the Marquis tell you we strolled on the terrace after our dance?" she asked.

It was an experienced guess.

"No, I haven't spoken to him, but it wasn't hard to figure out."

"Oh."

"Oh. Is that all you have to say?"

John clicked the ribbons on the horses' rumps, and they picked up their pace. He knew he sounded annoyed, and he was. He didn't understand it, but he knew he didn't want Westerland anywhere near Catherine.

"I'm not sure what else you expected me to say," she said.

"How about he kissed me or he tried to kiss me."

He heard her laugh softly, and he loved the sound of it as it wafted past his ear. It couldn't have aroused him more if she'd laid her hand on his leg.

"Well, I could say that."

He jerked his head around to look at her, and she smiled sweetly at him. They hit a bump in the road and bounced on the seat. Catherine had to hold on to the armrest, but he didn't slow the horses.

"But if I did it wouldn't be true. Lord Westerland was a perfect gentleman, and he didn't even try to kiss me."

"Truly?" John asked.

"Yes."

A milktoast just like I thought.

John smiled at her before turning his attention back to the road. "Good," he said and should have let the conversation drop with that, but being the man he was, he couldn't stop there.

"Would you have let him if he had tried?" he asked.

"I don't know."

"Catherine?"

"All right. I suppose I would have. It would have been educational."

He slapped the ribbons on the horses' rump again, and they went even faster through the streets of Mayfair.

"Educational? Excuse my cursing, Catherine, but how in the bloody hell would kissing him be considered educational?"

She twirled the handle of her parasol in her hand, and without looking at him she said, "I would then know if his kisses made me feel the same way yours do."

"And how is that?"

"My legs go weak beneath me, and I find it difficult to catch my breath when you kiss me."

That lifted his spirits. She made him feel the same way. "In all confidence I can say his kisses would not make you feel that way."

"How would you know about his kisses?"

"Because I know every man kisses differently."

"And ladies have told you this?"

"Yes," he answered truthfully.

"Do all ladies kiss differently, too, or do my lips feel the same as every other lady you've kissed?"

John hadn't expected this question, and for a moment he didn't know quite how to answer it. Just remembering his few moments alone with her in the closet had his manhood stirring to life again.

Finally he gave the only answer he could. "A gentleman doesn't talk about the ladies he has kissed, but I will admit your kisses are different from all the other ladies I've kissed." John chuckled and breathed a little easier. "You are a diamond like no other, Catherine. I have never had such a frank discussion with a proper lady before."

"Well, sir, I'll be twenty-one in the not too distant future. As you are aware, I got a late start and I'm not getting any younger."

"At twenty you are hardly old."

"Do you consider yourself old?"

"At thirty-one? No. Why do you ask?"

"No reason in particular."

John pondered that. There must have been a reason she mentioned it, and it must be the fact that Westerland was six years younger than he. He knew young ladies didn't like to be married off to older men, but damn—was he considered an older man at just past thirty?

Did she consider Westerland more dashing, more handsome than he? Did the younger man appeal more to her than he did? Is that why she wanted Westerland to kiss her? And when the hell did things like age start bothering him? He was not lacking for female companionship with the older ladies or the Season's debutantes.

He gave the horses another rub of the leather. "Do you think I'm old?" he asked.

"No, of course not. I consider you a very attractive young man."

"I wasn't seeking a compliment."

"Good. I wasn't giving one. I simply stated the truth. But you do seem a bit touchy about the subject, John."

"I am. I don't want Westerland kissing you."

He heard her soft laughter again, and he glanced over at her as they bounced along the street at a fast clip. Just hearing her laugh made him feel good.

"Why are you laughing now?"

"I was talking about your age, not about kissing the Marquis."

John felt as if his heart melted. How could he stay annoyed when she smiled at him like that?

"I guess I am *touchy,* as you say, about both subjects."

"There is no reason to be. You are not old and Lord Westerland didn't kiss me."

"Good to both," he mumbled.

The thought of him kissing you makes me jealous as hell.

John Wickenham-Thickenham-Fines jealous? That was something he never thought he would be about any woman. Before Catherine, if a lady seemed more interested in another man than she was him, John was quite willing to move on to someone else. Before Catherine, he had never wanted to vie for a lady's attention.

He noticed they were fast approaching a four-way crossing where they needed to turn left, and he almost had the horses racing. He'd been so caught up with his feelings and the conversation with Catherine that he practically had the team galloping down the street.

He pulled back on the ribbons, slowed the horses, and easily made the corner. The thought of Westerland kissing her drove him to distraction.

"Just don't do it," he said as he maneuvered the carriage through the busy traffic of carriages, horses and people crossing the street.

"Do what?"

"Let Westerland kiss you. Even if he tries."

"Are you worried I might like his kisses better than yours?"

"Hell no."

"Then why can't he kiss me?"

You belong to me.

"Because I don't want his lips touching yours," he admitted without any guilt.

"You might want to be careful what you say, Lord Chatwin. I think that is the second time you have said something to me that sounds remarkably like a jealous comment."

John felt a grin ease across his face. She was so delightful to talk to. She had a quick and entertaining wit. She was never shy or helpless with him. In fact, at times he thought her too damned independent for her own good.

"The second time you say? Maybe, but surely it's the first time for me that it might actually be true."

"Might?"

"I won't admit to any more than that, so be happy I confessed to that much."

She laughed and John realized she could get him hotter and make him feel better than any woman ever had. He'd always loved all women. Short, tall, heavy, slender, young, and even older ladies, but Catherine was different. He couldn't exactly put his finger on how or why, but there was no doubt that she was different and that excited him.

John directed the horses onto the park path and they fell in behind a long queue of carriages. The warm, sunny day had the park brimming with people on horseback, strolling, and sitting on the ground with their children, dogs, and picnic baskets.

"I'm going to park the carriage, and we'll find a place to sit down. That way I don't have to divide my attention between you and the horses."

Her eyes twinkled with a playful glare. "That is an excellent idea, my lord. I was aware that the more we talked about the Marquis and kissing, the faster you pushed the horses."

She noticed but hadn't said anything. She waited for him to realize what he was doing and correct it himself. He liked that about her.

John smiled to himself. What was there about her he didn't like?

"I was also thinking it would be difficult to kiss you and manage the team at the same time."

"So you plan to kiss me?" she asked.

"Most definitely. Why else would we come here?"

"I thought we came so that we can talk about my father."

"We'll take care of that, too."

"There are so many people in the park today. Someone would see you if you tried to kiss me."

"Not if I am careful, and I plan to be."

"You are a scoundrel, my lord."

"Thank you."

They went a little farther down the path before John pulled off to the side and set the brake of the phaeton. He jumped down and threw a coin to a street urchin who stood waiting to be asked to watch the horses.

John then walked around to Catherine. She rose and extended her hand for him to help her down, but instead of taking it, he reached up and caught her by the waist.

Without effort, he swung her round and set her on her feet, but not before making sure his hands settled comfortably on her waist, spreading his fingers wide to feel the gentle flair of her hips. He liked the way her body felt beneath his hands. Not too thin and not too thick.

The stirrings of passion hardened between his legs. He picked up the picnic basket from the back of the carriage, and they walked toward the grassy area in the park. They looked for a tree with a little shade, but all of them were already packed with people enjoying the warm afternoon.

Catherine assured him her parasol and bonnet would keep the sun out of her eyes and off her delicate complexion, but after a few more minutes of walking through the park he finally found a more secluded area that had a small tree for shade.

With Catherine's help, he spread the blanket on the ground, and then he helped her to sit down. Much to his dislike, he took a seat a respectable distance from her. Perhaps he could steal a kiss or two once the crowds in the park thinned.

"Would you like something to drink? I brought tea and wine?"

"Not right now, thank you, maybe a little later."

"Catherine."

"John."

They both managed to speak at the same time.

"Ladies first," he said.

"All right, I have a proposition for you."

"A proposition? Good Lord, Catherine, you are constantly full of surprises."

Her face was masked in innocence as she continued, "I have an offer I want to present to you and I'm hoping you will accept."

What would she come up with next? "Didn't anyone ever tell you that proper young ladies do not proposition men?"

She seemed to ponder that before she said, "Proper young ladies aren't supposed to talk about kissing, either. I'm not sure there is any other way to say it. I want you to do something for me, and in return I'm willing to do something for you. Is that not a proposition?"

"Yes, and I don't think I'm going to like this," he grumbled, "but what did you have in mind?"

John looked up and saw his old friend Chandler Prestwick and his beautiful wife Millicent strolling toward him.

"John, how are you?"

Damnation. What an inopportune time for them to walk by. He was obliged to stand up and greet them. He rose and then helped Catherine to rise. He took the time to properly present Catherine to the Earl and his Countess.

"I'm so pleased to meet you both," Catherine said. "Lord Dunraven, I've met Lord Dugdale and, of course John, so meeting you makes the circle of the Terrible Threesome earls complete." Without giving him time to answer, she then turned her attention to Millicent, "And, Countess, just last night Lady Lynette Knightington mentioned you while we were talking. She considers you a dear friend."

Millicent smiled at Catherine. "Lynette is one of my favorite people, Miss Reynolds," the Countess answered. "She was the first lady to befriend me when I came to London last year."

John could see that he didn't have to worry about Catherine. It was clear that within a matter of a few sentences she had charmed Chandler and his wife.

"Please call me Catherine," she said to the Countess.

"And you must call me Millicent. Anyone who is a friend of John's and Lady Lynette's is also a friend of mine."

Any other time John would have been happy to invite Chandler and Millicent to sit with them for a while but not right now. He wanted to know exactly what Catherine had in mind.

Chandler moved closer to John as the ladies continued to talk and in a low voice said, "It appears that the scandal over your horse is getting even bigger."

"You know, I never really minded the gossips like you always did, but this story has gone beyond the pale."

"Most men think it's sporting."

"No wonder. They're taking wagers down at White's and talking about a ghost riding The General. It's absolutely insane."

Chandler grinned. "If it's any help to you, my money is on Lady Veronica's ghost."

John felt like slugging his friend of more than fifteen years, but instead he just laughed. "We always could trust each other to be honest, but I fear you will lose your money this time."

"I have a feeling only you and Andrew know who rode that horse—other than the lady herself. Am I right?" he asked as his eyes drifted to Catherine.

That was the trouble with having a close friend. It was difficult to keep things from him. "I plan to keep it that way" was John's only answer.

Chandler nodded. "That's for the best, but to wager on a lady ghost was too tempting to pass up."

"You're going to lose your money, you know."

His friend laughed. "Yes, I know. Let's have a drink and catch up."

"We'll do it soon. Andrew and I haven't seen you since the Season started."

"I've discovered that I would rather spend the evenings alone with my wife than with hundreds of people at a noisy party."

"I won't argue that point. It was good to see you," John said, hoping Chandler would get the hint and move on, and he did.

He immediately turned to Millicent and they bid their farewells.

John helped Catherine to sit down again, and then he joined her on the blanket before saying, "Now let's get back to this proposal of yours."

"All right. I know that either Mr. Beechman or Mr. Chatsworth is my real father. I want you to help me find out which one is."

This was her proposal? John didn't know if he was relieved or disappointed, but he wasn't surprised by her request. He was ready with his answer.

"No. I don't pry into other people's lives for anyone."

She wasn't deterred. "But you haven't heard my entire proposition."

"I don't need to. I won't help you because I don't think you should do this. Catherine, there are some things that you are better off not knowing."

"This certainly isn't one of them. I realize that if you do this for me that I will need to repay you in some way, so I finally came up with something that might tempt you to help me."

"There is nothing that would tempt me."

Her brows drew together in a delectable frown that made him want to reach over and kiss the wrinkle from her forehead.

"But you said last night that my kisses tempted you. Were you untruthful when you said that?"

"No. Definitely not. They do."

Beyond my endurance to control myself.

She smiled. "Good. My proposition is that if you will help me discover which man is my father, I will in return give you kisses."

Her words hit him like a fist in the stomach. Did he hear what he thought he heard? Could she be serious?

"You want to pay me with kisses for helping you?"

"Yes."

"You only want to use me?"

She sat back quickly as if he'd struck her. "No, that's not the way I mean it."

"But that is exactly what you are saying. You don't want me to kiss you because of how I make you feel, you want only to let me kiss you for payment."

"No," she insisted again.

He didn't want her to know that his pride was wounded, but he had to say what he felt. "I have never had to bargain for any lady's kisses, and I don't intend to start now."

Catherine folded her arms across her chest defiantly. "You, sir, are deliberately misunderstanding me."

"I don't think I am."

At hearing his name, John looked behind him and saw Viscount Stonehurst and his lady wife, Mirabella, approaching them.

"Chatwin, over here. How are you?"

Bloody hell! Who would show up next?

Ordinarily, he would enjoy talking to Stonehurst, who was only a year or two older than John, but Catherine had just insulted him by wanting to pay him for his services with kisses.

Once again John rose and helped Catherine to stand and once again he made the appropriate introductions to the Viscount and Viscountess. Catherine chatted as easily with the two of them as she had with Millicent and Chandler.

It was hardly two minutes after she met them that she had charmed Stonehurst into telling her about the years he spent in America before he and Mirabella married.

John was impressed with the way she handled herself with his friends. She didn't seem intimidated by their titles as most young ladies would be. It was as if she and they had an instant rapport with one another.

And why shouldn't they like her? he thought as they talked. She was clever and beautiful but thankfully not as audacious and straightforward with them as she was with him. He hoped she was never that unconventional with anyone else. It was no wonder Mrs. Goosetree wanted to marry her off as soon as possible if she was as bold with her.

John couldn't believe how long Stonehurst and Mirabella stayed and talked. He tried to keep his mind on the conversation, but his thoughts kept straying to Catherine's offer to pay him with kisses.

She was unbelievable.

Finally John felt obliged to ask Stonehurst and Mirabella to join them. That is when they excused themselves and moved on.

Beginning to feel frustrated at the interruptions, John helped Catherine to sit on the blanket for the third time.

If there was ever a case for needing a drink, this was it. He opened the picnic basket and took out the silver flask of wine. He poured a glass of claret and handed it to Catherine and then poured one for himself.

He watched her take a sip while he took a drink. It was strong and cool, and he quickly downed another swallow.

"I like your friends," Catherine said. "You seem quite the popular fellow."

"Don't change the subject, Catherine. I'm still trying to believe your proposition."

He didn't like the way she made him feel used. He would have sworn to the King that she had been as overcome with passion as he'd been when they were in that closet. Now she was acting as if his kisses meant nothing to her but a way to get what she wanted.

In fact, he was having a hell of a time with it.

First she talked about wanting to kiss Westerland for educational purposes, and now she wanted to pay him with kisses. He didn't accept kisses for payment from any woman.

If she had been any other lady, he would have immediately taken her home and said good riddance. But he didn't want to do that with Catherine. She intrigued him with her free thinking. And despite what she'd just said, he liked the fact that he never knew what she was going to come up with next.

"I don't want to upset you, John." A serious, contrite expression settled on her face. "I'm sorry. That wasn't my intention."

John said, "I kissed you because I desired you, Catherine. I thought that was the reason you allowed me such freedoms when we were together."

"It is, John," she said earnestly.

She looked deeply into his eyes and reached over and placed her hand on top of his. Her touch warmed him like a fire on a cold night. He was tempted to grab hold of her hand, but it was only for a second or two that she touched him before she removed her hand.

"Please believe me when I say that is true for me. Deep

in your heart you must know that. But I need your help to find my father. Our embracing and kissing gave us both pleasure, and it is the only thing I have to offer you in return for your help."

He believed her. Her blue eyes had lost their sparkle, and her beautiful lips had no hint of a smile. Now she was the one upset, and he didn't like the way that made him feel.

"I don't need anything from you, Catherine. If I helped you, I wouldn't need any payment for it."

"I understand that now. I'm afraid I didn't think how my offer would sound. I suppose if you aren't willing to help me find my father, you won't be interested in the other thing I was going to ask of you."

All annoyance left him and he suddenly felt like laughing. How could she have him completely outraged one minute and dying to kiss her the next?

"There was more?" he asked.

"Yes, but I don't want to upset you further, so I won't say a word about it."

He couldn't let her get away with that. "Oh, no, you don't. I insist you tell me—"

"John, how are you?"

"Sweet damnation," he muttered under his breath as he looked up and saw Lord Colebrooke and his new wife, Isabella, heading their way.

This was murderous. He'd been to the park three times last week and never saw the first person he knew, but now today they were showing up every two minutes.

He took a deep breath, set their wine glasses aside, and rose before helping Catherine to stand. John remained as polite as he'd been with his previous two introductions, and Catherine enchanted the newly wedded pair just as easily as she had the others.

Thankfully Colebrooke and Isabella apologized for not being able to stay longer and visit, but they were on their way to an appointment. As soon as their farewells were said and their backs were turned, John reached down and emptied the contents of their glasses on the ground and put them back in the picnic basket.

"What are you doing?" she asked.

"We're leaving. I've had enough of these interruptions."

"I guess that means our delightful afternoon in the park is over."

"Delightful? You do have a way with words, Catherine. This afternoon has not been amusing in any way. Everyone I know seems to be in the park today. I want to go somewhere we can be alone."

He picked up his hat and stuck it on his head. He threw his gloves in the picnic basket and draped the blanket over his arm.

"Let's get out of here quickly before someone else stops by."

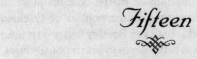

Fifteen

AS THE CARRIAGE bumped along the crowded streets of the city, John and Catherine remained painfully quiet. John was busy with his thoughts.

Catherine had gotten his attention, in more ways than one, and he needed to do some serious thinking about her. He liked the fact that she had a goal and she was sticking to it, even though the odds were not in her favor. If the man who fathered her didn't want to be found out, he would never own up to having been with her mother.

John wasn't sure Catherine was ready for such rejection.

What really had him thinking was the fact that he had never had an important goal like that in his life. His objective had always been to win the next card game, the next horse race, the next lady to court, or even the next mistress to hire.

He didn't know that he had ever had a goal that was truly worthy.

Why had it taken him so long to realize that? And why had it taken a lady with a very significant purpose to get him thinking?

Years ago his uncle pushed him to take his future and his title seriously by insisting he marry, take his place in Parliament, and get interested in the politics of England and the rest of the world. But even Bentley had grown tired of trying to force John to settle down to his responsibilities.

His uncle hadn't mentioned his duty to his title in years until yesterday. John had great respect for his mother's brother, but he had never given heed to any of the man's prodding to marry and produce an heir.

Suddenly, those things seemed a bit more important than they had just twenty-four hours ago. And John was re-thinking a lot of things, including Catherine's request for assistance.

He hadn't wanted to help Catherine in her quest only because he didn't like the thought of digging around in someone else's past—especially a gentlemen's past. There was an unwritten code that wasn't supposed to be broken. But he was now weighing that against Catherine's yearning to know the identity of her real father.

John realized Catherine was saying something to him and he turned to face her. She had a pensive expression on her face.

He said, "I'm sorry I didn't hear you."

"Yes, I could see that you were thinking. We just passed the last turn that leads to my street."

"That's because I'm not taking you home yet. We're go-ing somewhere we can be alone for a few minutes. The park was as crowded as Lady Waverley's party last night, and we haven't finished our discussion."

"Everyone knows the only reason to go to the parks is to see and be seen."

John returned his attention to his driving. "Not me. Not today."

He scanned the streets looking for anyone who might be familiar to him or Catherine. He didn't want someone they knew to see him turn down the next street, not with her in the phaeton with him. It wouldn't do for her to be seen with him in a carriage in the wrong section of town. He was taking a big chance, but he didn't know of any other way to get her truly alone. They certainly couldn't talk at ease under Mrs. Goosetree's watchful gaze.

He made a right turn and then another quick left. Halfway down the next street he took another right and then stopped the horses in front of a building that looked like a livery with two large doors, but there were no markings or names on it anywhere.

John jumped down and knocked soundly on the door. Within a few moments the door opened. John whispered to the old man who answered and then climbed back up on the phaeton.

The double doors were swung wide. John clicked the ribbons, and the horses took the carriage inside the large, empty, and windowless room that was lit by low burning lanterns hanging strategically from the walls.

Catherine's eyes grew wide with amazement as she watched the old man close them inside while John set the brake.

"Where are we?" she asked.

"We're in a building I own. The old man used to work for the Prince until he hurt his leg in an accident. He takes care of this place for me. He has a room through there"—he pointed to a door—"but for now he'll take a walk outside."

John watched as her gaze skimmed the bare, wooden walls to the dirt floor. He knew she could smell the cold-packed earthen floor, oil from the lanterns, and stale tobacco smoke. The only sound to be heard was the nickering of the horses and the rattle and jingle of their harness as they shuddered and tossed their heads in the air.

"I'm wondering what he takes care of. The room is empty."

John chuckled as he took off his hat and his gloves and laid them on the floor at his feet. "I see what you mean. Different men rent it from me for various things."

"What can they do with a vacant building?"

"Usually it's set up with tables for private card or dice games. Or it has been used for boxing matches and cock-fights. Things like that. Rory sets the room up according to what will be going on in here. I know it's not the best place to bring a lady and it's a bit chilly in here, but this was the only place I could think of where we could be completely alone and wouldn't be interrupted."

She looked around the room once again. "This is very private. I don't think anyone will find us here. And it's much bigger than Lady Waverly's closet."

"And we don't have to whisper," he added.

"Or have furniture sticking in our backs."

John chuckled. He hadn't minded the chair leg poking his back. Nothing bothered him when Catherine was in his arms.

Yellow light from the lanterns gave a beautiful glimmer to her skin. She didn't look or sound anxious, but for his own peace of mind, he asked, "You aren't frightened to be here alone with me, are you?"

She shook her head and smiled. "I trust you."

Those three words soared through him and made him feel so damn good it was ridiculous. No woman had ever had that kind of power over him before. That was going to take some getting used to.

"I'm glad you know I would never do anything against your will."

She smiled at him. "I do. I'm just surprised you want to be alone with me considering I upset you earlier."

John relaxed against the back of the carriage cushion and put his arm across the top of the seat. Catherine turned more facing him and pushed her hips in the corner between the back and the arm of the cushion.

"That's what I wanted to talk about. I guess I was wondering why you have such determination to find your real father when you obviously have great respect for the man who's been your father all these years."

Her expression turned serious. "I would have rather not known any of this. I was very happy thinking that the man who I lived with for almost twenty years was my father, and in truth I know he always will be. He was good to me, but that doesn't satisfy the yearning I have inside me. I want to know who my mother loved and why they never married. I want to know if I look like him, walk like him, think like him."

She paused for a moment and then said, "Perhaps I can best explain it by simply asking what would you do if you woke up tomorrow morning and discovered the previous Earl of Chatwin wasn't your real father."

"I have to admit I've never given anything like this a thought."

"I think you would feel as if you had been living a lie through no fault of your own and you would have a determination to find out the truth just like I do."

"Perhaps." That was all he was willing to admit.

"Most people don't have to think about a situation like this. You can't understand because you are an earl's son and you have always known your heritage. I need to know who I belong to. It has nothing to do with not loving the man whose name I bear. It has to do with how I feel about there being something in my past that I don't know the answer to. How can I not try to find out what that answer is?"

John swallowed hard. He would never have known she had these feelings inside her. He liked the fact that she didn't wear her troubles on her sleeve and that she kept them to herself.

"My mother loved a man enough to give herself to him. I'm the creation of that union. I deserve to know why he didn't marry her when she told him she was carrying his child."

"And you are sure she told him."

"As sure as I can be. In the last readable diary entry she wrote that she planned to tell him about her plight that evening. I want to know what happened when she told him. Did he feel nothing for my mother and only want to dally with her? Was he promised to another lady and felt he had to honor that vow? Was he just a coldhearted man who could ruin a lady and leave her with no thoughts of how she would cope?"

John listened intently. He truly wanted to understand what she was feeling. "What if this man doesn't want to know about you?"

She took a deep breath and shifted in the seat. "I've thought about that, and I realize that it is quite possible. However, I'm not going to worry about it because I'm doing this for me, not for him. I believe he knows he has a child, and as far as I know he's never looked for me. I couldn't have been that difficult to find for a man with means. How he feels about hearing from me is not as important to me as how I will feel once I know who he is."

"And how will you feel?" he asked softly, watching how the warming glow from the lanterns played on her delicate skin.

"I don't know. I hope to feel complete. Right now a piece of my past is missing. A very important piece. The only way I can explain it is to say I must keep searching until I have the answers."

She wasn't quibbling over what she had to do. She was resolute and that impressed the hell out of him.

"And what will you do after you've found him."

"Confront him with my questions. Ask him what happened between him and my mother that they never married."

"What will you do if he doesn't give you the answers you seek?"

"I don't want to cause him any trouble if that's what you mean. It is my desire to keep all of this private between my father and me. And I don't want any support from him. My father—the man I always thought was my father—left me a handsome income. I'm not looking for money. Just answers."

"No, I didn't think you wanted support from him."

"A lot of things will depend on how he reacts. I want to know what made him run out on my mother in her time of greatest need. I want to understand so I'm not constantly wondering why. I'm their daughter. I have a right to know these things."

"For your sake, when you find him, I hope he agrees with you, but no matter how he responds to you, what do you plan to do after this search is finished?"

She folded her hands in her lap and said, "I will go on

with my life and do what Victoria wants me to do, what all young ladies do. I shall look for a proper husband and get married."

"I envy you," John suddenly said, and didn't know why he'd been so truthful, but he wasn't unhappy he'd said it.

She gave him a look of disbelief. "What? You envy me? Why?"

"You know exactly what you want and you're going after it. And not only that, you're not afraid to do it. You have plans."

"I have no choice. I don't want to spend the rest of my life wondering who my father was."

"How do you think I can help you?"

"I need introductions to the men. As an earl they will willingly allow you into their house and you can introduce me to them so I can get to know them."

"Who are they?"

"Mr. William Walker Chatsworth and Mr. Robert Beechman."

This won't be easy.

"Those are two good family names, but I don't know how to say this other than to tell you that both men are strange ducks."

"I've heard of their idiosyncrasies, but I've also heard that Mr. Chatsworth enjoys visitors and card games. I'm very good at most games. If I could get him interested in a card game, then I could casually ask him if he remembers my mother and then take the conversation from there."

She was incredible. He had no doubt that in time she would find out all she wanted to know.

"How do you know he enjoys a good card game?"

"I've found out a few things on my own simply by asking questions."

"Indeed you have."

John's admiration for her grew. He reached over and picked up her hand and held it in both of his. Her skin was warm even though it was cool in the windowless building.

"I'm going to help you, Catherine. I consider it a challenge to help you find him, and I promise you we won't rest until we do."

The glimmer in her eyes turned into a bright sparkle. "John, do you mean it?"

"Every word of it."

He would find her father for her. He'd never wanted to really get involved with a lady or her problems until he met Catherine. But he was intrigued by the prospects of trying to get private information out of these two men.

"Thank you, John, thank you."

She reached over, threw her arms around him, and kissed him soundly on the lips.

The brevity, the chasteness of that one unsolicited kiss hit him so hard his trousers tightened.

As if realizing what she had done, Catherine suddenly pulled away from him and moved far to the other side of the cushion again.

"I'm sorry. I didn't mean to do that. I won't do it again. I promise. I don't want you to think I was trying to repay you for your help with kisses."

She looked so stricken for a moment that John had to laugh.

"I didn't think that. We've already settled that issue, but you said there was something else you were going to ask me to help you with. What was that?"

She gave him a doubtful look. "Are you sure you want to hear it?"

"Of course I do."

"I wanted to ask you to continue your interest in me for a little while longer—even after you tire of me and seek the charms of another lady. If you continued to pay attention to me, that would keep Victoria happy. She enjoys trying to outwit you and that would keep her so busy she won't be eager to marry me off to the Marquis or the first acceptable man who offers for my hand."

If only Catherine knew he had no interest in anyone but her she wouldn't have to ask that. And the last thing he wanted was Mrs. Goosetree trying to marry her off to Westerland or anyone else.

Where were all these notions coming from? He'd never thought about settling down to one lady. He'd always resisted the natural instinct to think about a wife, a home and a family. He'd never wanted that kind of life and he'd meant it. He'd scoffed at anyone who did. Why were those thoughts invading his mind now?

Catherine was making him rethink a lot of things.

"That won't be difficult at all. I will help you with both your requests."

Her eyes sparkled with anticipation. "Are you teasing me, my lord?"

He scooted over closer to her and cupped her chin with the tips of his fingers. "I wouldn't do that to you at a time like this. Not when you are so serious."

He saw relief wash down her face. Her expression sent his heartbeat racing against his breathing, and suddenly all his thoughts centered on the heat between his legs.

"I can't thank you enough for doing this."

"No more thanks. I'll need more information from you, but we can talk about that on the way home."

"All right."

"I'd like to read your mother's diary for myself. Perhaps there's some clue or something you've missed."

"I'll see you get it right away. John, I'm so—"

She looked as if she was about to thank him again, so he placed his fingertips against her lips to quiet her and said, "Don't give me any more gratitude. I'm filled up to here with it." He laid his other hand across his heart. "I don't want anything for doing this."

"All right," she whispered against his fingers.

It was time for him to get her home, but she was too close, and they were too alone. He was a man and he wanted to kiss her before they left.

The scooped neckline of her dress accented her beautiful breasts; goose bumps peppered his skin at the thought of touching her. Everything about her from her smile to the fragrance of her fresh-washed hair stirred him like no other woman ever had.

He wanted Catherine.

He moved even closer to her, and not allowing his gaze to leave hers, he placed an open palm on the front of her chest where his fingertips could caress the hollow of her throat. The heel of his palm rested on the fullness of her breasts.

"Did I tell you how lovely you are in the color blue?" he asked softly.

"No," she answered in the same quiet tone.

"I should have." He rubbed the cloth of her dress between his fingers. "I think the dye-maker must have been thinking about your eyes when he made this shade."

"I'll wear it more often."

"I'm going to kiss you because I want to, Catherine, and for no other reason."

"And I'm going to return your kiss for no other reason than I want to," she said, with her eyes conveying the message that she meant every word.

John pulled her up close and tight in the circle of his arms. Her breasts pressed against his chest as their lips met in a stirring kiss. His lips moved easily over hers, back and forth, softly, and deliberately slowly as if he were trying to take in her essence.

His hands skimmed slowly down each side of her neck and glided across the top of her shoulders and drifted down her arms. She leaned into the kiss and wound her arms around his neck and shoulders. His muscles tightened beneath her touch.

John heard her sigh contentedly against his mouth, and the fires of desire flashed through him like heat through an oven. He deepened the kiss, and she responded by opening her mouth. He moved his tongue inside and tasted the claret that had been left on her lips.

Her sweetness gave him a heady feeling.

Catherine matched him desire for desire and passion for passion. She responded with such fervor he thought he was going to lose control and start pulling off her clothing.

His kisses left her lips and moved down her chin to the soft skin on her neck just below her jawline where he could feel the frantic beat of her pulse against his lips.

He liked what he did to her. His tongue came out and tasted her skin.

Sweet glory.

The sudden intake of her breath thrilled and excited him. A strong shudder of desire to make her his swept through him.

She was so eager for his touch that he couldn't stop caressing her back, her neck, around her ears, and down the front of her dress to flatten his palms against her breasts. Soft, yet enticingly firm and fulfilling.

John had never felt such satisfaction from a woman.

She must have loved the way he touched her, too, because her breathing grew faster. Her lips continued to move seductively over his. His own breathing was gusty as his hands favored her breasts. He strained to hold himself in check and take it slow, but he was too hungry for her and she was too receptive for him to be a gentleman lover.

John wanted her to know that he desired her. He wanted her to know that she was different from all the others, but he didn't know how to let her know she was special other than to softly whisper her name over and over again.

The high waist of her dress fit tight up under her breasts, and with just a couple of movements of his hands he unbuttoned the first three buttons of her pelisse. He gently lowered the bodice of her dress and underclothing off her beautiful, rounded shoulders, freeing her breasts from her clothing. His gaze devoured her.

Over the years he'd seen women in all stages of undress, but he couldn't ever remember being as enthralled by any of them as he was with Catherine's beauty. Her skin was a lovely shade of creamy white. Her breasts were round, plump, and firm. Her brownish-rose colored nipples were hard as if they were waiting to be warmed by his mouth.

"You are as beautiful as I imagined you'd be."

"That is quite a compliment, my lord. Thank you."

He looked up into her trusting blue eyes as the palms of his hands skimmed back and forth across her nipples, making them peak tight with awareness. An uncommon yearning for something more raced through him as his hands lightly touched her delicate skin.

"I know that you are completely innocent, yet you allow me to look at you like this and touch you with no fear or embarrassment."

She smiled. "Does that confuse you?"

"Yes."

"How can I be afraid or shameful of something that feels so natural?"

He smiled at her. "I'm glad you are comfortable with me. That pleases me very much, too."

John dipped his head and took one rosy-tipped nipple into his mouth and suckled.

Catherine gasped with pleasure. The warmth between his legs tightened. She arched her back to give him better access.

John's manhood grew harder at knowing how wonderful he could make her feel.

He fondled one breast while he gently sucked and kissed the other. He felt her hands play in his hair, down his neck, and over to his ears, pleasuring him as he pleasured her.

Her touch was gentle and eager. He wanted to tell her to go lower to the hardness between his legs and satisfy his need for her, but he was concerned that her caress would put him over the edge.

Catherine's flesh pebbled beneath his mouth, letting him know that she desired him as much as he wanted her. John moaned softly from the gratification of touching her and from the pain of holding on to his control.

He desperately wanted to take her and make her his here and now and forever.

He had wanted her since he first saw her in the park when she demanded his horse. John wasn't fooling himself. He had already realized that it was more than just her loveliness that impressed him. She had a strength and determination that attracted him.

John lingered over her breasts, giving them his full attention. Anticipation made his body ache with a delicious longing. His mind told him to do what was natural and bury himself deep within her. His body responded quickly to his thoughts, urging him to take the lead and teach her everything he knew about loving.

He was hot and so ready for her that he ached. He needed to lay her down on the carriage cushion and make her his.

But that was madness.

She was a lady, not a paid mistress.

How could he find the strength to deny himself when she was so willing?

"I'm trying very hard not to go too far, Catherine, but you make it so difficult. You are the most satisfying woman I have ever touched."

"And I have never felt as wonderful as I feel here in your arms with you caressing me."

His arms tightened possessively around her as he looked down at her breasts. His heart and his body didn't want to let her go, but his mind knew he must.

"Why are you looking at me so intently?"

"I was just thinking how beautiful a pair of pearls would look against your skin."

"I have pearls that were my mother's. I'll wear them for you."

"No, don't. Not yet."

I want to pick out a strand for you.

The purely masculine sensations she created inside him had never been so alive, so compelling. He had never been so caught up by desire for a woman that it mattered who she was. Suddenly it was important who was in his arms.

And he wanted to buy her pearls.

That sobered him. He wanted Catherine. Not just a woman. Miss Catherine Reynolds. Sexual heat covered him like a blanket of hot coals as he tried to calm his breathing.

Yes, he wanted Catherine but not this way. Not here and not now.

Slowly he relaxed his hold and looked deeply into her eyes.

"I'd like to continue what we're doing, but I can't do that to you. I'm going to take you home."

Her lips relaxed and her lashes fluttered. "You make me feel so delicious that I forget everything but your touch."

"That's the way it's supposed to be."

He pushed some fallen strands of hair away from her face, and helped her adjust the front of her clothing.

"The last time you kissed me, Victoria noticed my lips were red and swollen," she said as she put her fingertips to her lips.

"How did you answer her?"

"Like this." Catherine caught her lower lip between her teeth.

John smiled. "You are very clever, Miss Reynolds. Very clever indeed."

"I'm afraid it's more of a habit than cleverness, but it worked just the same."

"Whichever it is, I'm glad she didn't figure out the truth."

"She is a bit overbearing sometimes."

"Some of the time. I think all of the time."

"But she does care for me in her own way, and I'm fond of her."

"I can see that you are, but I must admit that there is something about pulling the wool over Mrs. Goosetree's eyes that's very satisfying."

John laughed and Catherine laughed, too.

Sixteen

❧

"Was it a stalking horse, a Trojan horse, or merely a horse of a different color?" No, dearest readers, this comes straight from the horse's mouth. It was no ghost who rode Lord Chatwin's steed in the park that dark morn. It was none other than a lady in distress. Her name shall be omitted to protect her innocence. The lady and her companion were out for an early-morning ride when their groom was injured. Lord Chatwin happened upon them and offered his assistance. What was needed was his horse. The Earl handed it over, and as is often heard by many: The rest is history.

Lord Truefitt
Society's Daily Column

THE AIR WAS warm and the sky was a glorious shade of blue as John stopped the phaeton in front of her home. Catherine didn't know when she'd felt so good. Of course, that wonderful feeling that curled around her so tightly might have something to do with the way she still tingled from head to toe from John's passionate kisses.

She knew the day would come when he would discard her in favor of another, but she wasn't going to think about that right now. It would hurt her heart too much. All she wanted to remember was the taste of his sweet lips on hers and the touch of his hands and his mouth on her breasts, for surely there could never be another feeling that could compare to that.

There were two other reasons she was happy. John was going to help her find her real father, and he was going to continue to pursue her for a while. Nothing could make her happier than that.

John set the brake and jumped down from the carriage. He reached up and helped Catherine out with all the proper manners of a true gentleman. She admitted to herself that she would rather he be a rogue and take her firmly by the waist with his strong, warm hands.

"So you'll have a messenger deliver your mother's diary to me first thing tomorrow morning," John said as they walked toward her front door.

"Yes, and you will talk to your uncle, hopefully this afternoon, and see what he knows about Mr. Beechman and Mr. Chatsworth."

"Yes, if Bentley is home and doesn't have guests, I'll see what I can find out. And then I will look for you at Lord Baxley's party later in the evening."

They stopped in front of her door and their eyes met. Catherine felt the need to thank him for helping her but refrained from doing so. He'd made his wishes on that clear.

Looking up into his beautiful dark eyes, she simply said, "I enjoyed the afternoon with you."

He smiled at her. "Did you?"

She nodded. "Your friends are very nice. It was lovely to meet them."

His brow wrinkled with a mock frown while the smile stayed on his lips. "My friends? Is that what really made the afternoon lovely for you?"

She returned his smile with a teasing one of her own. "Perhaps there is something I'm forgetting?" She put a finger to her lips as if she were trying to remember. "Oh, yes, the wine was very good, too."

He moved closer to her as if he might bend down his head and kiss her right in front of her door, but instead softly he said, "You are a tormentor, Catherine, and I enjoy every moment I spend with you."

Catherine's heart soared. It was ridiculous of her, really. She knew he probably said things like that to every young lady, but she so wanted to believe this was the one time he meant it.

"I feel the exact same way, my lord. You torment me with your kisses and caresses. So before I go inside, do my lips look as if they'd been kissed?"

His voice lowered to a husky whisper as he said, "Very much so."

Her brow wrinkled. "What am I to do? Victoria might be fooled once, but she is too sharp to be fooled for very long."

A twinkle appeared in his eyes. "Then I suggest you walk into the house biting on your lower lip."

All of a sudden the door opened and there stood Victoria holding a sheet of newspaper in her hand. Catherine looked down and saw the name Lord Truefitt written at the bottom of the page.

She forgot all about her lips as her throat went dry.

Had Lady Lynette already given the information about her to the scandal lord?

Surely not. There hadn't been enough time, had there? Victoria didn't look as if she were upset about anything, not even the fact that Catherine was later returning from her afternoon ride than she should have been.

"There you are, Catherine. I expected you back sooner than this."

Victoria stood aside so they could step into the foyer. Catherine closed her parasol and untied her bonnet while John took off his hat.

"It's my fault we're late," John said, stepping in front of Catherine as if to shield her. "We were delayed because there were so many people in the park. Viscount Stonehurst and his lady wife, the Earl of Dunraven and his Countess, and the Earl of Colebrooke and his Countess saw us in the park, and they all stopped to meet Catherine. We lost track of the time."

Victoria looked surprised but pleased. "Oh, well, I suppose it's all right that she's late since she met so many of your friends."

Victoria looked at Catherine. "You remembered all their names, didn't you?"

"Every one of them, Vickie. I really have a very good memory."

Victoria turned from Catherine and toward John without making a comment about Catherine's memory. "Lord Chatwin, have you seen this today?" She handed him the sheet of paper. "It's Lord Truefitt's column."

Catherine froze. What did it say? There had to be a reason Victoria was talking about it, but what?

John returned the sheet to her without bothering to even glance at it. "I seldom look at these things, Mrs. Goosetree."

"Really?" she said with a hint of a challenge in her voice. "You should. You're often in it."

"My point exactly."

"Perhaps you'll want to read this one. Lord Truefitt says he knows who rode your horse that day in the park and it was no ghost."

Catherine held her breath. Lynette must have gone straight from the party to Lord Truefitt last night for the story to be in today's column. How else could it have been printed so fast?

"Is that what he says?" John asked with no real questioning in his voice.

Catherine was impressed with how John kept his gaze straight on Victoria's face and never blinked an eye. Catherine didn't know how he did it. Her gaze was steadily flicking back and forth between John and Victoria.

"Yes," Victoria said, laying the paper on top of the foyer table after John gave it back to her. "Apparently she was traveling with someone who became ill and needed assistance. For reasons not stated, the young lady needed to borrow your horse and you allowed her to ride it."

Catherine remained quiet, allowing John to answer Victoria. Catherine was grateful John remained calm and collected and didn't bother to give her so much as a glance. That would have been a sure way to admit guilt.

"Lord Truefitt is a writer, Mrs. Goosetree. I'm sure he knows how to tell a good story," John said.

"Is it a true story?" Victoria asked with a no-nonsense tone to her voice.

It was unusual for Victoria not to come right out and say what was on her mind, but she seemed to be playing a game with John. Was she testing him to see if he would tell the truth, or did she really not realize that this story was about them?

She knew John must be dying to know how it came about that the truth showed up in Lord Truefitt's column today. But she'd promised Lady Lynette that she wouldn't mention her name to anyone and she wouldn't. Not even to John.

"I have a rule that I never make comments on what the scandal sheets write about me, Mrs. Goosetree."

That was the perfect answer. She could see that Victoria liked his answer, too. Catherine started breathing easily again.

"There is no reference to the lady's name. Not even an initial. That's very smart of Lord Truefitt, don't you think?"

Or Lady Lynette.

"I have no comment about that, either," he said politely, still making sure his gaze didn't leave Victoria's face.

"Well, it's comforting to know that we don't have a lady ghost running around in the park stealing gentlemen's horses," she said with a rare hint of a genuine smile on her face and a seldom seen mischievous sparkle in her brown eyes.

John smiled, too, and Catherine realized that he had relaxed. "I will agree with you on that."

"Now Catherine must come in and get ready for the evening. Good day, Lord Chatwin."

With that pronouncement, John bowed to Victoria and turned to Catherine for the first time since they stepped into the house and said, "Thank you for a lovely afternoon, Miss Reynolds. Perhaps I'll see you at one of the parties this evening."

"Thank you, Lord Chatwin. I enjoyed the afternoon, too."

Catherine was impressed with how calm John remained

and how his eyes showed none of the turmoil she knew must be going on inside him. She had a feeling he would have plenty of questions for her later. Now, if only she could handle Victoria as easily as he had.

As soon as the door shut behind John, she took her bonnet off and laid it on the table beside her parasol. She looked up to find Victoria staring at her. Catherine took a deep breath, feeling confident.

"Lord Truefitt's column is about us, isn't it?" Victoria asked in a matter-of-fact tone.

Catherine didn't want to lie to Victoria. She would have to take the consequences of her actions. She had known that when she told Lynette what happened.

"Yes, but truly everything that morning was as innocent as it seems."

Victoria leaned against the foyer table and crossed her feet at the ankles, letting Catherine know she would stand right there and hear the entire story.

Catherine shored up her courage and told the story as near to the truth as she dared. She left out the part that she actually took the horse without John's approval and that she delivered it back to him the next morning. Victoria didn't need to know those things.

Her sister listened intently and didn't once interrupt her, but when Catherine finished, Victoria asked, "Why didn't you tell me about this before now?"

"You were so adamant that I shouldn't stop and speak to anyone that I feared you wouldn't understand."

"I'm your guardian protecting your reputation, your sister who cares about you, not an ogre."

Catherine had seldom seen this softer side of Victoria, and it heartened her. "Perhaps I was overly sensitive."

"Well, I suppose you handled things as best you could

under the circumstances. I guess Lord Chatwin could no longer endure the gossip about his horse and the ghost and decided to tell Lord Truefitt the truth—thankfully minus your name."

Should Catherine let Victoria assume it was John who told the gossip columnist, or should she admit to doing it? She couldn't let John take the blame for something she did.

Before she had time to speak up, Victoria said, "We won't worry about any of that now. What is in the past is past. As long as no one but the three of us ever knows that you were the one who rode his horse that morning. Do you think we can trust him on that?"

Was Victoria actually asking for her opinion?

"Yes," Catherine said, deciding to remain quiet about the truth of who told the story. "I am sure we can trust him."

"Good. That's my feeling, too."

Catherine suddenly realized she trusted John more than she'd ever trusted anyone.

"And should anyone mention this to you, I hope you will be as clever and evasive with your answers as Lord Chatwin."

"I will certainly do my best to measure up."

Catherine smiled. Victoria had surprised her again. She had thought Vickie would be outraged about her early-morning encounter with John, but instead she'd been very understanding.

For the first time since moving to London, Catherine felt as if Vickie was her sister and not her guardian.

*L*ATE-AFTERNOON SUNSHINE STREAMED into the room and cast shadows on the walls, the books, and the antique porcelain vase that sat on Bentley Hastings's desk. This made John's third trip into his uncle's office in as many days.

John settled himself in one of the comfortable uphol-stered wing chairs while Bentley poured their drinks.

It was luck that he'd caught him at home. Bentley invited him to join him in a splash of brandy after he'd re-turned his uncle's journal.

Now that John had agreed to help Catherine find her real father, he didn't want to waste any time.

How the doctored truth of the lady and his horse got in the gossip column still puzzled John. He wanted to know how in the hell Lord Truefitt had found out about his first meeting with Catherine. Other than her, he and Andrew were the only ones who knew the truth.

John would trust Andrew with his life. There was no way Andrew would have told Truefitt even if Andrew knew who the man was. And surely Catherine hadn't been in London long enough to know who the gossipmonger was and wouldn't tell if she did.

Maybe Lord Truefitt and Lord Pinkwater were one and the same. He laughed to himself at his own silly thought. He didn't believe in ghosts, but he had always wondered where and how Lord Truefitt got his information.

His uncle handed him the brandy and then took the matching wing chair opposite John rather than sitting be-hind his desk.

"I don't know why I've suddenly become so popular with you, John, but I'm not going to complain. I enjoy you coming over for a visit."

"Thank you, Uncle. I guess I haven't been to visit too many times the past few years, but as you can see, I'm changing that."

Bentley sipped his brandy. "Yes, but why? Something tells me that you have more questions for me."

His uncle was sharp enough to know there was more to his nephew's visits than family ties.

John swirled the liquid in his glass. He had to be careful what he said. He didn't want Catherine's suspicions about her father getting out among the *ton* any more than she did. While her true parentage didn't bother him in the least, it might give others cause for ridicule.

He looked over at his uncle. "I do need your help again, if you don't mind?"

"What kind of trouble are you in, John?"

"I'm not," John said honestly. "Believe me, what I'm working on doesn't even affect me or our family. I'm doing this for someone else."

"Who?"

"I know I recently asked you to trust me on what I needed to know about my father, and I'm going to ask the same now. I'm not at liberty to say who I'm helping. And even if you knew the name, I don't think it would keep you from helping me."

"Is what you're doing going to harm anyone?"

"No, I'm sure of it. This person does not want to cause any trouble and in fact wants this kept as private as possible."

Bentley sipped his brandy again. "All right. What is it you want to know?"

"How well do you know Mr. Robert Beechman and Mr. William Chatsworth?"

His uncle looked a bit surprised by the question. "I used to know them quite well. No one knows them anymore. They've all but dropped out of Society. They haven't kept up with their friends or their clubs."

"I know that much. I'm hoping you can tell me a little more about their past."

"Well, let's see. William Chatsworth was a good friend of your father's. Not as close as you are to Andrew, but close nonetheless. I'll tell you anything I can remember, but I need to know what exactly you are looking for. What kinds of things do you want to know? Are you interested in something like where they attended school or their family connections to the peerage? As far as I know, neither of them has any skeletons hidden in their closets, so I can't help you with anything like that."

John didn't know if that was good news or bad.

"Can we go back to the year seventeen ninety-eight as we did with my father? Do you remember if either of them were married?"

"You don't ask much, do you?" Bentley pursed his lips for a moment. "Let me think, over twenty-one years ago—I'm sure Robert Beechman would have been married. He's much older than I am, but I'm not sure whether or not William Chatsworth had married by that year. He probably doesn't even remember anymore. I can find out for you. He's gotten nuttier than a chestnut tree these past few years. How important is this question to what you need to know?"

John had no idea that Mr. Beechman was much older than his uncle. He'd met the man but had never really paid any attention to his age. Could Catherine's mother have been involved with a married man? That didn't bode well for Catherine's peace of mind.

It wasn't unheard of for a young lady to be swept off her feet by an older gentleman, but John was certain that information wouldn't make Catherine happy if it were true. No young lady would want to know her mother had been a mistress to a married man.

"It could be very important. I'm not sure yet. But you say you know for sure Mr. Beechman was married by that year."

"Yes. He had a son who would have been in his early twenties."

John's hand tightened on his glass and he leaned forward. "A son in his twenties? Are you sure we're talking about the same person? Where is his son? I've not heard of him."

"I'm not surprised you haven't. As best I remember, Mr. Beechman's son was killed in a hunting accident. It could have happened the year you asked about. I really can't remember."

"Had the son married?"

"No, no, I'm thinking that he was betrothed to a young lady, but I'm not sure of that detail and I'm really not sure of the year, either. Over twenty years is a long time to remember facts about someone I wasn't close friends with, and if it is the same year, remember that we spent half of it touring Scotland."

"But you are sure Mr. Beechman had a son who would have been in his twenties and he was killed?"

His uncle gave him a tired look. "Yes, I'm sure of that. His son was thrown from his horse and killed instantly. Though Beechman never said it, some of us believe that's why he never gets on a horse or rides in a carriage. It's been so long now that most people may well have forgotten he ever had a son."

Possibilities crowded John's thoughts and threatened to run away. He needed to do some serious thinking about this. He wasn't going to forget about Mr. Chatsworth but right now he would concentrate on finding out more about Mr. Beechman and his son.

"Thank you, Uncle. You've given me a lot to think about."

"I really didn't tell you very much. Is that all you needed?"

"You've given me a lot to go on. I'll do some further checking on my own."

"Just be careful, John. Most men don't like to have their past dug into, not even a man whose past is above reproach."

"I know and believe me I'm going to be very careful. I don't want to see anyone get hurt."

John turned up his glass and downed its contents quickly. Could Catherine's mother have been involved with the married father, or could she have possibly been involved with the son who was killed?

Seventeen

LATER THAT NIGHT, John left Lord Baxley's party and drove his phaeton over to White's. He wanted to sit in a dark corner and have a drink. Mrs. Goosetree had been her usual authoritarian self and had not let him have more than a few moments alone with Catherine before she whisked her away to another party with the parting statement that John had spent the entire afternoon with Catherine and if he wasn't ready to state his intentions concerning her sister, she had other young men to consider.

The lady was a tyrant. He had managed to tell Catherine that he'd spoken with his uncle and would be in touch with her later about his findings. Bentley had given him a valuable piece of information. John intended to study the diary and the possibilities that either Mr. Beechman or his son might be Catherine's real father.

Perhaps he would hire a Runner to find out more about

the son's death. A Runner would be able to look at old documents, newspapers, and ask questions without involving John, his uncle, or Catherine. He wanted to get this settled for Catherine as soon as possible.

And all of that was important, but mostly tonight John just wanted to spend some time thinking about Catherine and the breathtaking way she made him feel inside, the way she stayed constantly on his mind, his agitation when he saw her dance with other men, and the way he felt as if she belonged to him.

John walked into White's and handed his hat, gloves, and cape to a servant and headed for the taproom. He expected to find the place almost deserted at this time of the evening, as most men would still be at one of the multitude of parties scheduled for the night.

Lamps were lit but turned low in the room John knew as well as he knew the back of his hand. Tinkling of glass and rumbled chatter came from the few men who were scattered about the taproom. From a doorway he heard laughter and the sound of billiard balls smacking together. The smells of liquor and beeswax lay heavy on the air.

John signaled for the waiter to bring him the usual and was about to take a seat at an empty table when he noticed Andrew sitting by himself on the opposite side of the room staring into his glass.

Something was wrong. Andrew wasn't one to drink alone and never one to look forlorn.

John walked over to him and without bothering to ask for permission, he pulled out a chair and sat down at the table.

Andrew looked up and squinted at him with sleepy, bloodshot eyes. "Why don't you join me?" he said, even though John was already seated.

He immediately knew that his friend had had too much to drink for so early in the evening.

"I wasn't sure if you wanted any company. It appears you're having a rather good time by yourself."

He held up his glass in salute to John. "I am. It must have been my laughter that brought you over here."

And cynical, too? What was going on with him?

"Want to tell an old friend why you would be having such a jolly good time by yourself?"

"Are we?" His skeptical eyes belied his simple question.

John made allowances for Andrew's mood and tried not to read anything into his friend's words. "What do you mean by 'are we'?"

"We're old friends to be sure, but are we still good friends?"

It was unlike Andrew to be this way. He overindulged in the bottle once in a while. They all did from time to time, but Andrew was never maudlin.

"What kind of question is that to ask? Of course we are."

"Well, I haven't seen you since our *discussion* about Miss Reynolds in your uncle's library."

John should have known this had something to do with Catherine. And now that Andrew mentioned it, he hadn't seen him since their squabble in Bentley's office. They each had their say, and as far as John was concerned it was over. He hadn't given their brash encounter another thought, but apparently it was eating at Andrew.

Had Andrew taken an instant dislike to her or did he in some way feel threatened by her? John didn't like either possibility.

Andrew would just have to get used to Catherine being around because John had no intentions of giving her up.

"That would be your fault as much as mine, ole chap."

Andrew drank from his glass again. "I've been at White's the past two nights and haven't seen you."

I'm more interested in Catherine than White's attractions. She is the draw for me now. Not drink, cards, and friends.

"Really? I've been at several parties and haven't seen you at any of them."

"Touché," he said and again he saluted John with his glass. "Perhaps we've been hiding from each other."

Were they? No. They'd been friends too long to let a lady come between them. John's stomach tightened. He didn't like the thought that there might be some kind of tension between Andrew and Catherine, or Andrew and himself.

The servant placed a glass of port in front of John, but suddenly he didn't feel like drinking. He sat back in his chair when he realized the turn his thoughts had taken. Catherine had become a part of his life. And he wanted it that way. She was the first lady he had ever pursued that he wasn't willing to give up.

Andrew knew that. He'd seen it coming.

"I have no reason to hide from you and you have no reason to avoid me. We settled our discussion about Catherine, remember?"

Andrew half laughed and poured more wine into his glass. "And she's now *Catherine* is she? What a charming name."

He didn't miss a thing.

"We know each other well enough to be on first names with each other."

Andrew hooded his eyes with his lashes as he looked at John and asked, "Did Miss Reynolds tell you I had a conversation with her a couple of nights ago?"

"Yes, she mentioned that she'd met you. Why do you ask?"

Andrew sat up straighter in his chair and coughed. "No reason really. I just wondered if she told you we'd actually spoken."

"I assume Catherine considered you an acceptable gentleman. She has no fear of speaking her mind, and if you had behaved badly I'm sure she would have told me."

"I'm sure you're right about both those things," he said. "She's no wilting daisy. In fact, she's quite admirable."

Her self-confidence was one of the things that impressed him. She played by Society's rules and allowed Mrs. Goosetree a certain amount of authority over her, but she was not afraid to bend the rules when she considered it necessary.

"Well, Dunraven left the two of us last year, and it appears that you will be leaving me this year."

"No," John said and picked up his glass of port and took a drink. It was strong but almost sweet. Suddenly he was reminded of when he'd tasted the flavor on Catherine's lips. There weren't too many things recently that didn't remind him in some way of Catherine.

Andrew's cloudy eyes zeroed in on John's. "I'm right and I'm glad for you."

"That's your wine talking, Andrew, and it is nonsense. You don't know what you're talking about," John said, but knew he had no real conviction in his voice.

Andrew knew it, too.

"I saw a possessive look in Dunraven's eyes whenever he talked about Millicent, and now I see it in your eyes when you talk about Catherine."

It shows?

"I'm attracted to her. I'm not planning to marry her," John said and felt damned uncomfortable after the words left his mouth. He really didn't know what the hell he was feeling for Catherine.

"Oh, yes, you are. You're caught. You might as well admit it."

What was Andrew saying? Chandler Dunraven had actually fallen in love with Millicent and married her. John didn't love Catherine. He had no plans to marry her.

Did he?

No. He wanted her. She intrigued him. She enchanted him. Yes, he'd wanted to lay her in the carriage and make love to her, but love her? Wed her?

Whatever there was that made her special and different from all the other women he'd wanted over the years would pass soon. He was sure of it. It had to. John loved all women. He couldn't love just one. He couldn't.

"You're sloshed deeper than a frog in the Thames," John finally said. He reached over and took the bottle of wine that sat in front of Andrew and dragged it over by his own glass. "I can't make sense of anything a drunken man says."

"I might be well into my cups, dear friend, but you are lying to me and quite possibly yourself, too." He pointed a finger at John. "It's all right with me that you aren't ready to admit that; however, it doesn't change the fact I saw it in your eyes the first time you talked about her. It was different from the way you've talked about any other young lady."

A rumbling laugh passed John's lips. Andrew was right about one thing. Catherine had his attention like no other lady ever had. John couldn't hide anything from his old friend, but he didn't want to talk to him about Catherine. It was time to change the subject.

"Why are you in here drinking, Andrew? And don't try to make me think it has anything to do with me or Catherine. I'm not falling for that."

Andrew chuckled affectionately as he stared into his glass again. "You're right. It doesn't. You know me as well as I know you. What a hell of a pair we are."

"That's not going to change," he said, wanting to reassure his friend.

"I know."

"So tell me what's going on."

"I've just come to a very big decision in my life today, and I decided to celebrate the occasion."

"A celebration without me? That's a damned bloody thing to do. What's happened?"

"I'm going to be leaving London soon."

It was easy to see Andrew was serious about this.

John tensed. "What? Leaving? Where are you going and why?"

Andrew took another drink and wiped his mouth with the back of his hand before looking at John. "I'm not sure exactly how many places I will go or how long I'll be away. My main purpose is to visit all my estates first and then have a little chat with my manager."

"I don't think you've done either of those things since I've known you."

"I know and unfortunately it has not been a good thing for my finances. I've always had too much going on here in London to worry about the stability of my lands and holdings. As long as I had all the money I needed, I never worried about financial matters. But the time has come that I must take my responsibilities seriously and give them attention."

"That's a good thing."

Andrew's expression turned serious. "I'm in debt, John, and I barely have enough money coming in to cover my wagers."

It was no surprise to hear this, but it was to have Andrew finally admit it. There had been talk for over two years now that Andrew's finances were in peril.

"If you need a loan to cover—"

"John, no—I just need to find out why my income has steadily gone down the past few years. I should have taken the time to look into this the first year it happened, but the draw of London and my life here has always been too great. I didn't want any responsibilities. But now it's time."

"I can understand that."

"My manager kept promising me it would be better the next year and my solicitor was agreeing with him, but my finances have come to the point where I can no longer trust either of them. I have to go and see for myself what is going on."

"You know I'll help you if you need me."

His eyes brightened. "You could come with me. We could make it an adventure. We'll stop at every tavern we pass and bed the wenches."

The image of a big-bosomed tavern wench flashed across his mind and John cringed. Just as quickly Catherine's beautiful breasts came to his mind and a satisfying feeling of contentment washed over him.

Leave Catherine?

"No, I can't. It's not a good time for me."

Andrew shrugged. "So I thought. If you are going to marry Miss Reynolds, it better be soon if you want me to be at the nuptials."

"There will be no marriage," John quickly denied and

immediately wondered why he did. And was that guilt he felt for saying it?

"Damnation, Andrew, I'm attracted to her and I don't understand it. I think about her all the time. I enjoy being with her. I'm eager to be with her. I don't want her to dance with anyone but me, but marriage?" John shook his head.

"Yes, John, marriage. I think those are the things men usually feel when they find the lady they want to marry."

"That thought scares the hell out of me. I don't think that's something I want—"

"Mind if we join you?"

John looked up to see Wilkins and Phillips standing beside them.

"Not at all," he said.

In fact he was happy to have someone interrupt this intimate talk with Andrew about Catherine, but he wasn't happy to see Wilkins throw the latest column from Lord Truefitt on the table in front of him.

"Have you seen this?" Wilkins asked, pulling up a chair on one end of the table while Phillips took the chair on the opposite side.

"Probably all of London has seen it by now," John mumbled under his breath.

"I haven't. What's this?" Andrew picked up the paper and started reading it.

"Why did you hold out on us?" Wilkins asked.

"Yes, we're supposed to be your friends," Phillips accused in a seldom used annoyed tone.

John looked at them as if they'd gone daft in the head. "You are my friends. What are you two going on about? I have no control over what is written in that damned thing."

"You could have been truthful and told us it was a lady

who needed your horse that day in the park. We had to find out in Lord Truefitt's column."

Andrew laid the paper on the table and asked, "Why are you two giving him grief over this? Go play a game of cards or billiards and forget about it."

"But we've lost money on him twice now," Wilkins argued.

"How?" Andrew asked.

"There was that morning in the park when he lost the horse race with Westerland, and now we lost money again because we've just found out there wasn't a ghost riding his horse in the park."

"Bloody hell," John said. "You two didn't bet on that ghost wager here at White's, did you?"

"Of course we did. I think everyone has. You did, didn't you, Andrew?" Phillips asked.

John looked at Andrew and his friend smiled rather grimly. "Ah, no, I intended to, but I never got around to placing my bet. Good thing, too, don't you think?"

"It's your fault, Chatwin. When you said you didn't see what spooked your horse, I thought maybe it was a ghost or phantom or something of that ilk," Wilkins grumbled.

John had to force himself not to laugh, but he couldn't keep the smile off his face. These bucks would bet on anything.

"My, my, what do we have here? Isn't this a nice little chat among friends."

The Marquis threw a copy of Lord Truefitt's article on top of the one Wilkins brought.

The smile faded from John's face. He looked up and saw Westerland and two of his chums standing behind Phillips's chair.

"Don't bother to pull up a chair, Westerland, you won't be staying," John said.

Westerland sniffed. His thin upper lip curled in a sinister way as a grunt blew past his lips. "You certainly know how to make a name for yourself, Chatwin."

"I don't have to; other people seem to do it for me."

"You took the win from me, Fines, and I don't like it."

John picked up his wineglass with seeming indifference and took a drink. "I don't know what you're talking about?"

"Everyone is saying I didn't really win the race because you had to stop and help an unidentified lady who was in trouble."

"Since when do you listen to others? You won. Go and gloat about it somewhere else. I'm not interested in your shortcomings."

"This visit has a purpose. I'm here to challenge you to another race."

John looked up at Westerland again and realized that for the first time he had no desire to race him. He had no desire to race anyone. He wanted to help Catherine find her father. He wanted to be with her, not his friends and not his enemies.

"No" was all he said.

Gasps sounded all around him.

"You can't do that," one of Westerland's friends said. "You can't just say no."

"He just did," Andrew said.

"He's a marquis and he's challenged you. You'll be laughed out of London if you don't accept it," Wilkins said.

"I'll make it an official challenge." Westerland took his gloves out of his pocket and threw them down on top of the papers.

So the prig had thrown down the gauntlet. John still didn't care.

"We've already lost money on you twice," Wilkins reminded him in a whisper across the table. "You know The General can beat his horse. You need to show your mettle and shut him up once and for all."

Now, that thought was tempting.

Westerland laughed. "If you want to win your money back, you should bet on me, but Chatwin and I won't be racing for money. I have something more important in mind than money."

"What's that?"

"If Chatwin wins, I'll stop pursuing a certain young lady. If I win, he will stop pursuing her."

John made a growling sound in his throat, and he stood up so quickly his chair tumbled behind him and the table shook. Andrew, Wilkins, and Phillips jumped up, too.

John centered his gaze on Westerland's face and spoke quietly but menacingly as he said, "I'm not interested in your wager, your race, or anything else you have on your mind. As far as I'm concerned, you won fair. That's the end of it."

The Marquis didn't blink. "Are you afraid you'll lose the right to pursue the lady?"

"No. Don't try to bring her into something that's between you and me."

"She is between us. You could just stop pursuing her and let me have her."

I'll see you in hell first.

"Come on, Chatwin. You know you can win and we'll get our money back."

John scowled at Wilkins.

He swallowed hard. "You'll get the lady, too."

"What if he doesn't want her?" Andrew said.

For once John was glad Andrew spoke up for him. He was getting really close to smashing in Westerland's face, but he knew that was the last thing he needed to do.

"He wants her," Westerland said with a half laugh. "But the question is does her sister want him to have her? My father can offer her a lot more than you can."

"Let's forget it. He's a coward," one of the Marquis's friends said. "He doesn't think his horse can win. Let's go."

"I know you took the lady for a ride in the park today," Westerland said and then laughed before saying, "I'll take her for a *ride* tomorrow."

"When and where do you want to meet?" John said.

Westerland smiled. "I'll let you know." He then turned and left. His two friends followed him.

John drained his glass. Phillips and Wilkins clapped him on the back, congratulating him for accepting the Marquis's challenge.

Andrew gave him a worried look.

John signaled for another drink.

Eighteen

CATHERINE STOOD STRAIGHT and still on the small box in her bedroom while Madame Parachou pinned the hem of her latest gown. For once she didn't mind the fittings and constant chattering in French going on between Victoria and the modiste. Victoria liked to impress the older lady with her excellent command of the French language.

Their preoccupation with Catherine's dress gave her time to think about John. She hadn't seen him at all yesterday. Had they just missed each other? There were so many soirées given each evening, it was quite possible. Or could there be another reason she hadn't seen him?

She knew John wasn't happy the night before last when Victoria wouldn't let her stay at Lord Baxley's long enough to dance with him, but surely he knew she'd wanted to. She'd only seen him long enough for him to say he had spoken with his uncle and he would tell her about it when they were alone.

But that hadn't happened.

Yesterday afternoon she'd spent two torturous hours in the company of the Marquis of Westerland. Not only had he tried to hold her hand more than once, but he'd also reached over and kissed her as they passed a tall hedge and couldn't be seen by anyone.

John had been right when he said men kiss differently. The Marquis's lips were cold and dry compared to John's warm and moist lips. She hadn't felt any strength or confidence in the Marquis's touch, and she certainly hadn't felt any of the stirring sensations that flooded her whenever John touched her.

After the Marquis's kiss, she had quickly faked a cough so she could wipe her mouth with her handkerchief. His lips on hers was not something she wanted repeated. She decided that she would not see him alone again even if Victoria tried to insist.

The afternoon with the Marquis had made her painfully aware that John was the only man she wanted to be alone with.

When she and Victoria had returned from the parties last night, she'd lain awake in her bed remembering each kiss, each touch, and each whispered word that had come from John since they first met. And slowly she came to a very heart-wrenching conclusion. She knew that despite her bravado to the contrary, she had fallen hopelessly in love with John.

She hadn't expected to. She hadn't wanted to. But it had to be love. Why else would she shrink so fiercely from another man's touch, a handsome titled marquis? Why else would she feel such an unsatisfied hunger deep inside to be with John?

She knew it was foolish of her. John was known for loving all women, which she knew meant he loved no one woman. She had been warned about him, but her heart wouldn't listen.

She wanted to tell him of her feelings for him, but she knew if she did she would be added to a long list of heart-broken ladies who had tried to capture his heart and failed.

There was nothing she could do about her love for him but remain quiet. She feared if she even hinted that she loved him he would immediately stop seeing her for worry that he would be caught in a parson's mousetrap or a com-promising situation. She would never do that to him, but John didn't know that. All he knew was that marriage didn't fit into his life.

Right now she needed him to help her find her father. She was eager to know what his uncle had told him about Mr. Beechman and Mr. Chatsworth. She wanted to know if he'd had the time to read her mother's diary. She'd read it too many times over the past several months to believe she had missed anything, but she was pleased he wanted to look at it.

And she wasn't going to wait any longer for John to come to her. She had sent him a note this morning asking that he pay her a visit this afternoon. She had to know what he had found out so far.

"That's perfect right there," Victoria said in English. "There's no need to do anything more to it. Don't you think so, Catherine?"

Jerked out of her thoughts by Victoria's question, Catherine looked down at the fawn-colored gown with its three flounces and delicate lace trim.

She smiled and said, "It is lovely, Madame Parachou. You do beautiful work."

The dark-haired lady with small, wide-set eyes returned

her smile and in broken English said, "It is the lady who makes a dress beautiful and don't you forget it. Now, I must go. I will see you at my shop in a few minutes."

She picked up her sewing basket and headed for the door.

Victoria clasped her hands together under her chin and declared, "With you in this dress I think we may be able to win over Lord Dugdale."

That won't happen.

Catherine laughed. "Do you never think of anything other than making a match, Vickie?"

Victoria put her hands on her hips. "Not since you arrived in London. I've never been so busy and I'm enjoying every moment of it." Suddenly her eyes softened and she let her arms rest calmly by her side. "My husband and I, God rest his soul, were very happy together. But I never realized that I missed having a child until you came to live with me."

Warmth settled over Catherine at Victoria's heartfelt words. She stepped down off the platform and took Victoria's hand in hers.

"And I'm happy here with you, Vickie. Why must you rush me into marriage?"

"I must." Vickie squeezed her hand. "That is the way of things. Children grow up and they marry."

"I might not be ready to make a decision to marry by the end of the Season."

Victoria pulled her hand from Catherine's, the tender moment gone from her eyes and her expression firm once again. "What a horrible thought. I won't allow it. Seeing to your future is my only desire. Now, change quickly. We are going to Madame Parachou's shop to look at some divine fabric she just received yesterday from Paris. She said it is blue velvet."

"Oh, Vickie, may I beg off this outing? I'm rather spent

from all the parties and late nights. Besides, you are so much better at things like that than I am."

"You do look a little tired. All right, you spend the afternoon resting, my dear. I will see to the fabrics and designs for you."

Catherine sighed with relief. "Thank you."

Shortly after Victoria shut the door, Catherine donned a scoop-neck, gray-and-white striped dress. She had faith that if John received her note, he would come see her, and she was rewarded a short time later when her maid brought her a note.

Somehow she knew immediately it was from John. She tore it open and read:

> Plead headache or illness to get out of afternoon obligations. Go through your back garden to the mews. Promptly at half past two.

There was no salutation or signature, but Catherine knew who it was from. He wasn't coming to see her; he wanted her to meet him in secret. Her heart thundered in her chest at the prospect. He must have news for her about her father that couldn't wait.

Catherine looked up at the clock. She had less than half an hour to get out of the house unseen and on time.

She sent her maid on errands and then told their housekeeper that she didn't want to be disturbed. With anticipation building inside her, she quickly put on her bonnet and shawl. She quietly made her way down the stairs without seeing anyone and left the house by a side door off the parlor. Her stomach jumped with an unusual excitement as she casually walked around to the back garden as if she planned to take a stroll.

Catherine looked all around the grounds before she headed to the back where a tall yew hedge grew. No one was in sight, so she opened the gate and stepped out into the mews.

A large, fancy black carriage with gold and red accents was parked just outside the gate. The door opened and a hand came out and helped her step inside.

The carriage took off with a jolt, and Catherine almost fell into the plush, cushioned seat opposite John. The draperies that framed the small windows in the doors let in a little light. The compartment smelled of new leather.

Catherine suddenly realized she'd never been alone with a man in a closed carriage before, and there was something strange and alluring about it.

John was handsome in his dark brown coat and camel-colored waistcoat. She liked the way he always wore his neckcloth low on his neck and simply tied. He looked every bit the comfortable gentleman he was.

She had no regrets about loving him.

"Did anyone see you leave?" he asked.

"No, I don't think so. I was careful. I sent my maid on errands for the afternoon and Vickie is out of the house for the day."

"Good. That should give us plenty of time to accomplish our mission."

"Did you read the diary? Have you discovered something I missed? Do you know who my father is?"

His eyes told her his answer before he actually said the word, "No."

Her hope fell. "Oh."

"You were right about the diary. In the condition it is in I'm surprised you were able to piece together as much of the past as you did. But my uncle told me some fascinating things about Mr. Beechman, and I do have some hunches. We are going to act on one of them this afternoon."

Her hope soared again and she leaned forward. "What, tell me?"

"I spent the entire day yesterday reading old copies of newspapers."

"You did that for me?"

"When I told you I would help you, I meant it and I saw no reason to waste time. I thought about hiring a Runner from Bow Street but decided it would be faster to just do the work myself."

Her heart swelled with love for him even as she grew more anxious about what he'd discovered. "Thank you," she whispered earnestly. "What did you find out?"

"Enough information that we are on our way to pay a visit to Mr. Robert Beechman."

Her stomach felt as if it rolled, and suddenly the rocking of the coach seemed to intensify. Her hands tightened into fists in her lap. She tried to force herself to be calm and to relax as she asked, "Is he my father?"

John reached over and placed his hands on top of hers, and she immediately felt his comforting warmth. She looked down at his hands and realized she'd forgotten to wear gloves.

"I don't know, Catherine. He might be, but I think it's much more likely that your father is his son."

Catherine studied John's eyes as she breathlessly took in what he'd said. "The man who never rides carriages or horses has a son? Where is he?"

He squeezed her hands. "Had a son, Catherine."

Her low, deep breaths changed to short choppy ones, and she felt like her lungs couldn't catch up. "Are you saying he's dead?"

"Yes. He died in a hunting accident late in the year of seventeen ninety-eight."

"That is about the time when I was conceived."

"That's right."

She was not one given to bouts of weakness, but suddenly the coach was hot and stuffy. She felt light-headed and it was difficult to catch her breath. She sat back against the cushion and tried to get control of herself. The last thing she wanted to do was have an attack of the vapors in front of John.

"Mr. Beechman's son was just three years older than your mother. Their names were linked together in two gossip columns."

"You think this man was my mother's lover and my father?"

John's eyes were kind, steady. "I think it's possible. I'm hoping Mr. Beechman will tell us more. I sent him a note this morning saying that I would like to pay him a visit with a guest and he agreed." John paused. "But if this is too upsetting and you don't want to see him today, we can turn around."

She flinched. "What? No, absolutely not." She would not let her fear of the unknown keep her from finding out the truth. "I'm not going to miss this opportunity. I want to see him and talk to him now."

He smiled at her and sat back in his seat. "Good. The color is coming back to your cheeks. For a moment there I thought you might faint."

"Me faint?" she said indignantly, refusing to even admit how close she came. "Sir, I have never fainted in my life, and I don't intend to do it today."

He smiled. "Good. That's the Catherine I know."

As if by magic the roiling of her stomach subsided and her breathing slowed. "Now, tell me all you've discovered."

A short time later Catherine and John were welcomed into Mr. Beechman's home. The butler immediately showed them to the back garden, where he said his employer was waiting.

When they stepped outside, the first thing Catherine noticed was that the clear blue skies of yesterday had turned to a pale shade of gray. She smelled tobacco smoke and felt the heaviness of rain in the air. Mr. Beechman's garden was small but well tended, and vibrant colors of early spring blossoms filled his grounds.

And then she saw him.

Mr. Beechman rose from a chair at the far side of the house and beckoned them to come toward him. He was tall, slender, and impeccably dressed for a man who had all but given up Society. His hair was thinning, but it was a handsome shade of silver. This man was much older than Catherine had always imagined him to be, but then she never gave thought to the possibility that she might be meeting her grandfather instead of her father.

When she approached him, she immediately started searching for something about him that was recognizable, some kind of proof that his blood ran through her veins. She had to look no farther than his eyes. They were the same shade of blue as were her own.

She was glad she had brought her shawl, because she was feeling chilled, and as much as she hated to admit it she was nervous. Her throat thickened with hope; her heart felt light with anticipation that she might finally know her past and her mother's.

After introductions they joined him at the patio table.

Tea and small sandwiches were immediately brought out by a servant, but Catherine knew there was no way she could even take a bite of the beautifully prepared food.

All three of them were quiet until the maid poured the tea and left.

Mr. Beechman said, "I don't often get requests to entertain an earl or a young lady anymore. To what do I owe this pleasure today?"

John had suggested that he start the conversation and that she pick it up whenever she felt comfortable.

That is what he did by saying, "Miss Reynolds is new to London, but her parents grew up here. She wanted to meet some people who might have known her mother when she lived here."

"I don't know anyone anymore. I can't ride, you know, so I don't get out much. I still have a few friends who insist I attend their parties. Occasionally I go, but I don't stay long."

"Mr. Beechman, I wanted to ask about twenty-one years ago," Catherine said without any hesitation in her voice.

He picked up his teacup and sipped. His hands were as steady on the cup as his gaze was on her eyes, but Catherine didn't feel any discomfort at his staring.

For a moment she thought he was going to ignore her, but finally he said, "I don't like to talk about the past. I learned a long time ago you can't change it, so why try to relive it by going back over it."

Her hands remained in her lap, her tea untouched. "We can't change the past, but sometimes talking about it can help us understand it. I was hoping maybe you remembered my mother, Julia Wilson."

She saw recognition light in his eyes as his gaze searched her face. He pointed a stern finger at her and said,

"Yes, that's who you remind me of. Miss Wilson. Oh, yes, I remember her," he said, with no emotion in his voice. "But she didn't have blue eyes like you."

That's because I have your eyes.

"What else do you remember about her?"

Suddenly his expression softened. "Nothing. I didn't know her very well. I don't like to talk about the past. It can't be changed."

Catherine glanced at John and he gave her a slight reassuring nod. "But you must remember something else about her if you remembered the color of her eyes."

"She wanted to marry my son, you know," he said, as if the thought suddenly struck him. "She set out to capture his heart knowing that he was already promised to marry someone else."

Catherine moved to the edge of her seat. "But they didn't marry?"

"No, my son never married."

Catherine felt as if her heart stopped. "Why?"

"I don't like to talk about the past," he said again, and then he picked up his pipe that lay smoldering on the table and took a pull on it, but there was no fire in the tobacco. She looked at John again and he shook his head. No, she couldn't leave until she got more information from him.

"Tell me about your son," she said softly. "Was he tall and slender like you?"

"Yes," he said with the pipe held between his teeth and not seeming to look at anything but the air in front of his eyes. "He was a handsome fellow."

Catherine and John remained quiet.

"He came to me one afternoon on a day very much like today and said he must speak to me. I was out hunting with friends and told him I'd see him later. He said it couldn't wait. He must marry Miss Wilson. I told him I had already made the contracts for him to marry another. He was such a headstrong young man." Mr. Beechman took the pipe out of his mouth. "But I don't like to talk about the past. It can't be changed," he said for what must have been at least the third time.

There was a lump in Catherine's throat, but she managed to ask, "What happened to him?"

He looked directly into her eyes. "He got on his horse and took off like the devils of hell were after him. I was watching him leave when suddenly the horse went down on his front legs. My son flipped over the horse's head and never got up."

Catherine wrapped her shawl closer about her. She felt tears gather in her eyes. "Did your son tell you that Miss Wilson was carrying his child?"

He picked up his teacup and sipped. "Yes," he said in an unconcerned tone. "But I knew it was just a ploy to try to make me say yes to his wishes. I knew it wasn't true."

"Do I look like your son?" she asked.

Mr. Beechman looked at her and as calmly as if he'd been talking about the weather said, "Yes, that's who you remind me of. My son. He had eyes the same color and shape of yours. But you can't be my son's heir. He died a long time ago, and I don't like to talk about the past."

Catherine felt John's hand grab hers under the table. She blinked rapidly, forcing the tears to spread in her eyes and not roll down her cheeks. She looked at John and shook her head.

To Mr. Beechman she said, "I'm sorry about your son. Thank you for telling me about him."

"Yes." He chuckled, but it was a sad sound with no

laughter in his tone. "He was a headstrong young man, but I never talk about him anymore."

A few minutes later Catherine and John said good–bye and quietly walked back to the coach. Catherine felt as if she were walking with iron pots on her feet rather than her soft leather shoes. She felt odd, as if her spirit were disjointed from her body, yet her heart felt heavy and light at the same time.

She was satisfied that Mr. Beechman's son was her father, and that he had tried to do what was right by her mother. It pleased her that he hadn't abandoned her mother, and that gave her peace about him. But she didn't know exactly how she felt about her grandfather right now. That would take more thought than she was capable of at the moment.

John helped her step up and into the carriage. She heard him tell the driver to take his time on the ride back to her house before he closed them inside and took the seat opposite her.

Misty late-afternoon light filtered through the small windowpanes, giving off a gray glow inside the small compartment. Catherine liked being alone inside the coach with John. She felt comfortable and protected, yet inside herself she was restless. She knew there was something more she wanted.

And she knew what it was.

"I'm sorry it wasn't better news for you," John said.

Catherine looked at John. She didn't want to talk. She just wanted to feel. She wanted to be in his arms with his lips on hers, his hands on her body making her forget everything but his touch.

"Kiss me, John," she said.

His gaze fluttered softly across her face. "Catherine, I don't think that's a good idea right now. You're emotional. You need to—"

She didn't allow him to finish. She leaped onto the seat with him and wrapped her arms around his neck as she pressed her lips to his.

Nineteen

*H*E WAS HESITANT and for a moment she thought he might push her away, but suddenly his arms circled her and he crushed her against his chest.

He accepted her kiss for a few moments and then he became the aggressor. It was as if lightning struck between them and flames of desire exploded all around them. They couldn't kiss or touch each other fast enough, hard enough, or earnest enough.

As their breaths, mouths, and tongue mingled in desperate kisses, she whispered, "I know what I need."

You.

But she didn't know how to tell him that.

"Catherine, you know I can't resist you," he answered as his lips left hers and kissed their way down her neck to where the fullness of her breasts rose from beneath her dress.

Didn't he know she wanted him to possess her?

"Then don't."

"I must," he answered as he cupped her breasts, lifting them up and squeezing them gently as he moaned with pleasure.

His tongue searched her mouth, tasting her over and over again. Catherine trembled with a wanting she didn't understand, but she knew she wanted to be in John's embrace like this.

"I want to take you now and make you mine, but you know I can't."

Yes, she knew he was afraid she'd insist they marry if things went too far between them. Would he believe her if she told him she would never do that? She had such an intense desire to be this close to him that she would beg him not to stop if she had to.

His mouth stayed on hers as their tongues played together. Pleasurable sounds passed both their lips as he caressed her breasts and she ran her hands over his wide shoulders and through the back of his hair.

"I'm going to touch you, but don't be afraid of what I'm doing, all right?" he whispered into her mouth.

"You don't frighten me, John, you know that."

"But I've never done this to you before. Just relax against the seat."

How could she relax when she was coiled tight with unrequited passion for this man?

He leaned her back in the corner of the seat as he continued to kiss her lips, her cheeks, and her neck. His hand snaked down her hip and leg to the hem of her dress. He grasped the fabric in his hand and slowly slid it up, letting the tips of his fingers lightly caress her stocking-covered knee. When he made it to her thigh, he lingered, rubbing her soft skin gently back and forth and inching a little higher each time until he made it up to her waist.

Catherine trembled. She thought she might scream with madness if he didn't go faster.

She gasped with surprise not fear when he untied the drawstring of her drawers and parted them so that they fell away from her hips. Catherine felt as if her stomach were turning in on itself.

"I'm not going to hurt you," he whispered.

That never entered her mind.

"I know," she managed to say between gusty breaths of pleasure.

Slowly his hand slipped softly, warmly down her bare stomach to her most womanly part. He covered her with his hand as if he were protecting her. It was warm, soothing. She didn't know what he was doing, but it didn't matter because the thrill of his touch set her body on fire.

Catherine didn't know how or why, but she felt the need to lift her hips and press into his hand. She remained still even though she felt as if it were killing her to do so.

Her heart swelled with love for him that he could make her feel so good. She wanted to whisper those life-altering words to him, but she couldn't.

"Are you all right?" he asked.

"It feels so good it's hard to catch my breath. It's difficult to remain still."

"Don't try. Just move with the feeling, move with my hand."

She nodded.

"Close your eyes and enjoy the way I'm going to make you feel."

How could she feel any better than this?

She didn't want to close her eyes. She wanted to look at him with all the love and desire she had for him.

"What are you going to do?"

"This."

His fingers moved over her and her breaths suddenly became short and raspy. He stroked her pearl of desire in a soft, slow circular motion. The tingle was frantic. She had never felt anything so intense in her life. Her hips started moving with his hand. Faster. Harder.

The sensation built inside her so quickly her whole body suddenly exploded with sensation. She jerked and shivered as she cried out with pleasure. John covered her mouth in a searing kiss.

What she felt was too powerful to understand. His hand stopped and he cupped her. He held her tighter, softening the pressure on her lips, and on her core.

When the shuddering stopped, she gasped. She held him tighter for a wild moment thinking she could keep him forever in her arms. She wanted to ask him not to leave her. She wanted to ask him to marry her, but she knew she couldn't do that.

She pushed away from him, suddenly heartsick that a man who could make her feel so sensational didn't love only her.

John removed his hand from beneath her clothing and helped her pull down her skirts.

As her breathing calmed, she said, "I don't know what you did to me, but I've never felt that intense before."

He smiled. "Do you feel calmer and more relaxed?"

Satisfied but not content.

She nodded and asked, "Did you—did we—do what I think we did?"

He smiled as he readjusted himself in the seat and in his trousers. "No. You are still very much a virgin and I'm still very much—ah." He looked down at the bulge between his legs. "Let's just say you needed an emotional release and I provided it."

"Thank you." She moistened her lips and added, "But what about you? Are you—?"

"Don't worry about me. I'll manage."

He laughed and gently pulled her into his strong arms. She laid her head on his shoulder and she buried her face into his neckcloth. He seemed to know just when she needed his strength. The meeting with Mr. Beechman had drained her, and it felt so wonderful to be held in John's comforting arms.

She understood now how a woman could love a man so much she would trap him into marriage. But Catherine realized she loved John too much to do that to him.

"You're not crying, are you?" he asked as he caressed her back and shoulders.

She raised her head and looked into his eyes. "Certainly not. I'm not going to cry, but I am sad about what happened to my father and that he and my mother never had a chance at happiness."

"And how do you feel about your grandfather?"

"A man who admitted he wouldn't let my mother marry his son, a grandfather who looked at me, and I'm sure recognized me, but wouldn't acknowledge me? I don't know." She shook her head, and then said, "You do think he recognized me, don't you?"

He caressed her cheek with the backs of his fingers. "I don't know, Catherine. Maybe. Maybe he's too mixed up about the past to realize exactly who you are."

"He did seem a little touched in the head at times, didn't he?"

"Yes."

"My mother must have been devastated when she heard my father had been killed."

"I'm sure she was, but she married Patrick Reynolds and was happy, wasn't she?"

"As far as I can remember; I was so young when she died."

"You didn't tell Mr. Beechman you thought you were his granddaughter. Why?"

"I realized when I was looking at him, listening to him, that I would receive no pleasure or pain from telling him. After all these months of wondering and wanting to know the truth, the only thing I feel is relief that I know what happened. Comfort knowing my father didn't abandon me and my mother."

"Then you have the answers you sought and you can get on with your life."

She nodded, not even wanting to think about getting on with her life because that would mean without John in it. He now had no reason to continue to pursue her as she'd asked him to, but she couldn't bear to think about that right now, not after what just happened between them.

"I think Mr. Beechman knows who I am, but he can't admit it. I'm not sure he ever will."

"Perhaps old age has destroyed his mind," John offered.

"Or maybe he's slowly going mad because of guilt." She pondered both their comments for a moment before adding, "I'm going to come see him again and try to get to know him."

John looked surprised. "Are you sure? His mind seemed a little unstable to me."

"To me, too, but he is my grandfather. Maybe one day

I'll have the strength to tell him that a part of his son still lives. Do you think that would help him or hurt him?"

His expression softened again. "I don't know, Catherine, but I think it's admirable you want him to know. And I believe it's the right thing to do."

The coach stopped and Catherine pushed out of John's arms and straightened her dress.

"Thank you for all your help, John."

His gaze held fast on hers. "You know I don't want gratitude."

"I know."

"I'll get out first and make sure no one is around. You wait here."

John stepped out of the coach, but Catherine knew he was really stepping out of her life.

*H*E'D NEVER DONE that before. Pleasured a woman and not received satisfaction at the same time. But for the first time that he could remember, it hadn't been important to him to be pleasured. He was only thinking of Catherine.

That was new for him, too.

John leaned back against the softness of the carriage bench and propped his booted feet on the opposite seat. He folded his arms behind his head and stared out the window.

Catherine was good at hiding it, but he knew her emotions had been running away with her. Sexual release was the most satisfying feeling there was. Not finding her father left her unfulfilled; he knew pleasing her that way would comfort her.

And it had.

He'd watched her face, heard her sounds of surprise, wonder, and pleasure. He knew it had been good for her and that made him feel so blasted good. And he'd left her pure, well almost, for her wedding night. He felt damn good about that, too.

A sharp pain stabbed through him. He didn't like to think of Catherine marrying anyone. He didn't even like the idea of another man kissing her. Oh, hell—who was he trying to fool? He didn't even want anyone holding her hand when they were dancing.

So what was he doing allowing his friends to talk him into a race he didn't want to ride in and risk losing the right to pursue her? Racing horses no longer held any desire for him. He was angry that he'd allowed himself to be talked into it. He wouldn't give her up even if Westerland should somehow win.

Then he'd be considered a man without honor. What a hell of a mess. He'd allowed himself to be caught up in the moment and the challenge. He wouldn't lose anything to Westerland.

Especially Catherine.

What was he going to do? The race had already appeared in the wager book at White's. Men had already started betting on the outcome. His friends had money on the race.

He had to think of something. There had to be a way he could get out of this damnable race with his honor still intact and Catherine his.

Twenty

"As distance shows a horse's strength, so time reveals a man's heart." The wager book at White's is filling up quickly as another race has been planned between the Earl of Chatwin and the Marquis of Westerland. But this time it is not money these two gentlemen seek to win. They are racing for the honor of pursuing the hand of Miss Reynolds.

Lord Truefitt
Society's Daily Column

CATHERINE HEARD VICKIE calling her name before she burst through Catherine's bedroom door waving a sheet of newspaper in her hand.

"You won't believe this," Victoria said as she plopped down on top of Catherine's bed and fell back, spreading her arms wide, laughing.

Catherine rose from the stool in front of her dresser and looked at her sister as if she were crazy. "What on earth has happened?"

"This!" she exclaimed as she rose to a sitting position on the bed. "It's absolutely delicious. Lord Chatwin and the Marquis will be having another race, and you'll never guess what the prize is."

"Prize. It's usually money that they race for, isn't it?"

"Mostly, but this time, my dear, *you* are the reward!" She laughed again. "Oh, nothing could be more wonderful than this."

Catherine felt a pounding in her head. "What are you talking about? They can't race for my hand. Let me see that."

Victoria handed over the paper, and Catherine quickly read Lord Truefitt's column. This was outrageous. She read it again thinking it couldn't possibly be true, but it was. And Vickie was smiling like a cat that had just eaten a bird!

"Oh, no," Catherine whispered earnestly. "How could John do this to me?"

Catherine's mind went wild with thoughts. How could he do this after the way he helped her find her grandfather, after the way he'd touched her so intimately he reached her soul. She loved him deeply. How could he hurt her so? She had to remember he didn't love her. She could accept that, but she didn't want to believe he would be willing to give her up in a horse race.

Vickie kicked her feet happily as she sat on the edge of the bed and said, "Why are you looking so distraught, Catherine? This is the most wonderful news."

"For whom?" Catherine asked as her hands closed into fists, crumpling the paper, feeling anger, hurt, and stinging disappointment. "Certainly not me. What is wrong with you, Vickie? How can you think this is good news? I'm not a prize to be won."

"I will admit that when I first read it, I thought, how can they do this to me?"

"You?"

"Yes, me." She stood up and walked over to the dressing table and looked in the mirror. "After all the work I've put into matchmaking for you. I couldn't believe they decided to take it upon themselves to settle your fate without my participation."

Vickie was unbelievable.

She turned back to Catherine. "But after thinking about it, I realized that I've played Lord Chatwin's and Lord Westerland's game so well that I've outmaneuvered both of them. I knew this must be Lord Chatwin's doing. The Marquis is not smart enough to think of something as delicious as this."

Vickie continued to talk, but Catherine turned away and stopped listening. There was a ringing in her ears and a heaviness in her heart. All she could think was how could John have done this to her? She thought she knew him, but she didn't know him at all.

After their secretive outing yesterday they had talked, laughed, and danced last night at a party with no awkwardness between them. If he didn't want to pursue her, why didn't he just tell her? Why go to this elaborate scheme of horse racing?

Did he think this would be the best way to say good-bye without having to come right out and tell her? John could just see to it that he lost this race, and then he would be honor bound to stop pursuing her.

Her heart broke.

"But then I thought this is the best thing that could have happened to you," Victoria was saying. "The attention this will attract will be the biggest event this Season, maybe the biggest event since they outlawed dueling."

"Vickie, this is unacceptable."

"No, no, my dear. Everyone will think I had something to do with this, and it will be evidence of my matchmaking skills. Mamas all over London will want to seek my skills, and after I have you safely betrothed, I can take my time and choose only the best clients."

Catherine strained to understand Victoria. "This is about me. Not you. I don't want anyone racing for the right to pursue me. I won't allow it," she finished firmly.

Victoria looked confused. "But what do you mean? This will be a legal race between two titled gentlemen. You have no say in it."

"Watch me," she said, firmly knowing she had to do something but not knowing what to do. "If they race, I won't have anything to do with either of them."

"Of course you will," Victoria said as calmly as if they were talking about the weather. "There aren't that many eligible titled gentlemen. You certainly didn't win over Lord Dugdale. But we don't need to worry about that now. You will have to accept the pursuit of the winner. Because that is what will be best for you. Now finish dressing. There will be much discussion about this at the parties tonight, and we don't want to miss one delicious moment of it."

*I*T TOOK CATHERINE the rest of the afternoon alone in her room, but she finally came up with a plan of action. She would not just stand around and allow this travesty to happen. Not without having her own say in the matter.

One moment she would think she never wanted to see John again, and the next she couldn't wait to see him so she could tell him how outrageous this race was. And then at other times her love for him would rise to the surface of her heart and overflow, and she would think that there had to be a reasonable explanation for why he was doing this.

Perhaps he'd been coerced some way. Maybe the Marquis had called him a coward. Many things had entered her thoughts, but John was the only one who knew the answer.

The first party of the evening that she and Victoria attended was a nightmare for Catherine but a celebrated affair for Victoria who readily accepted accolades for Catherine's popularity.

Catherine was ill suited for such acclaim. Some of the young ladies looked at Catherine with disdain while others swarmed around her to ask questions about how she felt about the two most handsome bachelors in London racing to win pursuit of her hand. Catherine detested every minute of it and excused herself from the crowds as often as she could.

There were only two people she wanted to talk to.

And as soon as she and Victoria walked into the second party of the evening, Catherine saw one of them. She made a hasty exit from her sister and followed Lady Lynette to the retiring room that had been set aside for the ladies.

Catherine waited outside the door for Lynette and when she came out asked, "Lynette, might I have a word alone with you?"

"Yes, Catherine," Lynette said with excitement in her expression and her voice. "I've been looking for you all evening. I'm dying to find out what you think about the horse race for the pursuit of your hand. Let's find a place where we can have privacy."

They walked down the corridor, peeking into rooms until they found a cupboard that was lighted but empty.

They slipped inside, and as soon as the door was closed, Lynette said, "Now tell me how it feels to be the most sought-after young lady in London."

Catherine took a deep breath and answered, "Absolutely terrible."

"What? Why? You have an earl and a marquis wanting your hand."

"No, they don't want me, they each want to win over the other. I will not be their prize, and I need your help to accomplish that."

Lynette looked puzzled. "What can I do?"

"I've decided that I'm going to join Lord Chatwin and the Marquis in the race. I'm going to beat both of them, and then not have anything to do with either of them ever again."

"What!" Lynette exclaimed. "You can't do that. They'll never let you be a part of it. It's a gentleman's race."

"What are they going to do to me? Will they forcibly remove me from the starting point?"

"I don't know. They might."

"I think not."

"But even if they let you join them, how could you win? You don't have a horse, do you?"

"No. Not a very good one, but I'll hire the best horse I can find. Someone with a winning horse will come to my aid. I'm an excellent rider and I know how to make an animal give his best. I will join this race and prove to them what a ridiculous idea it is that they've come up with."

Lynette's eyes glimmered in the glow of the lamplight. "I don't believe this. It is just too delectable for words. Let me see, how shall I start Lord Truefitt's column. . . . 'You can lead a horse to water, but you can't make him drink,' or perhaps I should start with 'When a horse comes to the edge, it's too late to draw rein.' " Suddenly Lynette stopped and clamped her mouth shut. Her green eyes widened with fear. "Oh, dear, what did I just say?"

Catherine was aghast. "I think you just told me you're Lord Truefitt."

"No, no I didn't say that." She opened her reticule and pulled out a handkerchief and delicately dabbed at her forehead with a trembling hand. "No, I might have misspoken and implied it, but I never said I was Lord Truefitt." She looked up at Catherine with horror glowing in her green eyes. "Did I?"

"Lynette, it's all right. I am your friend. I will never discuss this conversation with anyone."

Lynette remained quiet.

Catherine laid a comforting hand on Lynette's gloved arm. "I have trusted you with my information, and now you must trust me to keep your secret. You have my word I will."

"I'm not really Lord Truefitt, but I know who she is. I work for her."

Catherine smiled. "I love it that Lord Truefitt isn't even a man. How ingenious of the lady, whoever she is, to write under a man's name."

Suddenly Lynette giggled a wonderful, feminine-sounding laugh that Catherine wouldn't have thought Lynette capable of because of her large frame and loud voice.

Catherine laughed with her.

"I've said way too much," Lynette said after their laughter. "I will get her in trouble and me, too. We'll both lose our jobs if anyone discovers who we are. You understand that, don't you?"

"I understand and no one will hear it from me. Even my sister thought it was Lord Chatwin who told Lord Truefitt the truth about what happened to us in the park that morning I rode his horse. I let her assume that and didn't tell her it was me who told you. Your secret is safe with me."

"Thank you. You are a dear friend."

"So now will you put in Lord Truefitt's column tomorrow afternoon that Miss Reynolds has decided to join their ill-conceived race and she expects to win? And after she does, she will not accept the attention of either gentleman."

Lynette reached over and gave Catherine an unexpected hug, and it made Catherine feel warm inside.

"Leave it to me," Lynette said. "I'll take care of everything."

Lynette and Catherine parted ways when they returned to the teeming party. Catherine immediately started looking for John in the midst of a hundred people, but instead she bumped into his friend Lord Dugdale.

"Miss Reynolds, it's nice to see you this evening."

"Is it?" she asked, not seeing any reason to be more than vaguely polite to John's unfriendly friend.

"Yes. I was hoping I could have a few minutes with you."

She studied his face. She didn't see the cold hostility she'd seen in his eyes the last time they'd talked to each other, but she wasn't in any frame of mind to be interrogated by him again.

"I really don't think we have anything to say to each other, my lord, so if you will excuse me—"

"Wait." He gently took her upper arm when she started to pass him.

She glared at him, and he quickly let her go.

"I'm sorry, I shouldn't have done that." He looked around to see if anyone in the packed room noticed his breech of etiquette.

Catherine knew the room was too busy with people talking, laughing, and drinking to have noticed his impropriety. The intensity of the noise was too powerful for anyone to have even heard their words.

"What I have to say to you is important. Hear me."

She started to deny him, but her curiosity got the better of her, and instead she said, "Very well, you can walk with me to get a cup of punch."

"Thank you, Miss Reynolds," he said.

Catherine couldn't help but notice they received many surprised looks and some outright stares as they made their way over to the punch table. No doubt everyone had heard about the race between Lord Chatwin and Lord Wester-land, and this was the first time she'd been seen alone with Lord Dugdale. Some of them had to be wondering what was going on.

Catherine smiled to herself. She would love it if more rumors started flying about her and Lord Dugdale. The way she was feeling right now, she would be happy to cause John even a moment of concern.

The earl handed her a cup of punch and took a glass of wine for himself. He escorted her over to a corner away from the other people in the room.

Feeling confident in what she'd decided to do about the race, she said, "Now, what can I do for you, my lord? Do you have more dire warnings or evil threats to give me concerning John?"

"Was I that bad that evening I met you?"

He looked sincere, but she wasn't in the mood to pacify him. "You were like a charging boar, and I was your prey."

"I hope you will forgive me. I'd had a little too much to drink that night and I—well, I didn't behave properly."

Catherine suddenly felt weary. She didn't need to see John. Not with the way she was feeling. One moment she was so angry with him she wanted to hurt him, and the next she was afraid she might break down and tell him she loved him.

She didn't want to do that. She couldn't bear it if he felt sorry for her.

She sipped her punch and looked back into Lord Dugdale's eyes. "What do you want?"

"I wanted to tell you that John is in love with you."

For a moment she couldn't say anything, but then she realized that he must be playing some kind of game. She wouldn't fall for it.

"How wonderful," she said in a false happy voice. "He loves me so much he's willing to risk losing the right to pursue me. You must think me an idiot, Lord Dugdale," she said and wished she was drinking champagne rather than punch.

"No. Look into my eyes, Miss Reynolds. I'm serious about this. John has been denying this almost from the moment he saw you, but I knew it from the first time he told me you had stolen his horse."

Catherine could not let his words get to her. He was trying to trick her, but why? Did he want her to say she loved him, too, so he could laugh at her or tease her?

Her eyes narrowed in on his. "Oh, yes, his horse. I should have known you wanted to talk about that."

"I'm telling you what I know to be true because I don't know if he will. I don't know if John realizes yet that he loves you, so I'm asking you to be patient with him."

"Sir, you have a bad habit of speaking for John. He does not need you to threaten ladies for him, and he doesn't need you to tell them he loves them. You need to learn to stay out of his concerns."

Catherine handed her empty punch cup to him and walked away. She would find Vickie, plead a headache, and go home. She didn't want to see John tonight. She needed to wait until she had collected her thoughts and decided just what she would say to him.

Should she show him her anger for what he'd done or should she show him her love?

Twenty-one

$\mathcal{I}$T HAD TAKEN him the entire night and half the morning, but John had finally come up with a plan and he was ready to get started. He grabbed his coat and jerked open his front door only to see Andrew walking toward him. John didn't have time to waste with Andrew.

"I'm glad I caught you before you left your house," Andrew said as he neared John.

John shoved his arms in his coat and answered, "Just pretend you didn't. I have a lot of things to do today, Andrew. I don't have time for a visit."

"Then perhaps you've seen this?" Andrew held up a sheet of newsprint.

"No, I haven't and I don't want to," he said, pulling his cuffs out of the sleeves of his coat. "I'm tired of looking at those things. I don't care what it says."

"Oh, I think you will this time."

"No, I won't." He took the paper from Andrew and

wadded it in both of his hands and threw it back into the house. It landed in the umbrella stand. He then closed the door behind him and started down the walkway toward his carriage.

Andrew fell into step beside him. "You're in such a temper, I should just let someone else tell you what's going on, but because I'm your best friend and I feel a bit guilty about some things, I'm not going to let that happen."

John stopped. "Guilty about what?"

"I may have been less than kind to Miss Reynolds in the past, but that's not important right now. It seems there will be a third rider in your race with Westerland."

"What? Another man wants in on this?" John swore under his breath. "I don't believe this. Who is he?"

"Not he, my friend, she. Lord Truefitt says that Miss Reynolds will be joining your race."

"What the devil?"

"And he goes on to say that she's excellent on a horse and expects to win. Furthermore, after she wins she won't allow either you or Westerland to pursue her."

John's mood turned dark. "Do not play with me about this, Andrew."

He put his hand over his heart. "I swear to you I'm not."

"Damnation." John turned away. "What the devil is she thinking?"

"Maybe that she doesn't want to be the prize in a game for two men who have nothing better to do in their lives than race horses."

But that had changed. John did have something better to do with his life now, and Catherine was the one who had helped him realize that.

Suddenly John chuckled.

Andrew shook his head. "You think this is funny?"

"No, of course not, but it doesn't surprise me that Catherine is taking matters into her own hands. She's like that."

"There's no way you will let her race with you, is there?" Andrew asked with a worried expression on his face.

John's stomach twisted at the thought. "Of course not, and I don't plan to give her up. I already have something in mind to stop this madness."

"What can you do?"

"I'm going to do what any good Englishman would do under these circumstances."

"Every Englishman I know would run the race and take their chances. It's a matter of honor now, but something tells me you're not going to do that."

"Hell no, I'm going to kidnap her."

Surprise lit in Andrew's eyes. "I don't believe it. You're going to run off to Gretna Green with her?"

John smiled at his friend and clapped him on the shoulder. "Nothing that ordinary, my friend," John said and walked away.

*I*T HAD TAKEN John all of the afternoon and way into the evening to arrange everything according to his plan. Now all he had to do was find Catherine and get her to agree with him. Mrs. Goosetree was fairly predictable about which parties she attended, and he felt sure he would find Catherine at the party given at the Great Hall.

He stopped just inside the door and looked over the crowded room. All he saw was a sea of color sprinkled with black and white. The room was packed with ladies dressed in silks, satins, and lace, and gentlemen dressed in evening coats with their white shirts and neckcloths gleaming in the candlelight. He'd be lucky if he found her in less than half an hour.

He stepped down into the large ballroom and started his search.

"Who's going to win the race, Chatwin?" someone called to him. John waved to him but didn't stop to talk.

"Lord Chatwin, my money is on you," another man said as he passed.

John smiled at everyone who spoke to him, but he didn't allow anyone to stop him as he waded through the people. He didn't know why it had taken him so long to realize that Catherine was the only woman he wanted to be with today, tomorrow, and forever. But what would he do if she didn't feel the same way?

He didn't want to think about that.

Finally he saw her talking to two other ladies near the terrace doors, and a smile of contentment came to his face. She looked beautiful in an ivory-colored dress that was embroidered with tiny blue flowers. The neckline was temptingly low. Tiny blue flowers had been woven into her hair. As he walked closer he saw that she wore a necklace and matching earrings made of sapphires, and while they looked beautiful on her, that was not what he wanted to see her wearing.

He made his way over to the small group and said, "Good evening, Miss Lawson, Miss Anderson, and Miss Reynolds."

He barely noticed the other two ladies other than to realize they spoke to him and Catherine did not. Her eyes were so cold they looked like blue ice. She didn't have to say a word for him to know she was angry, but he saw something else in her expression that bothered him even more. She looked wounded. Didn't she know he would never intentionally hurt her?

John's chest tightened. He didn't blame her. He should never have accepted that bet with Westerland. He was going to make it up to her.

"Did you hear that Catherine intends to join your race with Lord Westerland?" Miss Anderson asked.

John looked at the young lady and said, "Yes, I did," before turning his attention back to Catherine. "I'd very much like to talk with you about that, Miss Reynolds. Do you mind if I speak to you alone?"

Her expression remained cold. "I'm sorry, Lord Chatwin, it isn't convenient right now. Perhaps next year."

"This is a very important matter and I really need to talk to you now."

She took a deep breath. "Very well, excuse me, ladies."

He lightly touched the small of her back as they walked away, and he felt her cringe from his touch.

"I can't believe you have the nerve to even speak to me," she said.

"When I said I had something important to discuss with you, I meant it. This way," he said, pointing her toward the front door.

She looked at him. "Where are we going?"

"To get your cloak."

Her eyes questioned him as much as her one word, "Why?"

"Catherine, you told me a few days ago that you trusted me. Is that still true?"

He didn't like the way she searched his face, looking deeply into his eyes. He saw doubt in her expression that hadn't been there before. For his plan to work she had to trust him completely.

She glanced away. "I don't want to, but I do."

He didn't realize he was holding his breath until he let it out on a troubled sigh. He knew he loved her with all his heart, and he had made the right decision.

"We're going to get your cloak, and then we're going to walk out the front door together and get into my carriage."

"What? We can't do that. Someone will surely see us. John, I was perfectly happy to slip out the back garden to meet you in secret, but there are at least two hundred people here tonight. I can't just walk out the door with you. That would be madness."

They stopped by the servant at the front door, and John asked him to bring her wrap.

"I know, but you said you trusted me. If you do, you'll walk out with me."

"If you want me to escape with you, why are we waiting for my wrap? Someone will see us leave."

"That's the point, Catherine. I want someone to see us."

Her blue eyes sparkled with surprise. "I can't believe this. Why would you want someone to see us?"

"Because I want everyone to know that I've kidnapped you from this party."

"Kidnapped me? John, I don't know what you are talking about."

John reached for her cape and said, "We have to leave now. I see Mrs. Goosetree heading toward us. Do not hesitate no matter if anyone tries to stop us."

He took hold of her arm, and they ran out the door, down the steps, and toward John's fancy carriage. The footman held the door open while John helped Catherine inside. He then jumped in behind her and slammed the door shut as the carriage took off.

John heard Mrs. Goosetree calling Catherine's name.

They both looked out the small back window and saw Victoria and several other people standing in the street watching them speed away.

Catherine looked at John in horror. "Did we just do what I think we did?"

He smiled and placed her wrap around her shoulders. "Yes, we did."

"Are you mad? Have you gone insane?"

"Yes, I'm insanely jealous of you, and I don't want to risk losing you in a horse race. And yes, I'm mad, Catherine. I'm madly in love with you."

Yellow light from outside the carriage shone on her beautiful blue eyes that rounded in disbelief. "Don't tease me, John."

"I'm not. I love you, Catherine."

She shook her head. "No. You love all ladies. We are all the same to you."

"That used to be true until I met you. But you made me realize that I don't love all women. I have great respect for them. Beauty and age have never mattered to me. Every woman has a special quality, but you are the only lady I have ever loved."

Her eyes softened. "How can I believe you? You were willing to risk losing me in a horse race."

"No, from the moment I allowed myself to be goaded into that wager by Westerland, I've been trying to figure a way to get out of it."

"How can you? You will lose your honor if you don't race him."

He picked up her gloved hand and held it in his. "My honor is very important to me, but you are more important. I couldn't risk losing you, so I decided to kidnap you. Everyone will think we are heading to Gretna Green, and in truth we should be, but I have something else planned. Westerland will be angry as a wild boar that I've decided to take matters into my own hands this way, but he'll get over it. Besides, I've sent him a consolation prize."

"What?"

"The General is being delivered to his stables as we speak."

Her heart hammered and then fluttered. "That can't be true. You wouldn't give him your horse."

He nodded. "I have. I want you, Catherine. Nothing has ever been more important to me than you are."

"Do you think the Marquis will consider the matter settled?"

"He'll have no choice." The carriage stopped. "Come on. We're here."

John got out and helped Catherine descend the small step.

She looked around and then said, "We're in front of your empty building."

"Yes. Come inside and I'll show you."

John told the driver to wait for them, and then he knocked on the door and it opened. The caretaker walked out and John and Catherine stepped inside.

Catherine couldn't believe her eyes.

"I told you the room could be used for anything," he said.

She was stunned at the transformation in the room. The walls of the building had been draped in a blue velvet fabric. In the center of the room a large Persian rug lay on the dirt floor. A bed made with gleaming white sheets and pillows stood in the middle of the rug. Nightstands had been placed on each side of the bed, and they held beautiful silver candlesticks with flickering candles bathing the room in a golden light.

"I can't believe you did all this," she said, knowing that the whole evening had been unbelievable. She had actually run away with John. Victoria was probably out looking for her at this very moment.

His eyes locked on hers. His hand tightened on her waist. "I'd move heaven and earth for you, Catherine."

At that moment Catherine felt as if he'd touched the center of her soul, and she knew she'd done the right thing in trusting him and loving him.

She looked up at him with all the love she was feeling and said, "Show me what you have planned for us."

He walked her farther inside, closer to the bed. A side table held a bottle of wine and two glasses. He poured a little of the deep red wine into the glasses and handed one to Catherine.

"You have seduced me from the moment I first saw you. I thought it was time for me to seduce you."

"Do you not know that I have been."

"I've been hoping that all day."

He touched his glass to hers, and then they sipped from their glasses before he put them back on the table.

"You turned my world upside down, and now it's up to you to turn it right again."

"How can I do that?" she asked.

He picked up a black velvet box and took out a three-string pearl necklace. It glowed in the candlelight.

"May I?" he asked.

She nodded, still unable to believe that her dream of being with John was coming true.

He took off the sapphire necklace and fastened the pearls around her neck, letting his warm fingers lightly caress her before he bent down and kissed her nape. Shivers of desire filled her, and she turned into the embrace of his warm arms.

"I've always known the color of your skin was made for pearls," he whispered and pulled her up close to his chest. "Catherine, I've always known I'd give pearls to the lady I loved. I applied for a special marriage license today. Tell me you love me and that you'll marry me as soon as it can be arranged."

Catherine's heart swelled so big in her chest she thought it might burst. "Yes, oh, yes! John, I fell in love with you even though I tried very hard not to. Of course I'll marry you. I've been wondering how I could live without you."

"So do I have your permission to presume on our wedding night?"

His words and his expressions were so seductive the power of her womanly feelings flooded her. She put her arms around his neck and pressed her body close to his.

"Permission granted, my lord," she whispered as their lips pressed softly together in a long lingering kiss that was meant to relax and satisfy.

Their mouths mated, their tongues played, and their teeth nibbled as they enjoyed the freedom of being totally alone. As his lips moved back and forth across hers, she slid her arms under his coat and surrounded his body so she could draw from his strength.

Catherine had never felt so wonderful in her life. She'd never been so happy. The mystery of her father had been solved and John loved her and wanted to marry her.

Their kiss deepened as his hands gently pulled the pins and flowers from her hair and let them fall on the rug. As the length of her hair fell to her shoulders she felt his hands letting it sift through his fingers.

"Tell me you have no doubts, no regrets."

"None. I want to be yours, John. Take me and make me yours."

Her tongue darted farther into his mouth and their kiss escalated. His hands slid down to her breasts. He palmed them, fondled them beneath the silky fabric of her dress. She sighed softly as she enjoyed the pleasure his hands created inside her. Catherine didn't like the barrier of the clothing. She wanted to feel his hands upon her skin without her gown between them.

She turned her back to him. He moved her hair to one shoulder and kissed her nape as he unfastened the back of her dress. His lips were smooth and moist. Her whole body tingled as her gown slipped from her shoulders and fell to the rug.

Catherine stepped out of her dress and turned in his arms. She reached up and pulled on his neckcloth and untied the bow. His hands came up to help her unwind it and remove his collar. He then shrugged out of his coat, his waistcoat, and finally his shirt.

Catherine ran her hands over the fullness of his broad, naked chest. His skin was warm, smooth, firm.

"I like the way you look and the way you feel," she whispered.

He smiled at her and her heart melted. "I love the way you look and I love the way you feel."

He backed her against the bed, and she sat down on it. He took his time and removed her gloves, shoes, and stockings, lovingly touching her inner and outer thighs before removing her shift and drawers.

John shed his boots and trousers while Catherine watched him. In the pale light she looked at his desire for her showing in the full thickness of his manhood.

He laid her back on the bed and looked at her while his hands softly caressed her skin. She wondered if she should feel uncomfortable lying naked before John, but she wasn't. How could she feel inhibited with the man she loved, the man she was going to marry? She couldn't. It would be impossible.

John bent his head and kissed her stomach, burying his face in the hollow of her abdomen. His hand planed down her hip and her thigh to find that point between her legs that he sought, but he didn't linger there.

"Your breasts are so beautiful," he said

Catherine felt her nipples harden and pucker at his words.

"Thank you," she whispered.

He pulled the pearls down on her chest so that they lay in the valley of her breasts. He looked down at her and whispered, "I love you, Catherine."

Her chest felt heavy with admiration. "I love you, John."

He bent down and covered one rosy tip with his mouth and sucked while his hands slowly sculpted her breasts. The muscles in her abdomen contracted and quivered convulsively beneath the flaming heat of his touch. Desire hot and wild shot through Catherine, and she arched her chest.

He straddled her but held his weight off her by supporting himself with his knees. Her arms moved around his back to cup him to her.

"I need you so desperately, Catherine," he whispered into the warmth of her neck. "I thought I had lost you when I realized how stupid I'd been to accept Westerland's challenge."

"Don't think about that anymore. You have made me the happiest lady in London. Now make me yours."

He covered her lips with his, his chest against her breasts. His shaft lay snugly against her womanhood.

John slipped his hand between them and found the sweetness of her desire and slowly massaged it. He moved the tips of his fingers tantalizingly slowly against her. Within seconds she felt her hips lift and move with the motion of his hand. She couldn't keep her hips still when he touched her that way.

Waves of pleasure flooded through her as she felt strength in his hands, hunger in his kisses. His manhood lay nestled against her thigh and she felt his throbbing desire for her, and that touched her heart with more love for him.

"That feels so wonderful. Just like before."

"Enjoy it, Catherine, enjoy it," he whispered and she did until she knew she was going to explode. Suddenly she felt a hard pushing pressure she didn't understand. For a moment she was stunned and stopped moving, but his fingers never stopped.

"Move with me, Catherine, move with me."

The pleasure took over once again. Catherine forgot the pain and accepted the full thickness of his body inside her and realized she was once again moving with him. She heard his satisfying moans of bliss as he pumped and moved inside her.

She clutched his shoulders and lifted her hips to meet his and cried out her total release as John pushed deeper into her, burying his face in the crook of her neck and shuddering as he lowered his weight upon her.

His breathing was hard and raspy as she gloried in the heavy feel of his body on hers.

Catherine hugged John to her and whispered, "I love you, John, I love you."

He rose on his elbows with a smile. "I believe you, my love."

"You haven't changed your mind have you? About marrying me?"

He gave her a queer look. "How can you ask that? All of London saw me ride off with you in my carriage. I couldn't get out of marrying you even if I wanted to." He kissed the tip of her nose. "And I don't. Have no fear. You are mine forever."

She moistened her lips and said, "I just wanted to be sure I wasn't dreaming."

He slipped his arms underneath her back and pulled her up close to him. "You are not dreaming. I kidnapped you and seduced you. No one can take you from me including the formidable Mrs. Goosetree. Later we're going to get dressed and I'm going to take you back to her house, and in three days we will be married."

"I believe Victoria wanted me to marry you, but I don't think a fast wedding is what she had in mind."

"Do you think she will be furious?"

"Very much so." Catherine reached up and kissed him on the lips. "But I have a feeling that in time she will forgive you."

John chuckled. "You are mine, Catherine, and I will love you all the days of my life."

Catherine smiled contentedly. "And I will love you forever."

John rolled her over, placing her on top of him, and then he reached up and pulled her down to him.

Catherine thrilled to his touch.

Twenty-two

"Never look a gift horse in the mouth" might be the Marquis of Westerland's new motto, for he is now the proud owner of what was once the Earl of Chatwin's most prized possession, the General. But one could assume Lord Chatwin doesn't notice, for all his time is now spent with his blushing bride. It was revealed today that the last of the Terrible Threesome earls has left London with no word when he will return. If anyone knows more about the hasty departure of Lord Dugdale, please tell and all will be printed here.

Lord Truefitt
Society's Daily Column

Cupid can be such a little troublemaker...

A
Little
Mischief

by
Amelia Grey

An earl is at his wit's end when his sister joins Miss Winslowe's Wallflower Society—and winds up accused of killing London's most eligible bachelor.

0-425-19277-6

Available wherever books are sold or at
www.penguin.com

A recipe for success...

Start with one village girl turned
mysterious society columnist.

Add one aristocrat planning to expose her.

Mix in a cunning thief.

And you'll have one delicious Regency romance.

A Dash of Scandal
by Amelia Grey

"A wonderful, feel-good, captivating read."
—Heather Graham

0-515-13401-5

BERKLEY SENSATION
COMING IN OCTOBER 2004

Tempting Danger
by Eileen Wilks

Enter a bold new world where the magical and the mundane co-exist in an uneasy alliance—and a cop must balance her own life to stop a brutal killer.

0-425-19878-2

Hardly a Husband
by Rebecca Hagan Lee

Jarrod, sixth marquess of Shepherston, is asked by a childhood friend for help in the art of seduction. Jarrod is wary of a marriage trap—but love has a way of softening the hardest fall.

0-425-19879-0

Master of the Night
by Angela Knight

A tale of supernatural seduction from the author of *Jane's Warlord.* American agent Erin Grayson has been assigned to seduce Reece Champion. But she's been set up. Reece is not only an agent—he's also a vampire.

0-425-19880-4

The Kitchen Witch
by Annette Blair

When a single dad and TV exec hires Mellody as his babysitter, he knows she's rumored to be a witch—but when she magically lands her own cooking show, the sparks really begin to fly.

0-425-19804-9